Ghost to the Rescue

☙

Carolyn Hart

BERKLEY PRIME CRIME
New York

BERKLEY PRIME CRIME
Published by Berkley
An imprint of Penguin Random House LLC
375 Hudson Street, New York, New York 10014

ISBN: 9780425276570

Berkley Prime Crime hardcover edition / October 2015
Berkley Prime Crime mass-market edition / October 2016

Printed in the United States of America
1   3   5   7   9   10   8   6   4   2

Cover design by Jason Gill

For Suzie Fentriss and Henrie Close
in gratitude for friendship: past, present, and future

Chapter 1

Katie Davenport looked up at the stars. Would it make a difference if she asked? After all, she was thirteen, not a little kid anymore, looking up at the night sky and thinking that bright star was listening to her. But still . . . "Star light, star bright, / First star I see tonight, / I wish I may, I wish I might, / Have this wish I wish tonight. Please help my mom." Katie squeezed her eyes shut. "Star light, star bright . . ."

∽

Paul Wiggins pushed back the stiff cap atop his reddish brown hair. He was a man of his time: thick muttonchop whiskers, a luxuriant walrus mustache, starched high-collared white cotton shirt, heavy flannel trousers supported by suspenders, and a sturdy black leather belt. He turned from the broad window with its commanding view of the rail station platform and silver tracks. A folder rested on the corner of his yellow oak desk. He was rather sure the folder had not been there until this instant.

The folder's presence reminded him of the power of hopes and wishes that wing their way across starry night skies. He picked up the folder, smiled at a boisterous cover of unicorns, shooting stars, soccer balls, and laptops. He lifted the flap. A dossier contained a photograph of an attractive woman in her mid-thirties with frizzy brown hair and an expressive face. Ah yes, Deirdre Davenport, single mom, struggling author, job seeker. He scanned the facts. Deirdre Davenport was in a tough spot, though not the kind of trouble usually dealt with by members of his department. Still, heartfelt pleas mattered to him. "Star light, star bright . . ."

Slowly, he nodded. He knew the perfect person to send to the rescue.

♋

I welcomed the gentle slap of a swell, quite different from the towering waves that crashed over and sank the *Serendipity* on our ill-fated fishing trip in the Gulf. A steady backstroke carried me through warm salty water toward a beach similar to Padre Island. I took a breath of salt-scented air, then abruptly, as if galvanized, I picked up speed.

I had a sudden bright picture of Wiggins in my mind. Wiggins, the chief of the Department of Good Intentions, dispatched emissaries to earth to aid those in trouble. In my mind, I heard the sounder on his desk amplifying the clack of the Teletype. I reached shallow water and stood. True to my thought, a telegram sprouted in my hand. Breathlessly, I read the message: *Your advice and counsel sought. Come at once if possible.*

Wiggins is old-fashioned. The fact that telegrams have been supplanted on earth by texts and e-mails is of no interest to him. He sent telegrams when he was a stationmaster in the early nineteen hundreds. He sends telegrams now.

I moved fast, the sudsy, warm water splashing as I went. On the beach my ethereal form appeared in a fetching summer blouse and skirt. No need for towels and such. I simply thought as I wished to be and there I was, red curls shiny as a new copper penny. I waved to gain Bobby Mac's attention.

He looked across the water and waved in return.

I gestured toward the sky, pulled air deep into my lungs, and managed a creditable imitation of a deep train whistle.

Bobby Mac understood at once, gave me a jaunty farewell salute.

I waved a kiss to my husband. What a man. Bobby Mac is still as dark-haired and handsome as the high school senior who stopped a skinny redheaded sophomore in the hall one day, and said—blunt, forthright, and determined—"We're going to the prom." We've been going together ever since, good days and bad, happy days and sad. Someday, when we have more time, I'll tell you the secrets of a happy marriage. Number one? We laughed together. We're still laughing.

Right now, I had other fish to fry. One of Heaven's many delights is the ability to go anywhere in an instant. Think, and there you are. I hurried up the steps of a turn-of-the-century redbrick train station. There was no door. As I've explained before, Heaven doesn't run to doors. No one is shut in or shut out.

Heaven?

Do I see an incredulous expression? Hear a cackle of amusement at such naïveté?

It isn't my role to convince skeptics that Heaven exists, despite my firsthand experience.

Oh yeah? comes a sardonic reply. *So who are you and who stamped your ticket to the Pearly Gates?*

In a quick thumbnail, I am Bailey Ruth Raeburn, late of Adelaide, Oklahoma. That's right, late as in *dearly departed*, though that sounds a little too solemn for me. I prefer *happy voyager.* That was my attitude on earth as well. As for Bobby Mac, when he wasn't hunting for oil, he was fishing, and he never met a tarpon he wouldn't chase. That quest led to our arrival in Heaven when a storm in the Gulf sank the *Serendipity.* We were on the shady side of fifty when we arrived, but another of Heaven's delights is the ability to enjoy your very best age. Twenty-seven was a very good year for me, and that's how I now appear both here and when on earth. I'm a redhead with a spattering of freckles. Green eyes. Slender. Five foot five. A few revelations (not Revelations; that material is more suitable for saints, especially Teresa of Avila, who is as charming as she is erudite; and yes, I do know her. So there!): I love to laugh. I really, really try to follow the Precepts. (More about that later.) I have a taste for fashion.

Fashion. I'd made a quick choice on the beach. I wanted to look just so for my arrival here. I felt like June, the month of daffodils and daisies and dandelions. Yes, dandelions. I love their delicate toppings of fluff. Those feathery crowns inspired my choice of a gossamer-fine pale blue knit top over a white linen tank and white midcalf cotton pants and white wedgies that added an inch to my height. Admittedly, the colors favor a redhead, but I don't think it's vain to wish to appear one's best.

I hurried inside the station.

Wiggins gazed through the window at silver tracks winding into the sky, his genial countenance thoughtful. A thumb and forefinger tugged at his bristly mustache.

"Wiggins!" I caroled.

He looked around, smiled. "Bailey Ruth. It's good of you to come." He glanced at a gaily decorated folder on his desk, then at me, started to speak, stopped.

I sensed he was having second thoughts about his summons. Perhaps my costume was too frivolous. Wiggins admires restraint, i.e., he is fond of plain, unadorned—let me be utterly frank—hideously unattractive clothing as an indication of modesty and docility. As Bobby Mac would agree, perhaps too vehemently, *docile* has never been in my job description. However, Wiggins clearly must perceive a problem calling for my expertise. If my lovely costume was off-putting, I would—nobly—sacrifice for the cause.

With an inward sigh, I transformed my appearance: a prim dull green cotton blouse, a straight khaki skirt, flat black loafers, and my tangled red curls drawn back in a bun. My face is rather thin. I hoped I didn't look like a redheaded ferret. I felt my nose wriggle. Perhaps I'm too suggestible.

Wiggins's expression remained thoughtful, preoccupied.
The problem, then, wasn't my appearance.

I thankfully changed back to my summer choice.

Wiggins glanced again at the folder. "Deirdre Davenport
is certainly challenged, but perhaps her situation isn't serious
enough to warrant intervention. But that sweet plea by her
daughter touched me."

I looked at him with great fondness. "You are always
kind."

He endeavored to appear stern. "We can't be everywhere,
solve everything." He began to pace. "I am torn. My
resources are limited. Perhaps I am being foolish."

I avoided saying, *Huh?*, that favored reply in senior
English when I'd asked a football player to explain the significance of the corrida in *The Sun Also Rises*. "You know I
will be glad to help."

And, oh, how ready I was for an earthly adventure,
though I kept my mien solemn. Wiggins finds a taste for
excitement suspect, but, as I always say, why not have fun
along the way? It was a motto that served me well in life.
And since. Yet I must be circumspect. Wiggins expects his
emissaries to be, if not solemn, certainly serious and always
to follow the Precepts.

As if in response to my unspoken thought, he gave me a
questioning look. "You are always eager to be of help, but
this time can you follow the Precepts?"

Was this my cue? Quickly, I took a breath and sang—I
have a strong soprano—in a syncopated beat to a version of
"Zip-A-Dee-Doo-Dah."

GHOST TO THE RESCUE

PRECEPTS FOR EARTHLY VISITATION

1. *Avoid public notice.*
2. *Do not consort with other departed spirits.*
3. *Work behind the scenes without making your presence known.*
4. *Become visible only when absolutely necessary.*
5. *Do not succumb to the temptation to confound those who appear to oppose you.*
6. *Make every effort not to alarm earthly creatures.*
7. *Information about Heaven is not yours to impart. Simply smile and say, "Time will tell."*
8. *Remember always that you are on the earth, not of the earth.*

I squashed words together to get everything in, but I managed. If I'd hoped for a smile, I was left high and dry.

Wiggins's gaze was stern once again. "You must admit you have difficulty with Precepts One, Three, and Four."

Appearing was a sore point between us. It wasn't that I intended to flout the Precepts when on earth, but honestly, sometimes you have to be *there.*

"Wiggins." I was solemn, straightforward, and almost believable. "You know I never *want* to appear."

After a moment, he laughed, a wonderful, deep roar of laughter. "When I believe that . . . But you are the right person if this task should be undertaken. You are always creative."

I basked, unaccustomed to fulsome praise from Wiggins.

"And the problem"—he sat in his desk chair, picked up the folder—"is in Adelaide."

Whoops. I felt like a fast filly on the homestretch. Adelaide, nestled in the rolling hills of south central Oklahoma, was my town. I was sure it was June and there would be wildflowers, delicate blue and pale rose, and the smell of freshly turned earth after a rain, and the swoop of hawks against the dusky night sky. I loved returning to Adelaide. Of course, I still nurtured a faint hope that someday Wiggins would send me farther afield: Rome, Nome, Madrid, wherever. It was a great big world and I was ready. Would he ever have the confidence that I could succeed elsewhere? Perhaps if I acquitted myself superbly in this instance—whatever it was—my horizons would widen.

"Adelaide? Of course I'll help." I perched on the edge of his desk. "I'm ready."

"You were an English teacher. Another point in your favor."

I was transported to a hot classroom—not much was air-conditioned when I taught—and a clutch of restive football players, sitting, of course, in the back row. I could see them now: Jack, better known as Two-Ton, cadaverous Michael, mischievous Reggie. I'd won their hearts with Sydney Carton.

I took a deep breath and declaimed—and you don't know declamation until you've taught English—"'It is a far, far better thing that I do, than I have ever done; it is a far, far better rest that I go to than I have ever known.'"

Wiggins's face softened. "Redemption. Always beautiful. Always noble."

We shared an instant of silence in tribute to love's power to transform.

But his worried frown quickly returned. "Delicacy. Behind the scenes."

I placed my hand on my heart. "You can count on me. Delicacy." I broke into a soothing verse of "Delicado." I'd loved Dinah Shore's version. The song was after Wiggins's time, but he listened with a faint flicker of hope in his eyes.

"'Handle with care,'" he murmured. "Yes, decidedly so. A young mother, desperate for a job, and desperate as well for inspiration. Could you be inspiring?" He looked at me doubtfully.

"Can I be inspiring?" I crossed my legs. "Why, inspiration is part of my nature." There was the time I inspired a mass walkout from a city council meeting, but perhaps that wasn't quite what Wiggins had in mind.

He brightened. "To serve as a muse is a high calling though not the usual task set for an emissary. Think of the muses, Calliope, Clio, Euterpe . . ." He rattled off the names of the nine muses. "Keep them in mind."

The Teletype suddenly clattered. He swung about, grabbed a pad, made hurried notes.

Outside came the deep-throated wail of the Rescue Express nearing the station. The clack of the wheels sounded louder and louder. The acrid smell of coal smoke tickled my nose, elixir to a spirit ready to rumble. I came to my feet, held out my hand. "Quick. I'll go."

Wiggins glanced out the window, knew time was short. He pushed up from his chair, strode to the slotted wooden

9

container near the ticket widow, grabbed a red ticket, gave it a stamp.

I ran out the door, ticket in one hand, a sheet of paper with Wiggins's notes in the other. As I climbed aboard, Wiggins shouted, "She is seeking inspiration . . . her plight is desperate . . . bank account . . . Do your best . . ."

I stood in the swaying vestibule—on my way to Adelaide, on my way to Adelaide—and tried to decipher Wiggins's back-slanted scrawl: *Deirdre Davenport . . . single mother of two . . . bank account almost empty . . . writes clever mysteries . . . hasn't sold her last two books . . . must have a job . . . applied for a faculty position at Goddard . . . decision to be announced tomorrow. . . .*

∽

I settled unseen on the chair by the desk in a modest hotel room. The joints squeaked as the chair swiveled.

A young woman flicked a puzzled look toward the chair, then gave a little shrug. I liked her at once. Probably mid-thirties. Old enough to have lived and learned and lost. Frizzy brown hair needed a trim but was the color of highly polished mahogany. She had an air of leashed vitality, a woman with too many ideas to consider and tasks to accomplish and destinations to seek to think about herself and haircuts. Her long, expressive face puffed in exasperation with a touch of bitterness. She sat cross-legged on a saggy sofa, a laptop balanced on her knees. A cell phone rested on a coffee table.

A young thin voice talked fast. ". . . not started yet?"

Obviously, the phone was in speaker mode.

"Not yet, honey." Her tone was cheerful, but her expression was forlorn.

"Mom, don't you need to sell a book pretty soon?" The boy's voice was high and scared.

"Don't worry, Joey. I've had rough patches before. One of these days I'll be able to start."

"Look, Mom, I've been thinking about your book. I just finished the new book about Elvis Cole. You know—"

Now her smile was wide. "Robert Crais's PI."

"He is so cool." The young voice was awestruck. "Why don't you write a book like that?"

"I would if I could, but that's not the kind of book I write. My readers want lots of fun."

"Mom"—he sounded solemn—"you used to be happy all the time and you couldn't wait to get to work, but now—"

Deirdre's angular face drooped. But her voice was brisk. "Hey, Joey, I'm fine. I'll start a new book this weekend."

"You will? That's great." His voice lifted in relief. Then, a pause. "Can I come home early? Dad's girlfriend wears perfume that makes me cough and I heard her making fun of my glasses. Please."

"Baby, I'd come get you if I could. But I have to stay here this weekend. Try to have fun. Your dad loves you."

"Yeah." The boy's voice sagged. "Sure. Then why'd they go out and leave me here by myself?"

Her lips quivered and I knew she kept her voice bright with an effort. "Joey, you can handle it. Look, I'll drive down Monday and pick you up."

"Monday." It must have sounded distant to him. "Okay. See you then."

The call ended.

She came to her feet, face crumpling, hands clenched. She took one deep breath, another, another. "Come on, Deirdre. You told Joey to handle it. You handle it. You don't have any choice."

I liked the sound of her name, *Deer-druh*. I liked the way she lifted her chin. I liked her staccato speech.

She clapped her hands on her hips, stared across the room at her image in the mirror. "Handle it, babe. So you owe money everywhere in town. So you spent next month's house payment to send Katie to camp. So you haven't sold your last two books and you've got two hundred and forty dollars in your checking account and you're maxed out on two credit cards. Think positively. That's what you tell the kids. *Jay will pick you for the job. Jay will pick you for the job.*"

She whirled, flung herself onto the sofa, grabbed the laptop, glared at it. "You're about as cold as the grave scene in *Doctor Zhivago*. I told Joey I'd start a book this weekend. Sure, and in my spare time I'll pop a plan for world peace and write a treatise on the mating habits of piranhas. I try to write and nothing happens. Is it crazy to talk to yourself? But there's nobody else I can talk to. Wesley likes being single and he has a girlfriend with too much perfume. I can't tell Joey and Katie that I'm broke and desperate, but they know I'm stressed. It's like I have coyotes running circles in my head. Bills, Jay, the kids, whether I make the cut, get the job. I can hear Jay now, his voice smooth as honey: 'My decision is momentous for our faculty, our students, the state's writing community.' Oh yeah, pompous ass. Momentous for me and Harry, too. Trust Jay to insist that he's still struggling with his choice. Too bad he's got carte blanche. Maybe nobody else on the faculty cares."

She looked down at the laptop, her face creased in a tight, frustrated frown.

Without warning, the door swung in. A man stepped inside, closed the door firmly behind him. Six feet tall, he was well built, knew it. His T-shirt was tight. Faded jeans hung low on his hips. He was barefoot. He leaned back against the door with all the assurance of a tousle-haired Hollywood bad boy and that was the look on his face—suggestively seductive brown eyes, lips parted in a sleepy smile. "Hey, Deirdre." He carried two champagne glasses and a magnum. "Time for a little celebration." His dark eyes ignored her face, grazed slowly down her body, lingered on her long, bare legs. "Nice."

She came to her feet, stood quite stiff and still. "How did you get in?"

"The kid at the front desk doesn't know who's in room 206. I told him I was Jay Knox"—emphasis on his last name—"and I locked myself out. So here I am. And here you are." He drawled the last sentence.

"The clerk should have asked for an ID." My tone was hot. I clapped a hand over my lips, but it was too late. My husky voice could always be heard in the last row.

He gave her a sleepy smile. "I like the new voice. Deeper than usual. Kind of throaty. Sexy. As for ID, I may have mentioned my uncle. Useful that he owns this place." He spoke with easy assurance, accustomed to the deference a small town accords certain families.

Knox? Like pieces slotting into a puzzle, I remembered

Jeremiah Knox, the long-ago beloved dean of arts and sciences at Goddard. His wife, Jenny, was a volunteer for children, reading, the arts. Whatever needed to be done, Jenny Knox was ready to help. I had a hazy memory they'd had several children. This would be a grandson. He was handsome in the Knox manner, sandy-haired, broad face, generous mouth, but there was a hint of dissolution in the curl of those full lips. Even the best oak tree can spawn rotten acorns.

"Yeah, I like that voice. Say something else, Deirdre."

Deirdre knew she hadn't spoken. She looked back and forth, turned to glance behind her.

Jay's laugh was easy. "It's okay, sweetie. Nobody here but you and me. I like it that way." He started toward her.

She said sharply, "Jay, I'm not dressed—"

Actually, Deirdre was more fully dressed than women today appear at swimming pools, and was quite attractive in an azalea pink cotton sateen shirt tunic and adorable light feathery mukluks. Of course, the tunic only reached her upper thighs, and she had long, well-shaped legs.

"—and you need to leave." Her tone was flat, her gaze cold.

"Less is more." He placed the champagne bottle and glasses on the coffee table in front of the sofa, but he never took his eyes off of her. He took one step, another. She stood her ground. "Jay, I'm asking you to leave. Now."

He reached her, stood too close. "Come on, Deirdre. You're no kid. The night's young. We can have fun." He reached out with both hands, gripped her arms, pulling her close.

"Let go." Deirdre's voice rose.

He gave a hot, low laugh. "Loosen up, lady. Maybe I

forgot to mention all the duties in your job description. That is, if you get the job. How bad do you want the job, Deirdre?"

She strained backward. "Let me go."

I was at the door. I yanked it open as, colors swirling, I appeared—but, of course, I had already been inside the room.

Jay stood with his back to me, hands clamped on Deirdre's arms.

Deirdre stared past Jay at me. Her eyes widened. Her lips parted. She tried to speak but no words came.

I looked over my shoulder as if speaking to someone in the hall. "I'll take a rain check on a drink. I promised Deirdre I'd drop by. She offered to help me"—I was at a momentary loss, but after all, as Wiggins recalled, I had taught high school English—"with the transition from chapter four to five. She's so generous to new writers." By the time I closed the door and moved toward Deirdre and Jay, he was standing a few feet away, facing me, a startled look on his face.

"Professor Knox," I burbled as I hurried forward, gazing at Jay in delight. "I've heard so much about you." This was usually safe, though I knew only enough about him to write a single-word description: *jerk*.

Deirdre blinked several times, perhaps trying to erase the memory of colors moving and coalescing.

I glanced at the mirror. Surely she approved of my ivory cotton-knit tunic with the most elegant medallion trim at the neckline and six to eight inches of an intricate design at the hem. Black leggings and black strap sandals with faux stones were a perfect foil for the ivory. And, of course, for red hair.

I held out my hand to Jay, loved the flash from the large faux ruby ring that echoed the red stones on the sandals. "I'm"—I hesitated for an instant. St. Jude was the patron of impossible dilemmas, and that seemed a good appraisal of Deirdre's status—"Judy Hope." Surely Wiggins would be impressed.

I glanced at Deirdre.

Her expression was glazed, but she came through. "Judy"— she managed a strained smile—"I'm glad you were able to . . . drop by." She was torn between sincere gratitude for her deliverance and mind-stretching incredulity at my arrival.

"I'm so eager to talk about the transition." I hoped this would help her get past her wooden speech.

"Transition," she repeated as if the word had no meaning, her gaze still focused on me. "Oh. Oh yes, of course. Transition! We had a good discussion about leading into a new chapter. I know we can make some progress." She turned to Jay. "I know you'll forgive Judy and me if we get right to work." She hurried to the coffee table, grabbed the champagne bottle by the neck and the glasses in her other hand, thrust them at him. "I'll see you in the morning."

He took the bottle, tucked it under his arm, the glasses in his left hand. He moved in an easy slouch, gave her a steady stare when he reached the door. "Tonight. Cabin five." He spoke casually, but the message in his eyes was clear: *You want the job? Show up.*

Chapter 2

I'd like to say Deirdre was delighted when the door closed behind him.

Instead, she stared at me and slowly backed away, a step at a time. "You . . . weren't there." Her voice was shaky. "The doorway was empty. Nothing. And then"—she waved her hands—"colors shimmered. There you were. You can't be here, but you are. I see you. I must be crazy." She clasped long slender fingers to each temple.

"You're not crazy at all. I wasn't there. Then I was." I was glad to reassure her.

She gave a ragged laugh. "That's swell. Not there. Then here." She stumbled to the sofa, sank down in one corner. "It's stress. I'm trying to come up with a book. Maybe you're part of a book." There was a desperate hope in her voice. "Yes. A book. There's this cute redhead—"

I smiled. What a dear girl.

"—who is Johnny-on-the-spot when Jay's acting like an ass." She stopped, looked grim. "It was worse than that. I'm afraid if you hadn't come . . . But you did. Look, did you ask for a key at the desk and maybe the light was funny when you came in . . . ?" Her words straggled to an end.

"It's better not to worry about things we can't change."

I saw the realization in her eyes that the light in the doorway had been fine. She'd seen colors and the colors were me appearing and that was not an experience she understood.

I was brisk. "Everything works out for the best. I was able to come and intervene in what had the makings of an unfortunate event."

"Very unfortunate." Her voice was thin. She gave me a long, careful look.

I resisted fluffing my hair. A quick glance in the mirror reassured me. I looked as nice as could be.

"Judy Hope," she said experimentally. "You aren't wearing a name tag."

"Should I be?" I was truly curious.

"Are you here for the writers' conference?"

I beamed at her. "I'm here for you. I want to help you with your stress. What's the problem?"

She squeezed her eyes shut for a moment, opened them.

I smiled again.

Her breath was a little quick. "Judy Hope. Okay. As they say, when somebody gives you a gift, say thank you, even if you don't have a clue about why. Thank you. You arrived in time to save me from a fate I wouldn't wish on any job seeker—"

"Job seeker?"

"If you're here to help me, you missed out on the basics. Problem? I guess I can sum it up in two words. Money and sex. I need a job. Specifically, I applied for a new opening in the English Department at Goddard. . . ." She looked at me questioningly.

"Goddard College, the pride of Adelaide."

"Okay. Anyway, it's a job to teach creative writing. Who gets picked is up to Jay Knox. You just met him. I should get the job. I've actually sold books. Harry Toomey, the other finalist, wrote a thriller, which he self-published. The book has a slick cover on the outside, but the prose is plodding— *clump, clump, clump*. The words have the zing of stale soda. Jay looked me right in the eye and pointed out that self-pub's the wave, the new force in publishing, and has a lot of appeal. That's true if you want to suck in people who pour their hearts into a book and pay somebody to print it and think that's publishing. For anyone who wants to build a career as a novelist, it's a dead end nine times out of ten."

"You believe it's exploitive?"

"I do. And what really makes me sad is when a self-pub book's really good and could reach readers but the author doesn't know how to make the right connections. There are always exceptions, but, trust me, Harry isn't one of them. Oh, you don't care about any of this. Anyway, I'm the headliner tomorrow at eleven at the annual Goddard College Writers' Conference." Her voice indicated a quote: "'Knock 'em Dead with a Killer Beginning.' And Jay will announce the new faculty member tomorrow." Her eyes were intense. "I have to get the job. I'm out of options, out of money, and I can't ever seem to get a new book started."

I said gently, "If you've done it before, why not this time? What's wrong?"

"If I knew, I'd fix it. I try to write and I can't even come up with yada yada yada. I think I have an idea and you know what happens? I set it up: the protagonist is a nice girl, her boyfriend's dumped her, she comes home to the small town, going to open a bakery or a pottery store or maybe a cat hotel. Cats are big. We've got a cat. His name's Cassius, so now you know what he looks like. She can have a cat hotel, the cats tell her things. But that night somebody throws a rock through her window. She hurries to the window."

I leaned forward, expectant.

She brushed back frizzy curls. "She looks out and there's this ghostly form and she hurries downstairs and out on the porch . . ."

"Yes?"

"That's the problem. Nothing happens! I don't know who she is or what she looks like. I don't know why anybody cares if she's back in town. I keep trying and nothing happens. It's like I have a dead squid for a brain." She lifted long, thin fingers, gently massaged her temples. "I write—used to write—light, funny books about zany characters. Before my brain turned to Jell-O and the neurons stopped connecting. I'm absolutely desperate. I thought maybe if I meditated, that would help. I let my mind empty out and I focused on one idea: *I need inspiration. I need inspiration. I need inspiration.*"

I clapped my hands together. "That's why I'm here."

"But I need a hilarious character, like something out of Janet Evanovich or Parnell Hall."

I was a bit short on hilarity at the moment, but perhaps practicality would be helpful. "If the job at the college doesn't work out, you can look for another job."

"You don't understand." She sounded exhausted. "If I make Jay mad, he'll make sure I don't get a job anywhere in town. One of his sisters works at the Chamber of Commerce, another runs a charitable foundation, a brother's the assistant managing editor at the *Gazette*, his aunt heads up human resources at the hospital. Anywhere I'd try to get a job, there would be a Knox. They're all wonderful people, but they have one blind spot and you just met him— handsome, spoiled, 'whatever I want I get' Jay. He's the baby of the family and nobody in the family or in town ever admits Jay's a louse because the Knoxes are wonderful. End of story. I don't have enough money to move anywhere." She ended on a defeated sigh.

I'd definitely chosen the right name. I hoped St. Jude was at my shoulder. Deirdre's back was against the wall, no money coming in, bills to pay, expenses to meet. It was easy to say, *Look for another job*. But obviously, in her mind, the Knox family had plenty of clout. As for well-paying jobs, those are on a lot of wish lists. It's easy to get huffy and say to take any job, but if the pay doesn't match the bills, where are you?

Speaking of jobs, mine was clear. "Every problem has a solution." I hoped I didn't sound like my well-meaning high school geometry teacher who lost that cheery certainty before I exited his class.

I plopped onto the sofa beside her.

Deirdre stiffened, pressed hard against the side of the sofa. She glanced toward the closed door, no doubt recreating in her mind the riveting moment when I appeared.

I waved a hand in dismissal, admired the pale rose of my nails. Possibly, the ivory blouse demanded carmine.

Deirdre stared at my fingernails, now brilliantly red, and blurted out, "Maybe I didn't know how easy I had it. I'm broke. Jay wants to trade the job for sex. But that's real. Sleazy but real and I'm a big girl. But you!" She reached out tentatively, touched my arm, yanked her hand away as if her fingers burned. "You are really there. Or"—she drew a ragged breath—"if I'm imagining you, I ought to be in a sideshow. Come one, come all! Look at the woman who sees people who aren't there!"

I patted her knee. "Deirdre, take a deep breath. You're fine."

She jerked like she'd encountered a jellyfish, drew herself together as if ready to bound from the sofa.

"Please," I urged, "sit back and relax. I'm here to help you and I'm as real as can be."

She stared with saucer-shaped eyes, but, even though her muscles were rigid, she remained seated.

I had to be accurate. "For the moment."

"*For the moment.* If I'm really quiet, will you go away?"

I was patient. "Deirdre, let me help you."

She gave me a forlorn gaze. "You're the rescue squad? Who are you? Where did you come from? How did you get here? How soon will you leave?"

I was afraid I smelled a whiff of coal smoke. Surely Wiggins understood this woman was in dire need of a champion.

And in dire need of reassurance. I was crisp. "I'm Bailey Ruth Raeburn. I used to live in Adelaide. When I was alive."

"Alive?" Her voice cracked.

"Before I went to Heaven."

She made a despairing sound. "If I wrote it all down . . . it wouldn't sell. Nobody would believe me." A quick breath. "You told Jay you were Judy Hope."

I smiled modestly. "I'm not making any claims, but St. Jude is the patron of"—actually *impossible* was his specialty, but she might find that discouraging—"people in difficult situations. And Hope is a key virtue."

"Bailey Ruth. Judy. What do I call you?" A frantic head shake. "What am I saying? How can I have a conversation with somebody who isn't real?"

"I am real for the moment." I felt this was a profound insight. "As for names, if we meet in public, call me Judy. When we're alone, I'm Bailey Ruth."

"Judy. Bailey Ruth." She still sat as rigid as a post.

"Let me put your mind at rest. . . ." I described the Department of Good Intentions and Wiggins and his concern that she was stressed and that's why I was there. "Wiggins speaks highly of you."

She continued to sit as stiff as a starched crinoline.

"Pretend you're in Miss Silver's drawing room and her wonderful calm demeanor assures you that everything is going to be all right." My voice was soothing.

She looked at me blankly. "Who's Miss Silver?"

I was shocked. "You call yourself a mystery writer and you don't know Miss Silver?"

Now she was ruffled. "I've had six books published.

Secret of the Scarlet Macaw, The Dragon Hissed, Dance of the Derelict—"

I hastened to interrupt. "That's wonderful. But all mystery readers know Patricia Wentworth's Miss Silver."

Her smile was quick and apologetic. "I'll look her up." Then her wary expression returned. "But let's stick to the subject. You say you're going to help me. How?"

"Yes. It's really very simple. I intend to inspire you." But first I needed to solve her job situation. Then she would relax and be able to write. "Tell me about you."

She streaked fingers through her frizzy curls.

I wondered if she indeed resorted to old-fashioned permanents or if her hair naturally bristled.

"Okay." She made a production of the word, a low *o*, and the emphasis on a higher-toned *kay*. "Life story of Frazzled Middle-Aged Multitasking Mother with Writer's Block for Woman Who Doesn't Exist but Here She Is. I'm—"

Her cell phone rang.

She shot me an apologetic look, yanked it. "My daughter. She's at camp. I'd better take it. . . . Hi, honey. I thought you'd be in bed by now. . . . Your voice sounds kind of muffled. . . . Oh, Katie, don't cry. . . . Of course it's not a problem. I wanted you to go to camp. I had money put back for that. Now, you get to sleep and don't worry about anything. Everything's fine here. . . . That's my girl. No more tears. Promise? . . . Good night, honey. Sleep tight. Don't let the bedbugs bite." She turned off the phone, looked at me. "They're camping out and she called me huddled inside her sleeping bag, sobbing because the camp costs so much and she knows I don't have the money and maybe she should just come home now and maybe they'd give us some money back."

"Kids know when we're in trouble."

"You got that right." She looked bleak. "I'm panicked about money and now my kids are panicked."

"So you need this job."

"In spades. And I'm thirty-six. It isn't easy to get a job at my age, especially when you haven't worked for a long time. I was a reporter for the *Gazette*, then I quit to stay home with the kids. My ex-husband walked out last year. I write mysteries but they only make enough money for a down payment on a car, like the Mazda he's now driving in Dallas, or to pick up three months of house payments. I haven't sold any books lately. The *Gazette* doesn't need me and the pay there is only okay if you're single. Now I'm a single mom without any savings. This great job opened up at Goddard and I applied. I'm qualified. Sort of. I don't have an advanced degree, just a BA, but I've been a reporter, had six books published. I can teach writing. Between us, you can't teach how to take an idea and turn it into a story that pulls in a reader like Poe's maelstrom."

I nodded approvingly. One of my favorite short stories.

Deirdre managed a lopsided grin. "I can do what writing teachers do, talk about character and plot and development and transitions. The neat thing is, I'd be on the faculty and I love to talk about writing and I like kids and the pay's great and I'd have health insurance. But—"

I knew the answer. "Jay Knox makes the pick."

"It's up to Jay. My fate's in the hands of a guy who wouldn't know work if he fell over it. All Jay's ever done is play and now he's playing at academia. I told you about his family. They're top-notch. Everybody likes and respects the Knoxes. He has a special in at Goddard because his grandfather was a wonderful dean. When they decided to emphasize a creative-writing curriculum, Jay got the job. He has"—her tone was grudging—"had a couple of books published. Thrillers. But he got the job because he's a Knox. I've heard rumors about Jay. Happy hands with coeds, and willing ones get A's. A lot of people know he's a louse, but nobody wants to publicly accuse him. When I applied, he was a little too familiar but I thought I could handle him. I thought he'd be careful about sexual harassment. The law is clear. No hanky-panky to make a secretary keep her job. Except when it happens. Some guys still figure you need the job too much to squawk or you're afraid nobody will believe you or you just don't want a hassle. Anyway, Jay made it pretty clear. I show up at cabin five tonight or he picks Harry." She gave me a despairing look. "How can you possibly change his mind?"

I tried to look calm and reassuring, though I hoped St. Jude had an ear cocked. Changing Jay's mind would rank as a miracle. I never lay claim to miracles. A different department altogether.

"I'll have to persuade him. So"—I looked around—"why are you and Jay at a hotel?"

She spoke rapidly, perhaps hoping if she satisfied all questions, I—somehow—would depart. ". . . Silver Lake Lodge . . . Goddard English Department sponsors a writers' short course here every summer. . . . Jay Knox is the director. . . . People come from all over . . . some agents and editors. . . . I'm headlining tomorrow: 'Knock 'em Dead with a Killer Beginning.' In the afternoon, my talk is 'Turning on the Lightbulb.'"

I nodded approvingly. "It is just like turning on a lightbulb. Bingo. An idea and it blossoms." That's what Deirdre needed. An idea.

She looked rueful. "That's the irony. I can't start a book and I'm supposed to tell the students how to come up with ideas. But"—she plunged both hands into her unkempt curls, looking like a poodle on a bad hair day—"I didn't pick the topic."

I quickly changed the subject. "Back to Jay Knox. He selects the new faculty member?"

"Right. I talked to a couple of other professors as well when I interviewed, but Jay has the final say." Her face was bleak. "He'll announce his choice in the afternoon session tomorrow. Right now my chances are nil. Unless—"

"I'll deal with Jay." I spoke hastily. "What motivates him?"

"In addition to sex?" Her tone was wry. "I don't know him well enough to say. I know some stuff about him. He worked on the *Gazette* after my time, wrote a couple of thrillers. One of them got a movie deal. That helped get him the job in the English Department, that and his family name. He's on tenure track. He'll probably get tenure. He's already turned his position into a cushy deal. He does consulting on the side. He takes money from writers for 'advising' them and what he really does is set up deals with agents and editors. I guess it pays pretty well. He has a classic Thunderbird. The Knox family isn't rich, so Jay has to have a paycheck. The entrée to agents and editors is part of the draw this weekend and Jay's clients have the inside track."

"He takes money to connect writers to agents?" I frowned.

Deirdre shrugged. "He's careful. He doesn't take money from Goddard students but they don't have any money anyway. He takes advantage of writers who will do anything to make connections. Three or four of Jay's protégés are here this weekend. Most conference attendees are just thrilled to attend panels and maybe catch a word with an editor or agent in the bar."

I glanced at the clock. Almost ten. "I need to talk to people who might unload on him."

"Hoping for a little quid pro quo?" Deirdre asked.

I needed leverage to deal with Jay Knox. Heaven would frown on using information to coerce him, but I would be doing a great service to womankind if I discouraged Jay Knox from using his power to sexually harass subordinates. I was circumspect in my response. "Let's say I hope to gain some insight into his character."

Deirdre turned her hands palms up. "I know the guy, but I don't *know* him, if you know what I mean. I'm just trying to get my foot in the door. I don't know the faculty. I've met Maureen Matthews. She also teaches creative writing. I like her a lot. She was quick and funny and very nice to me. But I don't know the people running the conference. Maybe you can talk to somebody down at the bar. There was a big crowd when I came upstairs. I didn't know most of them. I guess they're attending the conference, especially the ones who have that lost, hungry look in their eyes. I understand. They're desperate to sell their books."

"How about faculty members?"

"The chair of the department was there. Dr. Randall's a big guy, thick shock of white hair, tidy white mustache, florid face. He fills out a seersucker jacket like an old fullback. Jay's agent is Cliff Granger. Tall, thin, a four-hundred-dollar sport coat. Cliff usually looks bored and supercilious but he has smart green eyes. Jay's editor is Jessica Forbes. She's imposing, silver hair drawn back in a bun. Here"—Deirdre reached for a brochure on the coffee table—"everyone's photo is in the program." She handed the leaflet to me.

I looked at each in turn as Deirdre described them.

Deirdre was unsparing. "Jessica has a pleasant face but I get the feeling she'd put her grandmother on an ice floe for a best seller. Harry Toomey's pudgy, his clothes are too tight, his hair looks like it needs a good wash, and he has a little mustache that reminds me of peach fuzz."

I popped to my feet. A convivial gathering at the bar sounded like a perfect spot to begin my quest. I never doubted that Jay Knox had a history, and I was going to dig it up. "Don't worry about a thing, Deirdre. I'll nose about a bit. You get a good night's rest. I have a feeling tomorrow will be a new day." Some things we can count on.

She rose, too. "Thanks again, Bailey Ruth. It's been nice knowing you."

Obviously she had no confidence I could assure her of winning the job. Her parting sentence even suggested she had no interest in meeting again.

I smiled with my hand on the knob. "You can rest easy, my dear. Tomorrow I'll have much to report."

I stepped out into the hall, closed the door. I hoped Deirdre would get a good night's sleep. It was my intention to be thoughtful of her sensibilities by waiting to disappear. I made certain no one was in the passageway. I was midway gone, colors dissolving, dissolving. . . .

The door opened.

Deirdre stared at the fading colors, flinched, covered her eyes, slammed the door shut.

Had she intended to call me back? Or had she succumbed to curiosity? Whichever, she was now forced to accept the fact that I was exactly what I claimed to be, an emissary from the Department of Good Intentions, here on her behalf, sometimes seen, sometimes unseen.

In an instant I was hovering in the night sky. Light spilled from the front of Silver Lake Lodge. The two-story plantation-style structure once housed a big family, who had fallen on hard times. Since then the house had been a bed-and-breakfast, a bar and dance hall, and now, with the addition of two wings, a small hotel. Six cabins were nestled among cottonwoods, white oaks, and weeping willows. A winding path dotted with an occasional lamppost led to the lake and a fishing pier. The wooded area was dark and quiet, but lights illuminated the entrance. More light spilled out onto a back terrace.

The bar was noisy. Loud voices and outbursts of raucous laughter indicated the attendees were having an F. Scott Fitzgerald moment. Or moments. People stood two-and three-deep near the bar. All the chairs at a half-dozen small tables were filled. Several soft leather sofas and chairs were occupied. I saw flushed faces, heard rapid speech. Glasses were lifted, refills ordered. Everyone was having a grand old time, so this was likely a good venue to find out more about Jay Knox.

Most of the revelers were causally dressed. Polos and short-sleeve shirts with slacks were the norm for men. The shirts weren't expensive. Trust me, I know. As for the women, I closed my eyes in a delicate shudder. Perhaps Deirdre should incorporate a tactful version of dressing for success in her presentation. I reopened them and the vision didn't improve. Did women writers have no fashion sense? All that black! Blouses, slacks, shoes. Dear Heaven, it was summer.

I spotted the four-hundred-dollar sport coat, a blue window-pane with notched lapels and a two-button front over a navy turtleneck. Its wearer stood at the far end of the bar, but he wasn't engaged in conversation. I came up beside him, unseen. Invisibility has its perks. He was half-turned on the high stool, his gaze flicking from group to group. Standing next to him, I was aware that he radiated tension. I gazed at his profile. Supercilious, as Deirdre said, but more than that, a man under intense pressure.

The occupant of the next stool stepped to the floor.

A plump woman darted for the vacant seat, beating out a thin, angular woman with eyes like a barracuda. The winner caught her breath, turned toward Cliff Granger. Her face had the hopeful look of a puppy seeking a treat.

Cliff's smooth face and high forehead immediately reminded me of Franchot Tone; world-weary, a sophisticate, and, at this moment, disdainful.

The woman said hesitantly, "Mr. Granger." Her voice was uneven; obviously it had taken all her courage to speak to him. "I wonder if I could talk to you for a minute about my book—"

"Panel tomorrow at eleven. I'll take questions then. Individual appointments in the afternoon." He turned away.

She stared at his shoulder, then slid off the stool, eyes shiny with tears, lips quivering.

I don't like people who kick puppies.

His half-full drink sat on the bar, golden liquid and glittering ice.

I lifted the glass an inch or so and flung the contents with force.

Liquid splashed across Cliff's lap. He jerked, stared at the bar.

The bartender was perhaps a foot away, bald head damp with perspiration, fielding orders with an automatic smile.

"What the hell's going on?" Cliff glared at the bartender. "Why'd you knock my glass over?"

The man on the next stool was staring at the glass, his face perplexed.

Perhaps I am too tidy. The empty glass stood upright. I'd flung the contents, put the glass down. In the world of physics, a glass whose contents spewed should be lying on its side. That's what usually happens when glasses are pushed over.

"That glass." The man's words were slightly slurred. He wrinkled his nose, peered. He looked like a befuddled owl, beaked nose and no neck. "The glass came up in the air a couple of inches and then it tipped toward him. All by itself." He paused, repeated belligerently, "All by itself. The glass lifted in the air, then it spilled. Stuff slopped all over him.

Then"—he spaced the words slowly—"the glass came back down on the bar."

Cliff glared at him. "Did you knock my glass over?"

The little man with the big nose and no neck slid off the stool, stood wavering. "I think I don't feel very good." He turned unsteadily and stumbled away.

Cliff swiped a cocktail napkin across the front of his sport coat, his jaw rigid.

The bartender was solicitous, handing him a clean cotton towel. "Here, sir. Guess that guy's elbow caught it." He tried for some levity. "Looked like he'd seen a ghost."

I listened for the clack of wheels on silver rails. Would I ever master my impulsive nature? Precept Five blazed in my mind like neon: "Do not succumb to the temptation to confound those who appear to oppose you."

The man who had occupied the now-empty bar stool shot a furtive look over his shoulder, hurriedly lurched around a potted fern. I hoped his room wasn't too far away. On the bright side, it is a human necessity to transform what happens into a better reality. Instead of a UFO, it was obviously a weather balloon. That rattle in the attic was the weather, not an ax murderer. The wind caught the ball. It wasn't a slice. That sudden vivid sense of an unseen presence? Hoo-hah, nobody believes in ghosts.

Cliff Granger mopped at his soggy jacket and trousers, then was abruptly still, his face turned toward the archway leading into the bar. He slapped the wet towel on the bar, was off the stool. He moved purposefully through the crowd.

A tall, imposing woman stood there, white hair pulled

back in a bun, smooth oval face. Deirdre had described Jessica Forbes's face as pleasant. I would add commanding. Her face had character, deep-set dark eyes with a penetrating gaze, long thin nose, rather thin lips, a firm jaw. She surveyed the gathering, gave a slight head shake, turned to go. She reminded me of a Persian cat: fastidious, not finding the company to her liking.

Cliff Granger was one of several people hurrying toward her, but he arrived first, bent toward her, spoke rapidly.

I joined him.

Jessica's posture was revealing. She stepped back a pace, stood straight and still, met his gaze with a dismissive look.

". . . had a chance to reconsider. Look, Jessica, I'll send you—"

"More dreck?" Her voice was deep.

"Jessica, I've got some good stuff. I'll—"

She cut in, that deep voice cold and deliberate. "You sent me six manuscripts that a desperate dog wouldn't pee on. If you have good stuff, am I your go-to dead-letter drop for rubbish?" Her look was appraising. "I heard about your new wife, young and expensive. So I get it, you need to make money. Flooding editors with lousy books isn't the answer. Or are you just a shill for Jay Knox's manuscript mill? Maybe you better have a heart-to-heart with Jay. I'll look at one more, Cliff. This one better have a killer beginning, a roller coaster middle, and a Technicolor finale." With that she moved past him, the *Queen Mary* leaving a barge in her wake. She strode around a potted plant and was gone.

Face grim, he walked back to the bar, slid onto a stool.

A woman shyly approached, spoke to him. He shook his head, rudely turned his back to her. Her face flushed.

So much for my hope for a tête-à-tête with either Jay's agent or his editor.

The noise was increasing. As was said long ago in a very different context: Loose lips sink ships. Maybe I could find out enough to capsize Jay Knox. But I needed entrée. . . .

I looked around the crowded area. From Deirdre's description, I easily spotted the chair of the department. Dr. Randall was bigger than I'd imagined, likely six foot one or two, heavy shouldered and stocky, which made him a giant in the gathering. I wondered if writers ran smaller than average. White head slightly inclined, he listened with a patient smile to a bony woman with flying hands. Silver bracelets jangled on one arm. I could hear their tinkle even above the roar of conversation and hoots of laughter.

I made a quick decision.

In an instant, I was in the ladies' room. I stepped into a stall and appeared. It wasn't my intent to show up the dowdiness of the attendees. Certainly not. But in my new role, I needed to be comfortable and, for me, comfort begins with appearance. I stepped out of the stall and appraised myself in the mirrors over the washbasins. Truly lovely: a classic thin-weave jacket with flared lapels and matching tank in pale jade with white straight-leg pants and white woven leather sandals. I felt complete as a bronze link long-loop necklace with a medallion of St. Jude appeared. I took only a moment to fluff my hair.

I pushed through the door into the powder room.

An older woman seated on a leather bench turned a startled face toward me. She looked and her eyes began to resemble pop-outs. She held a lipstick in one hand that remained frozen in the air.

Obviously, she had been in the restroom area and been certain no one was there.

I am rarely at a loss for words.

"I don't . . ." she began slowly.

I flashed a friendly smile. "I didn't see you when I came in. I must have been thinking about something else. And you looked quite deep in thought. Plot lines coming together?"

Her relief was endearing. "I guess. . . . Yes. I have a problem in chapter six."

I was at the door. "If all else fails, your heroine walks into her room/office/garage and lying on top of a bench are three small brown parcels." The door sighed shut behind me.

I walked fast. I wanted to catch Dr. Randall. He wouldn't share any negative information about Jay Knox. It would not be to Randall's advantage to admit any clouds loomed on the academic horizon. But I needed to speak to Randall first to carry out my plan. I also walked fast because Wiggins surely wouldn't approach me in the middle of a crowded bar—

I felt a tap on my shoulder.

I stopped, looked around. My heart sank. No one was near me. Despite the hubbub, I heard a growl in my ear. "Front drive. The magnolia tree."

"Wiggins, let's visit later." I couldn't see him, of course. I looked up and about, generally spoke as though addressing a small platform a few inches above my head. "You know I treasure our talks." Was that laying it on too thick? But as Mama always said, "You can never tell a man often enough how wonderful he is." Mama also always told us kids that a positive attitude turned a detour into a new adventure. "I'm making excellent progress."

"Progress? A glass rising in the air, the contents splashed?" In his outrage, Wiggins's volume increased as he spoke. "That woman in the powder room?"

I was a bit surprised Wiggins had ventured into a powder room. "Isn't the décor lovely?"

"Bailey Ruth, can you give me one good reason why—"

I heard the clack of wheels, the distant *whoo* of the Rescue Express.

"—you shouldn't be on board?"

"Because . . ." I felt rather desperate, then said in rush, "you are much too kind and wonderful to abandon Deirdre. She's desperate for inspiration. I'm sure the minute I solve Deirdre's job problem, why—whoosh—she'll be able to write again, and perhaps I can help with the job—"

The sound of the whistle was fading, the clack of wheels on the rails farther away. Wiggins was no longer near.

I gave a huge sigh of relief.

I became aware that the Woman in the Powder Room stood riveted only a foot or so away. She said shyly, "I'll bet you're working out a scene, aren't you? I use different voices for different characters, too."

That explained Wiggins's departure. I gave a cheery laugh. "Exactly. I say dialogue aloud to make sure I have the right cadence. Now I know I'm on the right track." The latter in case Wiggins was lurking. "How is chapter six?"

"I'm hurrying right up to my room. I can't wait to get to my laptop. I can see it now"—her eyes had a faraway look—"Sanduska—that's my main character—has been to the dentist and when she gets back to her office, do you know what's sitting in her chair?"

"Three brown paper—"

She dismissed brown paper packages with a wave of one hand. "A triangle, a square, and a hexagon! Isn't that cool?"

My late geometry teacher would be thrilled, but I failed to see the attraction to readers. The Woman in the Powder Room had already turned away, muttering to herself. "The triangle's purple, the square . . ."

My gaze skittered about me. No one appeared to have noticed anything unusual. I took that as a good omen. I turned and headed straight, or as straight as one can maneuver through a crowded bar area, for Dr. Randall. A ceiling spot illuminated his dramatic bush of white hair. His florid face might be a trifle redder than usual, likely hypertension, but he held what I guessed to be a glass of seltzer and his pale blue eyes were bright and observant and quite sober.

The bony woman—iron gray hair, tortoiseshell glasses, a baggy black sateen blouse, jeans, and high-top tennis shoes (I repressed a shudder)—was still planted solidly in front of him, her face poked forward, her voice didactic. ". . . and then my character—the lawyer, not the minister—goes around the corner and there's an explosion. He's knocked against the wall. Through the smoke, he sees a gazelle." She paused, eyed him with intensity.

"A gazelle. How remarkable. Definitely high tension."

Randall lifted his arm, looked down at his wristwatch, clearly a man planning to slip-slide away.

I spoke briskly. "Dr. Randall, I'm glad I found you."

If ever a man welcomed Heavenly intervention, it was the besieged academic. He welcomed me heartily. "Oh yes. Very good to see you."

I managed to slide a shoulder in front of the writer while giving her an appreciative smile. "So sorry to interrupt, but I'm a few minutes late for my meeting with Dr. Randall." I sounded very official.

"Oh." She looked deflated, started to turn, paused. "Perhaps tomorrow I can finish telling you about my book."

"Tomorrow," he said firmly, "will be a very full day. I doubt you'll have a moment between sessions."

She moved away, gray head poking this way and that, likely in search of another audience to regale.

I nodded toward the archway, which was framed by potted palms. "Perhaps we might step over by that palm"—it was a highly visible location where we could easily be observed by anyone in the bar. I wanted to underline my standing with Dr. Randall—"and I'll explain?"

He shot me a wary look.

"I'm very interested in the work of your wonderful department." Obviously he feared I might also have a plot and the staying power of a limpet. But I can appear almost angelic (not wishing to presume, but it is what it is) when necessary. Once when the car (yes, I was driving) went forward into the garage door instead of backward to the street, I exclaimed, "Now that's a surprise!" and beamed at Bobby Mac. He laughed, and said, "How can you look so innocent? 'Me, drive the car into the garage? Can't believe you'd even think that! Hey, must have been two other guys.'" Of course, it helps to have a husband with a sense of humor.

I turned and Dr. Randall followed. I stopped beneath a ceiling spot and spoke briskly. "I'm Judy Hope. From *Rabbit's Foot*." I wasn't surprised that he looked blank. "We're a new online magazine set to launch next month. Everything's under wraps until we come out with a big announcement next week. We're based in Austin. Top secret."

"*Rabbit's Foot*?" He was trying to wrap his mind around it.

"For luck, you know. Everybody needs a rabbit's foot, especially if they Want to Be in the Know." I can speak in caps with a flourish. "We're launching with a big article on unlocking the world of writers. Your conference has a great reputation. I intend to do an in-depth interview tomorrow with Jay Knox." If that sounded as though I'd spoken to Jay and the interview was set, everyone must interpret what they hear as best they can. "Tonight I'm rounding up personal views of him. Perhaps you can point me to some people here who know him well."

Randall's light blue eyes gleamed with interest. Free positive publicity charms most college administrators. He launched into a detailed description of the English Department and the creative writing section. I was attentive and admiring. He was expansive by the time he pointed out possible sources for me.

As he spoke, I studied them.

Maureen Matthews, Jay Knox's second in command, according to Randall, was a fortyish brunette with a haggard beauty, high cheekbones, a beautifully sculpted jawline. She wasn't engaged in conversation, but instead lingered at the edge of a group, apparently listening.

Liz Baker, a recent graduate, sat at a small table half-hidden in the shadow of a rubber tree. She appeared tense and wary, hands folded into tight fists. Occasionally, she flicked an uncertain glance at her companion. He was young, too, sandy-haired, slender, sullen. He held an almost empty glass in one hand, stared at it. On happier days, Liz Baker would have had a delicate charm, with her thin face and fine features framed by dark brown hair. Her clothes were inexpensive and simple but attractive, a sleeveless white cotton shirtdress with scalloped edges and white sandals, a welcome change from the sea of black on the older women.

Harry Toomey, Deirdre's competition for the faculty job, leaned back in an overstuffed chair. He looked expansive and slightly drunk. Lank brown hair straggled on each side of a moon face with a wispy mustache. He was forty pounds overweight, much of it bulging against a tight pea green polo.

". . . and that's Jay's agent, Cliff Granger, fourth from the end of the bar. I don't see Jay's editor, Jessica Forbes, but I'm sure you can find her tomorrow."

"I definitely will." I started to turn away, then said brightly, "Oh, by the way, I'll do a special inset about the new creative writing teacher. I've asked around and everyone is thrilled. Deirdre Davenport's a marvelous choice."

Randall looked startled, then pleased. He assumed I had learned Jay Knox's choice by talking to him.

I put a finger to my lips. "But hush-hush until tomorrow, right?"

I hurried away. I'd made a start in positioning Deirdre as the de facto appointee. It wasn't a trump card but it might play well when I confronted Jay Knox.

I looked in turn at Maureen Matthews, Liz Baker, and Harry Toomey. Maureen didn't look especially approachable, but she looked highly intelligent, skeptical, and observant.

I chose Maureen.

Chapter 3

Maureen Matthews turned as I spoke to her. "Ms. Matthews, I'm Judy Hope. Dr. Randall suggested I speak to you."

She gazed at me politely, her violet eyes inquiring. She was taller than I, slender and lovely in a rose print linen dress with a bateau neck and a graceful midcalf length. She listened without comment as I described *Rabbit's Foot*. ". . . and if I could visit with you for a moment, I'd be most grateful."

She smiled and nodded, a faculty member dutifully responding to what she saw as the department chair's wish.

We found a small table around the corner from the bar, quiet enough that we could speak comfortably, and ordered wine.

"I suppose"—her tone was casual—"you only focus on the positive aspects of a program."

I lifted my chin, said firmly, "I report what I find, good and bad. Otherwise we would have no credibility."

She nodded and I thought I saw a flicker of a satisfied smile. "Yes, of course. That's understandable. Goddard is extremely fortunate to have someone of Dr. Randall's caliber. He is a superb . . ."

I drew out a notepad from my purse, looked attentive, and made notes. Maureen was extremely positive, as would be expected in speaking of a superior, but I thought her admiration for the department chair was genuine.

". . . and he is always alert to creating a curriculum that addresses what students need to know. That means a great deal to students." She nodded in approval. "Now, how can I help you?"

There was quick intelligence in the depths of her violet eyes. More, there were sensibility and intuitiveness and perception.

I chose my words carefully as I met her gaze. It was as if she drew in my words, arranged them, analyzed them, foresaw possibilities beyond my understanding. ". . . and if you could give me a sense of Jay Knox's character?"

"Jay's character." I heard a slight tremor in her low, soft voice, though her haggard face remained as it had been, quite lovely but clearly a faded beauty.

"Jay is young. Perhaps you can gain a better picture of him from someone nearer in age." She smoothed back a tendril of midnight-dark hair. "I suggest you speak to one of our recent graduates." She paused as if thinking, her glance roaming the area. "I see Liz Baker." She nodded toward the small table a few feet from us.

Liz now sat alone, misery evident in the droop of her narrow face. One hand turned a half-empty glass around and around.

Maureen's face was unreadable. "I believe Jay offered editorial help to Liz." Maureen's voice was uninflected. It was as if she wished to be clear that this was a casual suggestion, possibly helpful, possibly not. "You might talk to her, gain some knowledge about Jay's work with hopeful authors."

"I'll do that. I understand Jay heads up the creative writing section and you work for him."

The hollows deepened in her cheeks. "It would be more accurate to say we both work in the same area." There was coolness in her tone.

"Is he a good teacher?"

She shrugged. "I couldn't say. Jay and I teach our own classes. Students are in a better position to judge professors."

See no evil, hear no evil, speak no evil. She was not only intelligent, she was very, very careful. Yet I sensed an undercurrent of emotion. Did she like Jay, dislike him? Was I imagining this undercurrent?

She gazed at wine that gleamed like gold in the glass. "Excellent Chablis." As if an afterthought, she said, "You might want to talk to Professor Lewis. Ashton Lewis. He has strong opinions about faculty standards." Her voice again was uninflected. Again a flicker of a smile.

She took a last sip of wine, put the glass on the table with finality. "It's been a pleasure, Ms. Hope."

"One last thing," I said hurriedly before she could rise. I offered a conspiratorial smile. "I'm sure you're in the know about the new faculty member in creative writing."

Her lovely face was suddenly still and watchful. Obviously, she had no idea.

I leaned closer, whispered. "Deirdre Davenport appears to be an excellent choice." Would it matter to Jay Knox if he learned that the conference was burbling about Deirdre's expected appointment? It couldn't do any harm.

Maureen's response surprised me. She gave me a sudden, kind smile. "We will all be pleased to welcome Deirdre." With that she rose, and murmured, "Good night."

I came to my feet and looked after her thoughtfully as she walked away.

Maureen moved with grace, the long skirt of her linen dress emphasizing her slenderness.

I puzzled over the fact that her response to Deirdre's supposed selection surprised me. Why? Abruptly, I understood. Her quick, kind welcome for Deirdre was her only unscripted moment. Obviously, Deirdre posed no threat to her. She had no animus toward Deirdre. On the flip side of that understanding was a realization that Maureen had indeed spoken carefully to me and that she had intended to achieve a definite result. She wanted—

A warm sweaty hand gripped my elbow. "Is it true?" The light tenor voice was slurred, the words thick.

I looked into reddened brown eyes on a level with mine. Harry Toomey blinked rapidly. "I heard you talking to Maureen Matthews. Did Jay pick Deirdre?"

Had Harry overheard our conversation? I looked past him to a row of ferns in a waist-high planter. If he heard, he must have followed us to this quiet area. He was well aware Maureen was second in command to Jay. I faced him. His eyes shifted away from my searching gaze. He knew he'd eavesdropped. He knew I knew. Was this habitual with him?

"Actually," I spoke with force, "there's no official announcement—"

"But you're here to write things up." He labored with the sentence. "Did Jay tell you—"

"I haven't spoken to Jay. I simply heard someone say that she would be announced, but we'll have to wait until tomorrow to find out."

Thin lashes fluttered over those red-veined eyes. He turned and walked to the little table where I'd sat with Maureen and slumped onto a chair.

I followed, aghast at what I'd done. It was as if he grew smaller as I watched, round face sagging, eyes stricken, mouth slack, shoulders drooping.

"Mr. Toomey." I sat down opposite him.

He looked at me and his words came in a rush. "Jay told me my book was good." His bleary eyes had the lost and lonely look of a child crying at midnight when no one comes.

Oh my, oh my. "You put your heart into your book." My voice was soft.

"You know who I am?" There was a tiny note of hope in his voice.

I understood his thoughts. Despite several drinks, despite a tongue that couldn't quite enunciate clearly, he was connecting—to him—the dots. I was a writer for a new online magazine. If I included him in the grand piece, this could be his big break. If I featured his book, someone—an agent, a publisher, Hollywood—would knock at his door. Burgeoning eagerness and terrible vulnerability glistened in those bleary eyes.

Any minute coal smoke might envelop me. But there wasn't a Precept forbidding care and comfort for wounded souls. As for hewing to truth—oh, well. That was an ethical concept I would definitely ponder, preferably when aboard the *Serendipity* on a gorgeous day. Beauty is truth, truth beauty, according to John Keats. I would hold to another truth: There is a spark of the divine to be nurtured in all creatures. I set out to nurture.

Leaning forward, I confided in a low voice. "Of course"— warm emphasis—"he said your book was good. That's why the choice will be so difficult. I'm sure if he chooses Deirdre it will likely be based on the number of books she has had published."

"He said"—Harry's voice trembled slightly—"that I had great capacity to grow, and he could use my example to inspire students."

Harry Toomey didn't realize the import of Jay's comment. Jay using Harry as an example of successful self-publishing was an entirely different matter than Jay adding Harry to the faculty because of his success at self-publishing. Had that been the case, Jay would have told Harry, "You will inspire students." I felt a whoosh of relief.

Was I parsing Jay's words too carefully, seeing only the outcome I desired? I didn't think so. Jay might have trouble with his trouser zipper around vulnerable females, and he would use what power he had when he wanted sex, but he had the wit to recognize that his own reputation was enhanced if he surrounded himself with successful professionals.

Anyone on tenure track considers how each and every act will affect that decision. Despite his threats to Deirdre, I felt sure he intended to announce her selection tomorrow.

As soon as the announcement was made, Deirdre could relax, though I'd advise her to always have someone else present when she had occasion to be in Jay's office. I had no doubt she'd handle him with ease. Soon she'd begin a new book and I would report a successful mission.

If Wiggins focused on the moments when I'd appeared, I could point with pride to the Woman in the Powder Room, full of zeal for her book. As for the fellow at the bar, surely Wiggins would spot me one mishap. And this interlude with Harry Toomey certainly was evidence that I could spread solace with élan. I'd be meticulous before I boarded the Rescue Express and inform Harry of the shocking news of *Rabbit's Foot*'s demise but assure him that I'd greatly enjoyed hearing about his book.

Harry was scrabbling in a book bag. He pulled out a book, thrust it at me. "Here's my book. It's a trade paperback. What do you think of the cover?"

I glanced down at a garish orange cover. The title straggled in a slant down the page, letters in alternate colors: purple, pink, cerise, juniper, taupe . . . *Grabbed* by Harry Toomey.

"Hey"—he was pumped—"doesn't the title *grab* you?" The man was besotted with his own cleverness. "Here, I'll read the first paragraph." He pulled out another copy, flipped the book open. "'Jenkins jumped. But the kick caught him in the gut. Arrgh. Down he went. The years flashed through his mind. When he was four. That hand that grabbed the feather, took it away, dripping blood . . .'"

Startled, I asked, "The feather dripped blood?"

He blinked, his rhythm broken. "It was the hand."

"Of course. And so impressive when read by the author. More feeling. But that's all I want to hear. I must read *Grabbed* for the full effect." I clasped the book to my chest (that would probably be *bosom* in a historical romance, but I refused to succumb to the environment) and quickly stood.

He stumbled to his feet. "But I want to tell you all about the book."

I didn't doubt his intent. "That would be wonderful, but I have several more appointments."

Once again his too-warm, moist hand caught my arm. His voice was less thick. "You said you heard someone say it was Deirdre. Who?"

I gently but firmly removed his hand. "It was one of those conversations. I can't sort them all out now. A while ago."

His face folded in thought. "Jay told me my book was good. I was sure that meant he'd chosen me. If I were on the faculty, I know an agent would look at my book, take it, find a publisher who'd see how wonderful it is. I'm not going to believe he picked Deirdre unless he tells me. He owes me that much if everybody's talking about Deirdre getting the job." Harry turned away, moved past me, walking with caution but with obvious determination.

I watched as he reached the patio door. I was sure he intended to go and see Jay Knox. I hoped Wiggins never thought to add a Precept about unintended consequences. But Harry wouldn't change Jay's decision. And if Jay wondered that the word was out, that might be all for the good.

The crowd had thinned. There were even some empty

stools, but the noise was up several decibels. I didn't see Dr. Randall. Cliff Granger raised his glass, downed the rest of the contents, swung off the bar stool, moved toward the archway.

Most of the revelers were middle-aged, a lot of women in black tops and pants. I didn't see many youthful faces. The slender student, the one with whom Jay Knox had spent quite a bit of time according to Maureen Matthews, the one who'd sat miserably with a sullen escort but was now alone, came to her feet. She took a deep breath and hurried toward the exit.

I didn't follow Liz. I was certain I'd correctly guessed Jay Knox's decision. He was going to appoint Deirdre. He might be angry that she'd pushed him away tonight, but he wouldn't jeopardize his standing in the department by appointing Harry. In fact, I imagined he'd only included Harry as a presumed finalist in order to have some leverage with Deirdre. In any event, Jay was likely involved right this moment in a conversation with Harry Toomey. I congratulated myself. I'd done good work tonight in discovering that Jay Knox would name Deirdre because she was the candidate with publishing credits.

I strolled to the ladies' room. The powder room was unoccupied. As I disappeared, I didn't know when I had felt more carefree. Tomorrow would see Deirdre announced as a new faculty member. After appropriate celebration, I would see what inspiring thoughts I might share with Deirdre. Shoulder to the wheel. Keep on keepin' on. Write *what if* on a sheet of paper and let ideas surge. Once she began to write, the Rescue Express would swoop through the sky and I would swing aboard.

Until then . . .

I popped from spot to spot, peeking in on those dear to me.

My daughter, Dil, looked comfortable in silky blue pajamas. She was smiling as she read. But it was strange to me to see her red hair streaked with silver and her face touched by age.

I glanced at the title: *Secret of the Scarlet Macaw* by Deirdre Davenport. Definitely a good omen.

Suddenly Dil peered over the top of the book, sniffing. "Mike, do you smell perfume?"

Her husband lowered his newspaper, looked puzzled.

Dil flashed a quick smile. "Just my imagination. I thought I smelled a fragrance that Mother loved, a light gardenia."

I found my son, Rob, in his workshop, even though now it was near midnight. He'd always loved working with wood. His pale reddish hair was also flecked with silver. He looked intent, content. There was a plaque on the wall, which I was sure he'd made, a quote from Lao Tzu:

> *If you are depressed, you are living in the past.*
> *If you are anxious, you are living in the future.*
> *If you are at peace, you are living in the*
> *   present.*

I touched my fingers to my lips, blew a light kiss.

Rob lifted his head and a sudden sweet smile touched his face. He bent back to work, humming "Rock and Roll Music," which I always sang with gusto when stirring up brownies.

∽

I made a last survey of Silver Lake Lodge. I was visited by a sudden inspiration. In the powder room, empty at this late hour, I appeared. I hurried into the lobby, found a house telephone. "Cabin five, please."

The phone rang several times. I was a little surprised Jay didn't answer. He had been emphatic that he intended to remain in the cabin and await Deirdre's arrival. Perhaps he'd given up, wandered into the gardens, taken a stroll down to the pier. I decided to leave a message. "The buzz is out that you selected Deirdre Davenport. You'll be pleased that Dr. Randall is absolutely delighted. Your choice reflects the mature judgment"—if Jay assumed this sentiment came from Dr. Randall, why, it simply illustrated how easy it is for anyone to jump to conclusions. It was my own observation   "expected from a candidate for tenure. It would be a shame"—this was a warning to Jay—"if you disappoint him." I hung up.

This corner of the lobby was empty. I disappeared.

Windows in the two wings of Silver Lake Lodge were mostly dark. I made a circuit of the cabins. Though the curtains were tightly drawn, a thin streak of light seeped from the edges in cabin 5.

I wondered if Jay Knox had listened to my message.

Perhaps I'd find out tomorrow.

∽

I arranged the bolster on the bed just so. The room gave no hint that I had occupied it last night. I took a final glance in the mirror. Perhaps my ensemble would inspire some of the women attired in black—a hip-length, bateau-necked Italian silk blouse brilliant with red, orange, and indigo blocks. Picture a macaw. Add indigo slim-legged cropped pants and orange sandals. Bright, bright, bright.

Breakfast was served on the patio. Many tables were filled. Women in black engaged in intense conversations over bacon and eggs. ". . . only a thousand-dollar advance . . . but I've already had six hundred and eleven hits. . . . They promise to send e-mails to ten thousand book clubs. . . . was one of those unsigned reviews . . . Men always get more money. . . . told me no dead monkeys . . ."

Deirdre sat alone at a table for four near a goldfish pond. She appeared pale and worn, her angular face drawn in a tight frown. She looked as doomed as a poker player holding nothing higher than a ten.

I slipped into the chair next to her, gave her a bright smile. "I always told my kids, long faces make dreary places."

Without warning, she reached out, poked me. "You again."

"I'll be gone soon. Everything's working out." I beamed at her.

Deirdre looked like a castaway on an atoll with no ships on the horizon. She stared down at her plate, jabbed a fork into scrambled eggs, but made no effort to eat.

I didn't understand the gloom. "My dear, I have everything under control." I felt puffed by understandable pride. "You will be announced as the new faculty member by Jay this morning."

"Jay's going to announce me? But he can't." She stared at me, her face incredulous.

I was startled by her response. "I'm sure—" I looked across the patio at two men whom I knew and broke off in midsentence, tried to catch my breath.

Adelaide Police Chief Sam Cobb was just as I remembered him, a large powerfully built man with a thatch of graying dark hair, a strong face. He wore his usual baggy brown suit. At his elbow was Detective Sergeant Hal Price, white-blond hair, brilliant blue eyes, crisp blue shirt, khaki trousers, tall, lean, ruggedly handsome.

Sam listened to a small man who scurried along beside them talking fast, gesturing wildly. Hal's gaze automatically ranged around the terrace, a police officer attuned always to his surroundings. Abruptly, he stopped short and stared across the terrace.

At me.

We'd had several encounters. My heart belongs to Bobby Mac, but that doesn't mean I am oblivious to an attractive male. In a purely academic fashion, of course. Just as I wouldn't expect Bobby Mac to pass Ava Gardner on a beach and not notice. In a purely academic fashion, of course. If Ava was before your time—trust me, no man ever averted his gaze.

It wasn't my aim to entrance Hal, although his admiration was sweet. In fact, I hoped that Hal would find a winsome young woman who would win his heart. I would be the first to raise a toast.

Hal still stood and stared.

Sam Cobb stopped and looked over his shoulder, frowning.

A waiter with a tray walked between me and Hal.

I disappeared.

"Will you please stop doing that?" Deirdre unsteadily

returned her coffee cup to the table. "Here, not here, here, not here. Make up your mind."

"I'll explain later."

In an instant, I stood at Sam's shoulder, caught a scent of woody cologne.

"You spot something, Hal?" Sam looked inquiring and slightly impatient.

Hal stared for a long moment at the table now apparently occupied only by Deirdre, then started forward. "I thought I saw"—he paused, dropped his voice—"that redhead. The one who comes and goes."

Sam gave him a sharp look. "Officer Loy?" Sam sounded both incredulous and eager.

"I looked across the patio and there was a woman sitting with a redhead. The woman"—there was a change in his tone—"very attractive, now seems to be sitting by herself, but I could swear I saw a redhead." His voice dropped lower. "The redhead looked like Loy."

I had occasion in the past to appear as Officer M. Loy in one of those fetching French blue uniforms. The dark stripe down the side of each trouser leg adds flair. The name was a tribute to Myrna Loy, famed for her role as Nora Charles to William Powell's Nick. Dashiell Hammett's Nick and Nora were immortalized in *The Thin Man*.

Sam was on full alert. "Go find her."

Hal slowly shook his head. "She was gone when I looked again. There wasn't time for her to have walked away." Hal kept his voice even.

Sam gave a slight shake of his head. "I get you. If she's gone, she's gone. Let's get out to that cabin, see what we find."

Their escort walked beside Sam, his words coming in short bursts. "I haven't been there yet. I called nine-one-one as soon as housekeeping told me. One of our sharper old gals saw the front door open to cabin five. She heard the air-conditioning running, so she went up on the porch to see if anyone was around. She looked inside and said there was a man lying on the floor. She said she thought he was dead and it looked like somebody clobbered him. The unit's occupied by Jay Knox, he's the guy running a conference here this week. The lodge belongs to his uncle, Walt." The path wound among clumps of honeysuckle and weeping willows that fronted several cabins.

The men came around a bend. A middle-aged woman huddled in the shade of a willow, determinedly not looking toward the steps to cabin 5. A cleaning cart was parked in front of the cabin. The maid held a duster in one hand. The other plucked at feathers, and a little pile lay on the ground by her feet.

A young woman with pale blond hair in tight ringlets strode to meet Sam and Hal. She was trim in the Adelaide police uniform. Her name tag read: *Officer S. Anderson.* "I've called for the ME. Nobody's been inside but the maid." She yanked a thumb toward the open door. "She said—"

Sam held up a broad, callused hand. "We'll talk to her. I'll take a look."

I was already inside. The overhead light blazed. The curtains were still drawn. I imagined the light had shone all night, but the only occupant of the room would never have noticed.

Jay Knox lay on his right side on the floor near the coffee

table in front of the sofa. A huge purplish blue patch discolored his left temple. That was the only sign of injury. No blood, just that uneven dark blotch.

Sam and Hal stood in the doorway. Sam's heavy face was somber. No matter what he had seen as a police officer, his expression made it clear that murder sickened him. Life was too fragile, too precious to be deliberately destroyed.

Hal understood that moment of quiet, waited to speak until Sam turned toward him. "I'd say he was caught by surprise." Hal peered down at Jay. "No bruises on his hands. No signs of scratches."

Sam studied the wound. "It would take a pretty heavy weapon to make that mark, something smooth, rounded." Sam didn't step closer for a better view. He wouldn't approach the body until death was officially declared by the medical examiner. For now, his brown eyes moved carefully from left to right. The movement of his head stopped. In a quick motion, he pulled a small flashlight from his shirt pocket, one of those tiny ones with a laser beam. He turned on the bright light, pointed the beam toward a shadowy patch at the base of the television cabinet.

The beam illuminated a champagne bottle lying on the floor. "I thought I saw something." Sam looked from the bottle to the body. "If somebody grabbed that bottle by the neck and swung, it's as good a weapon as a two-by-four."

"Right." Hal gazed around the living room. "Nothing appears to be out of order. Furniture's upright. No signs of disarray." He walked to each window, returned. "No sign of a break-in."

"I'd say he wasn't expecting trouble." Sam's brown eyes

studied the coffee table. "Maybe he had a visitor who said something like, 'How about a drink before I go?' and picked up the bottle. The glasses are on the coffee table. Maybe he—or she—held the bottle by the neck. Pow."

Hal's bright blue eyes gleamed. "It could have happened that way. The visitor walked up to him, holding the bottle by the neck, and made a quick pivot, full force behind the swing, the barrel of the bottle hitting the left temple." He looked down at Jay. "A hard blow there ruptures the temporal artery. Quick. Deadly."

"Think you can do my job?" The tenor voice behind Sam and Hal was cocky.

The two men moved aside for Jacob Brandt, the brash young medical examiner who was smart, quick, and flip. His Flaming Lips tee was too big, his age-whitened jeans had a hole in one knee, but his eyes were appraising as he looked at the body. The physical investigation of the scene couldn't begin until he certified death.

He pulled a pair of crumpled plastic gloves from a pocket, knelt by Jay. He slid on the gloves, touched a bare arm. "Rigor mortis well advanced. Dead eight to ten hours. From appearances, looks like blunt trauma. I'll tell you more after the autopsy." He popped to his feet, yanked off the gloves, stuffed them in a pocket. "Have at it, guys. Got to get to the morgue." For once his face looked bleak. "Happens every summer. Somebody loses track of a toddler. Pool in the backyard. God, you'd think they'd learn." He turned and strode away, head down, face drawn tight.

A careful investigation began, officers measuring, photographing, searching. I recognized Judy Weitz, a self-effacing yet impressive detective. She knelt, took a close-up of the body with a video cam. Slowly she rose, took one step back, filmed, took another step, filmed. When she could move no farther, she would have the body in the context of the room, its position clear, every piece of furniture and all visible objects recorded in specific relationship to the body.

Sam stood in the doorway with the overwhelmed hotel employee. I guessed he was the manager.

The man pulled at the neck of his shirt, looked queasy.

Sam pointed at the body, likely seeking formal identification.

But I was focused on two items. Each posed possibly horrific problems for Deirdre Davenport.

The champagne bottle lying in the shadow of the television set was almost certainly the same bottle that Deirdre grabbed by the neck and thrust at Jay last night in her room. I glanced at the glasses, sparkling in the morning sunshine streaming through a window. Deirdre had also picked up the glasses. The bottle and the glasses would be fingerprinted. Jay's fingerprints and unknown prints that belonged to Deirdre would be lifted and preserved.

If there came a reason for the police to request her fingerprints, the match would be made. Sharp, probing questions would follow. When did you hold the bottle? What was your relationship to Mr. Knox? Had you and Mr. Knox quarreled?

Unfortunately, I foresaw a reason the police would go to Deirdre. I looked at the telephone sitting at the end of a wet bar. The red message light blinked, blinked, blinked. Now I knew the answer to my casual interest in whether Jay got my message. He had not. But that message was a place for an investigator to start. Sam Cobb would want to know all about Deirdre. It wouldn't take long to discover she was vying for a job, that she desperately needed a job. How much longer would it take Sam to determine Deirdre's whereabouts last night? Had anyone seen Jay carrying the champagne bottle, walking toward her room?

I hovered over the phone with its incessant blinking red light. I looked at Sam. He was facing the wet bar. Sam was talking to the hotel clerk, but Sam was always aware of his surroundings. He was also watching the investigation unfold. He would see a telephone receiver rising in the air of its own accord. But there would be a phone in the bedroom.

I was at the bedside table. I lifted the receiver—

"Hey." The voice was deep, commanding.

Startled, I dropped the receiver. It clattered on the bedside table, plummeted over the side, hung dangling a few inches above the floor.

Hal Price crossed the room in three long strides. He fished a handkerchief out of his pocket, gingerly lifted the receiver. In an instant, he was punching buttons. He listened, and I knew he was committing to memory the message I'd left for Jay.

Why had I not remembered Precept Five? Of course, I rationalized, I hadn't intended to confound Jay with the message. Oh drat. Honesty compels me to admit I definitely intended to confound Jay. I was trying to make certain he selected Deirdre. I wanted to warn Jay: *Watch out, buddy, you're boxed in. Dr. Randall expects Deirdre Davenport to be selected.*

Instead the message was going to embroil Deirdre in a murder investigation. And her fingerprints were on the champagne bottle. . . .

Hal punched *speakerphone*.

I heard my voice. I must admit it's rather distinctive, low and husky.

Sam was in the doorway, looking sharply around.

Hal pointed at the phone. "A message left at 11:28 p.m." He played the message.

Sam's expression was hard to decipher. "Sure sounds like her."

I knew he meant Officer Loy.

Hal nodded. "Yeah. Uh, Sam? When I came in the bedroom, the receiver was kind of like, up in the air."

Sam nodded. "When we finish here, see what you can find out about this Deirdre. Check the front desk, see if she's a guest. When you're out and about, keep an eye peeled for *her*." He didn't have to specify. I knew Hal would definitely be on the lookout for me.

Hal replaced the receiver, turned to go.

Judy Weitz entered the bedroom, her gaze roaming from the side table to the beds to the chest. "Chief, I've checked the victim's pockets. No cell. We didn't find a cell phone anywhere in the living room. How about in here?"

Sam's eyes were intent. "Good thinking, Judy. Everybody has a cell. Check in here—drawers, floor, everywhere, then scour that room again. Let me know."

Outside, a crowd was gathering. It was already hot, the scent of fresh-mown grass hanging in the air, the smell intensified by the heat of blazing sunlight, a summer day in

Adelaide. Onlookers stood in the shadow of white oaks and a gnarled magnolia. Voices were subdued, but the watching eyes were excited. An officer looped crime-scene tape around a stanchion, moved to stick another metal pole in the ground.

Rapid footsteps clattered on the sidewalk. Maureen Matthews hurried around the bend. She was dressed for the conference, a silk blouse with a delicate crochet at the throat and a long, slim skirt, both in sunrise pink. She stopped at the turnoff to cabin 5, her way barred by the tape, and looked at a burly officer. "What's happened?"

"Sorry, ma'am. Crime scene."

"Crime?" Maureen looked past the balding, red-faced officer. She took a deep, uneven breath, forced out the words. "Who . . . ?" She lifted a hand to her throat.

"Sorry, ma—"

Maureen broke in. "I have to know if something's happened. That cabin . . . Jay Knox should be there." Her voice was shaky. She stared at the open door of cabin 5. "Professor Knox is scheduled to speak at ten o'clock."

The officer reached up, flicked a switch to the mic clipped to his shirt pocket. "Chief, lady out here says she has to know about the occupant of the cabin. He was expected to speak at some program."

Maureen stared at the officer, pressed her fingers against her cheeks, began to tremble.

℘

Her slender hands planted on the windowsill, Deirdre stared down at passing blue uniforms and at clumps of interested watchers. The sunlight was unsparing to Deirdre, her expression drawn, her eyes sunken.

I felt a wrench inside. I didn't have to ask. The hollowness in her eyes meant she knew the reason for the gathering below. She knew Jay Knox was dead. That was why I'd shocked her when I said he would announce her selection today. I grasped at a straw. Maybe she'd talked to someone, been told that Jay Knox was dead.

But I blurted out sharply, "How did you know?"

She jumped, looked wildly about. "That's all I need—a voice out of nowhere, a voice of doom. But hey, things can't get any worse. Are you here or in my head? I don't know that it matters. All I know is I am dumb and I am in big trouble. I should have called the police." She turned away from the window, walked to the sofa, and dropped in one corner, clapped her hands over her eyes. "Come out, come out, wherever you are. If you have handcuffs, I won't be surprised."

I swirled present, enjoyed the flash of colors in the mirror on the wall. I took an instant to admire my blouse, then I settled on the sofa beside her.

She reached out to touch me, flinched. "The voice. Then you come. Maybe I can just tell the police I'm nuts. Maybe I am nuts."

"Why should you have called the police?"

She rubbed knuckles along a suddenly quivering chin. "I went to the cabin last night. It was awful, Jay lying so still with that awful bluish mark on his face. I looked and looked but he wasn't breathing. Nothing. His chest was still. I knew he was dead." A ragged breath. "I was in school with his big sister. Cathy thought he was magic, and maybe he was as a little kid. None of them knew how he bullied people. He could be an ass, but everybody said, 'Oh Jay, he's such a kid. But so much fun. So handsome. So smart.' He was dead. On the floor. I thought I was going to be sick. Then I realized what it might look like, my being there. I thought about my kids and what the police might think and I turned and ran. I should have called the police. I've always told my kids, 'Do the right thing and you'll be all right.'"

First things first. "Did anyone see you at the cabin?"

"I don't think so. But probably somebody was lurking in a bush and the cops are on their way up here right now."

The cops would be here soon enough.

"Anyway, I should have called the police. If they'd known sooner"—her voice was small—"maybe they would've caught whoever"—she took a breath—"hurt him."

I shook my head. "I'm sure it wouldn't have made a difference. But you will need to be ready for the police."

"Maybe no one noticed me." She looked brighter. "And I don't know anything that would help. Maybe I'll be okay."

"I'm afraid not." I was regretful. "Surely you saw the weapon?"

Her blank look was my answer.

"The champagne bottle."

I watched the words register, her eyes widening, her lips parting.

"Oh no." She sagged against the sofa. "I didn't think it could get worse. This is worse. Much worse. Are you telling me Jay was hit with the champagne bottle?"

"It hasn't been proven yet, but the bottle was lying on the floor a few feet away from the body. The police will check the bottle against the wound, but right now the assumption is that the bottle was the weapon."

"The bottle that I picked up." Deirdre's hand touched her throat. "That tears it."

Her fingerprints on the weapon was bad news, but even worse was the fact that Deirdre had gone to the cabin. If that was discovered, she would become a serious suspect. Her presence at a murder scene had to be dealt with.

Deirdre spoke through stiff lips. "What am I going to do?"

"Tell me exactly what you did last night."

Deirdre jammed her hands together, looked both defensive and beseeching. "I was upset. I couldn't relax. I kept thinking about Jay and tomorrow and the job and I finally decided I was going to have it out with him. I got dressed. I decided at that point I didn't have anything to lose by talking to him."

If only I had returned to Deirdre's room last night. I had no doubt she'd intended simply to talk to Jay, but leaving her room to go to his cabin wouldn't look good to the police.

Deirdre was somber. "I wish I'd gone sooner. Maybe whoever killed him would have been scared off."

"I think it is better you weren't there any earlier." I kept my tone mild. A murderer would not have been diverted by Deirdre's arrival, and she might well have put herself in danger. "What time did you go?"

"About eleven."

"Did anyone see you leave your room?" I suspected I already knew the answer. It might have been eleven p.m., but attendees at conferences don't roll up the sidewalks at nine.

Her expression was resigned. "Oh, sure. Before I got halfway down the hall, two doors opened. Almost everyone in the place is here for the conference. A tiny little woman darted out, said she was thrilled to meet me and if I just had the teeniest minute she had a copy of her manuscript in her room. I told her I was sorry but I was on my way to meet with Professor Knox—"

I pictured handcuffs.

"—and I got away from her. That worked, so I told the second woman the same thing."

I could imagine Sam Cobb's skeptical reaction. A lone woman going to a man's cabin at a late hour suggested more than a chat. But what was done was done. "Did you go straight to the cabin?"

"Yes." Deirdre nodded, her eyes dark with memory.

"Did you see—"

A tinny voice blared. "All hotel guests and staff—"

The announcement, with attendant buzzes and rattles, issued from a grille above the bed.

"—are asked by the Adelaide Police Department to proceed to the main auditorium immediately. Repeat, all hotel guests and—"

Chapter 4

The auditorium was housed in a one-story structure east of the gardens and cabins. A signpost pointed the way from the main path. Women in black and an occasional male in brighter colors streamed through the doors. High, excited chatter in the auditorium sounded like starlings stirring in treetops.

I hovered on high.

Dr. Randall stood by the steps at the foot of stage left. White head bent, face somber, he appeared to be in deep conversation with Chief Cobb. Maureen Matthews watched and listened. She was pale, her haggard beauty drained. Last night Maureen had delicately, blandly pointed me toward Liz Baker and Professor Ashton Lewis to gain information about Jay's character. I felt sure she had done so with malice aforethought, which suggested the young woman or Jay's colleague had reason to dislike him and Maureen harbored a grudge of some kind.

I estimated the audience, which half filled the auditorium, at about 125. Several rows from the back, Cliff Granger's smooth face seemed curiously untouched by the circumstances. I saw no evidence of sadness or even dismay. Yet he must have known Jay well. But perhaps the relationship was solely business. Next to him, Jessica Forbes gazed steadily at the stage, a woman who appeared in complete command of herself, poised to deal with whatever happened. Her expression was serious, as befitted the circumstances, but again there was no evidence of personal distress.

Harry Toomey was two rows behind them. He wriggled, as if unable to relax. His right knee jounced, jounced, jounced. One hand scrabbled at his indeterminate mustache.

Last night Liz Baker had sat in the shadows with a sullen companion. This morning she huddled in a seat, slid a nervous glance at the sandy-haired man beside her. She again wore a dress. Instead of the sleeveless white of last night, she wore a navy knit with a placket at the throat and short sleeves. Her companion looked grim, but it wasn't the grimness of bereavement. The thin, tight line of his mouth indicated anger. She looked tense, perhaps frightened. What had been their connection to Jay Knox? Or was the connection only to her?

Did one of these people know the truth of Jay's death? Or was his murderer a conference attendee unknown to me?

I linked his murder to the conference because his death occurred at Silver Lake Lodge, not at his home. The use of the champagne bottle as a weapon suggested immediacy, some trigger that dictated murder at that particular moment.

I thought about Jay and what this day should have held for him. He was scheduled to announce his choice for the new faculty position. He had clients, writers whose manuscripts he promised to connect with an agent or editor.

And there was Deirdre.

Deirdre sat stiffly in an aisle seat in the fourth row from the back. She was especially attractive in a printed patchwork dress with alternate white and black patterned squares. She was thin enough that the dress flattered her. Her frizzy hair, a rich mahogany, was drawn back in a ponytail. Her long, expressive face had an appeal of openness, spontaneity, intelligence, but, at the moment, her eyes looked huge and she watched the stage with a look of uneasiness.

The crowd began to shush. There was a sense of expectancy and an underlying frisson of nervousness overlain with quivering morbidity. Obviously rumors had spread, flourished. The attendees knew a man had been killed in cabin 5 and many likely knew the victim was Jay Knox.

The department chair mounted the steps, walked to the podium. Chief Cobb, solid and muscular, followed. Professor Matthews was a step behind, her face empty, one hand holding tight to the long loop of a gold chain necklace.

Dr. Randall gripped the sides of the speaker's stand. His florid face was grave. "Ladies and gentlemen, I am Gilbert Randall, chair of the English Department. It is my unpleasant duty to inform you that Professor Jay Knox, director of the conference and assistant professor of English, has been the victim of foul play. After consultation with the police and with Professor Matthews, the decision has been made to proceed with the program. As the police will explain, Professor Knox's death does not appear to be the result of robbery or a random attack, which reassures us that our conference attendees are not in danger. Adelaide Police Chief Sam Cobb will explain the investigation." He stepped back, nodded at Sam.

Bulky and powerful, Sam strode to the podium, looked out at the quiet audience.

I hoped Adelaide's citizenry appreciated Chief Sam Cobb. Despite the wrinkles in his brown suit, he was a man anyone would notice and judge important, not as the world so often judges, by surface charm or fineness of raiment, but by his presence—confident, commanding, stalwart. His broad face was calm and thoughtful. Big and sturdy, he radiated the right kind of power, that of a man who lived the creed of the Old West: A man's word is his bond. In another day, he would have pushed through the doors of the saloon to face the outlaw, ready for confrontation, ready for danger.

Sam's voice was deep and resonant. "Thank you for your attendance this morning. I am Sam Cobb, chief of the Adelaide Police Department. We informed Dr. Randall that this crime does not appear to be the result of theft, nor does it appear to be random. From the circumstances surrounding the crime, we believe the victim, Jay Knox, likely knew his attacker. Mr. Knox died last night as a result of blunt trauma to the head. We have no reason to believe that anyone in the hotel is in any danger of attack and those of you attending the conference should feel confident of your safety.

"Since it is likely that Mr. Knox knew his attacker, we are interested in information about Mr. Knox and anyone seen with him at any point yesterday. We look forward to your assistance. If you have information about Jay Knox or who might have committed the crime, please come to conference room A at the close of this announcement.

"As for the details as we now know them, housekeeping notified the manager at ten minutes after nine this morning that a man was dead in cabin five and his death appeared to be murder. Police were summoned. The victim was formally identified as Professor Jay Knox. The medical examiner estimates that death occurred last night between ten p.m. and midnight. The cause of death was blunt trauma. We are seeking information about a bottle of champagne—"

Deirdre's slender shoulders hunched.

I must speak to her about body language. But I understood her reaction. Public mention of the champagne bottle would soon set the police on a trail that led directly to her. When unidentified prints were found on the bottle in addition to Jay's, she'd pop up as suspect number one.

"—found at the crime scene. There is no evidence a break-in occurred at cabin five. This leads investigators to conclude that Professor Knox's attacker was permitted to enter the cabin and that his guest was very likely attending the conference. No hotel staff was summoned to the cabin during that time period or had any reason to be in the cabin. Professor Knox's personal belongings did not appear to have been searched. His billfold was lying on a chest in the bedroom. The billfold contained money, credit cards, and other personal identification. Anyone with information about . . ."

I dropped down beside Deirdre, whispered, "It will be better if you go to the police to mention the champagne bottle."

Deirdre said hotly, "Don't surprise me like this."

A woman in the next row turned, a finger at her lips. Slowly her face changed from censure to bafflement as she saw the empty seats near Deirdre. "Who were you talking to?"

I think it gave Deirdre great pleasure to appear surprised. "Me? Talking? What on earth gave you that idea?"

I waited until the puzzled face turned away, and whispered lightly but firmly, "Go to conference room A. You have to explain the champagne bottle."

She looked despairing. "What am I going to tell them?"

I thought fast. "Tell them he offered the champagne to celebrate your selection for the job. You write fiction. It's time to produce."

❧

Conference room A was quite a bit more cheerful than the interrogation rooms at the police department. Instead of dingy beige walls and a scuffed linoleum floor, this room was mellow, with pale ivory walls and golden parquet flooring that had been buffed to a high shine. Windows overlooked the garden.

Chief Cobb sat behind a small table. Detective Judy Weitz was at his right with a recorder. Detective Weitz always looked professional, her broad face impassive. She still needed a makeover, with billowy brown hair just this side of frowsy and an unadorned, unflattering white blouse, but her blue eyes were perceptive. It would be a mistake to underestimate her.

Deirdre sat in a straight wooden chair pulled to face the table. A shaft of sunlight turned the reddish glints in her hair to streaks of flame. In our short acquaintance, I had never seen her look so appealing. Her face was too long, the line of her jaw too strong for conventional beauty. Instead of softness, there was intelligence, eagerness, and honesty. You could picture her climbing a narrow trail, hitting a tennis ball with a strong forehand, dancing the night away, turning with a beguiling smile to a man . . .

Oh.

At this moment there was no trace of the uncertainty and stress she'd exhibited this morning with me.

Deirdre's gaze slid toward the windows, once, twice, three times, stayed there.

Hal Price stood with his back to a window, hands loose at his sides. His white-blond hair gleamed like a Viking helmet in the sunlight. His dark blue eyes never left Deirdre's face, a man glimpsing a dream, a man responding to unheard music, a man whose heart and mind sensed a haven for now and tomorrow and always.

The cynics would laugh, the realists dismiss, the sophisticates ignore. Love at first sight? A romantic fantasy. But I was watching the immediate attraction between a man and a woman, two strangers looking at each other and somehow knowing this could be the beginning of magic.

"Ms. Davenport?" Sam Cobb's voice was impatient.

Deirdre slowly turned, looked at Sam. "Oh yes." Her tone was vague.

Sam's face was expressionless, neither welcoming nor hostile. "You're Deirdre Davenport." He'd planned to talk to Deirdre because of the message I'd left on Jay's phone. "You have something to tell us?" He was intensely interested in the fact that she had approached the police before she was summoned. Perhaps he wondered if she expected to be interrogated, hoped to give an impression of innocence by contacting them.

Deirdre nodded. "Yes, sir. It's about the champagne bottle. Or at least about a champagne bottle Jay was carrying when he came to my room last night."

"He came to your room?" Sam's gaze never left her face.

A faint flush touched Deirdre's cheeks. She lifted her chin. "Yes." Her tone was clipped. "It was about ten. I wasn't expecting him. He said he thought we should celebrate and he put two glasses and the bottle on the coffee table. Before he could explain—I was sure he meant I'd been chosen for the new faculty spot—a conference attendee knocked and she wanted to talk about her book. Jay understood I needed to visit with her, so I handed the bottle and the glasses to him and he left."

Judy Weitz's level stare was skeptical.

Hal Price, his blue eyes dazed, his strong square face open and direct, said admiringly, "That was awfully good of you to see the attendee after hours."

Deirdre gave him a grateful, enchanted glance. "Since I'm a presenter at the conference, it's part of my job to encourage—"

Sam cleared his throat. "Name of the writer?" He wanted a witness to confirm her story. Unfortunately, that witness couldn't come forward. Instead, the police would soon be hearing from people who saw Jay at her door, then saw him leave, his face tight with anger. And there would be the woman who stopped Deirdre in the hall. That witness would explain that Deirdre begged off talking to her because she was on her way to meet with Jay. The evidence linking Deirdre to Jay would continue to mount.

Deirdre jerked her gaze away from Hal. She hesitated, said slowly, tentatively, "She said her name was Judy Hope."

Sam jerked his head toward Detective Weitz, who made a note. Sam would be doubly interested when a check revealed no one of that name registered for the conference or was staying in the hotel.

"Good job," I whispered to Deirdre.

Her body tightened, then she forced herself to relax. She didn't look around for me and continued in a fairly strong voice, "I didn't remember meeting her during the day but I must have. Otherwise, she wouldn't have said I'd promised to see her, would she?" Her tone was bright. "Anyway, there she was. This really attractive redhead—"

Deirdre had no choice but to describe me.

The chief's eyes glinted. Hal's eyebrows rose.

"—really cute and lively, green eyes, lots of curls, freckles, moves quickly—"

Sam looked at Hal, jerked a thumb toward the door. Sam didn't have to say a word. Hal knew what he meant. Check the register for Judy Hope.

Deirdre took a deep breath. "But I saw Jay again. He called and asked me to come to the cabin to celebrate—"

This was the tricky part, Deirdre's visit to cabin 5. I hoped she was convincing.

"—and I agreed. I suppose it took me five minutes or so to walk there. I knocked. Jay offered me some champagne but I refused. We spoke for a few minutes and I was really happy to know I was going to be named to the faculty. I thanked him, said good night, and came back to my room."

The chief slowly nodded.

My heart sank. I don't think he believed her.

"Did you see anyone near cabin five?"

Deirdre was abruptly much more convincing. "Not a soul. It was really quiet. I didn't see anyone. Or"—she gave a small shrug—"if I did, I didn't notice. I was thinking about the good news."

"Right." Sam nodded. "Thank you for coming to see us, Ms. Davenport."

When Deirdre reached the door, he spoke again, his voice heavy. "If you remember anything else, come and see us."

In the hallway, Deirdre walked fast toward the lobby.

I didn't need to look at her face to know she was scared. I was terribly afraid she had good reason to be scared.

∽

I studied the day's schedule on a placard placed on an easel in the lobby.

> *10:00 a.m. Opening session—Director Jay Knox, main auditorium*
>
> *11:00 a.m. "Knock 'em Dead with a Killer Beginning"—Featured speaker Deirdre Davenport, main auditorium*
>
> *11:00 a.m. "Be Authentic"—Maureen Matthews, conference rooms B and C*

Noon. Break for lunch

1:00 p.m. "An Editor's Heads-up"—Featured speaker Jessica Forbes, main auditorium

1:00 p.m. "Truth, Not Spin"—Professor Ashton Lewis, conference rooms B and C

2:00 to 4:00 p.m. Prescheduled appointments:

> *Conference room A. "E-book Magic"—
> John Kelly
> Conference room B. "Pitch Your Novel to
> an Agent"—Cliff Granger
> Conference room C. "Marketing Your
> Book"— Pam Fisher*

6:00 p.m. Cocktails on the terrace

7:00 p.m. Barbecue buffet on the terrace

The placard was low-tech. Modern hotels run more to electronic boards with a continuous feed of information on activities. Conference room A had been scratched out and D substituted.

Attendees once again streamed toward the terrace. The ten o'clock session would begin soon with, I assumed, Maureen Matthews taking over for Jay. Hal Price was on the auditorium steps, scanning those entering. If he was looking for a redhead, he was going to be disappointed.

I went inside, hovered above those settling into seats. I looked for Liz Baker and her companion and Harry Toomey. I spotted Liz talking to a genial-looking older woman. Liz was now unaccompanied but she still looked stressed. I was thorough in my search. Harry Toomey was not in the auditorium.

I waited long enough to hear Maureen Matthews announce Deirdre as the new faculty member. "We are excited to welcome Deirdre Davenport, a wonderful writer who will join our faculty this fall. She will be a great asset to the department. It would be my pleasure to introduce her to you now, but she is assisting the police in their investigation. She is speaking at eleven, and I know you will offer her your congratulations. . . ."

Now, Harry's absence truly interested me. Last night he had set out to talk to Jay Knox, hoping that Jay hadn't selected Deirdre. Had Harry spoken to Jay? Had Jay told him Deirdre would be the new faculty member? Had Harry stayed away from this morning's session because he knew he had been passed over? That seemed very likely.

∽

I found an empty conference room and appeared in a prim, high-necked, slightly shapeless gray knit dress. I tried a black wig. Ghastly. I considered various colors—brown, silver, gray—finally settled on a blond pageboy. I added dark glasses with purple frames. As an added touch, I eschewed makeup. The purse was a boring shoulder bag in black leather. I squeezed my eyes in concentration, then opened the bag. I smiled when I drew out a black leather folder, opened it, and saw an ID card for Detective M. Loy. My smile wavered as I studied the image. I consoled myself that the harlequin frame sunglasses would draw a viewer's eyes, not ghostly pale skin.

I doubted anyone who had glimpsed Judy Hope in the bar last night would recognize her in this guise. I was ready to work.

∽

I waited patiently in a line at the front desk. Two clerks on duty were answering questions, checking people in, dealing with disputed charges, registering complaints.

When I faced a frazzled brunette, I flipped open the ID. "Detective Loy. Homicide. I need some room numbers."

Excited by her proximity to a murder investigation, she quickly provided them: Harry Toomey in room 217, Liz Baker in 311, Ashton Lewis in 302, Maureen Matthews in 326. Cliff Granger was in cabin 6 and Jessica Forbes in cabin 7—finer quarters for the New York visitors.

I carefully wrote down the numbers in a small notebook from the purse—Heaven does provide—thanked her, moved away. I took the stairs to the second floor. At room 217, I knocked firmly.

The door jerked open. Harry Toomey had the air of a man freshly shaved and showered, a man looking forward to his day.

I felt momentarily at a loss. I'd hurried up here to see him because he skipped the session where the new faculty member was announced. I assumed he'd followed through on his plan to see Jay last night and had learned that Deirdre was the choice. I thought he would be skulking in despair.

Obviously, he wasn't. Yet I knew he'd left the bar to go see Jay. From his demeanor, I wondered if he had heard about Jay's murder. Perhaps he'd ignored the summons to the auditorium. He looked at me politely.

"Police." I spoke in a crisp, commanding tone, though I kept my voice in a slightly higher register than normal. I held out my black leather folder.

He scarcely glanced at it, but I definitely had his attention. The watery brown eyes looked at me warily. "You want to talk to me?"

"Yes, sir. About Jay Knox."

His face creased. "Man, that's a shocker." His tone was perfunctory. No sad songs for Jay here.

"From information received, we know that you talked to Jay Knox last night." I estimated the time of his departure from the bar. "Between ten thirty and ten forty-five."

His light brown eyes narrowed in thought. "That sounds about right. I'd been in the bar, talked to this lady about publishing. She'd heard that Jay was going to announce Deirdre Davenport as the new faculty member. I guess I was surprised. I thought he'd picked me. I decided to go see him, but I only stayed a few minutes."

I was firm. "We know quite a bit about your contacts with Jay Knox. If you are cooperative, we can talk here and it won't be necessary to go downstairs." My tone suggested it would be much easier for all concerned if we spoke here. I smiled and stepped forward.

He backed away from me. "Sure. We can talk here." He was eager to be agreeable.

I closed the door behind me. "You can sit in the chair."

He sank onto the oversize office chair, designed for a man six foot four inches tall and weighing two hundred and fifty pounds. Harry's worn running shoes didn't quite touch the floor.

I slid the leather folder into a pocket, pulled the notebook out of my purse. I stopped a foot or so away, remained standing, looked down over the rim of the sunglasses. "We'll be taking your fingerprints this afternoon to confirm the fact that you visited cabin five. Please describe your actions."

He talked fast. "I don't know anything that will help the police. I talked to Jay for a few minutes—"

"The subject?"

"Well, I'd been in the bar and there was a woman who'd heard that Deirdre Davenport was going to get the new faculty job. I thought I'd go ask Jay. See"—and suddenly there was pathos in his eyes—"I'm self-published." He looked at me doubtfully, wondering if I understood.

I nodded. "The new big wave in publishing."

He was suddenly animated. "Exactly. Any writer can have a book now." He looked down at the top of his scuffed Adidas. "But only a few self-published books ever really succeed." He sounded discouraged. "Writers need a real publisher, somebody pushing the book, getting orders from wholesalers and stores and libraries. I thought if I got the faculty job, I'd have a chance to talk to editors and agents. I know my book can sell, get the backing it needs, if I have the right contacts." His eyes were bright. "That's all I need, somebody to place my book."

I wasn't interested in Harry's analysis of publishing. "You went to see Jay." I held the pencil above the pad. "You took the path from the terrace. Did you see anyone on your way to the cabin?"

"I wasn't paying much attention." He was vague. "Some people were sitting by the pool. The path twists and turns. I didn't run into anybody. There are some side paths with benches. I heard somebody laughing. It's around the third turn that you can see cabin five. The lights were on so I went up and knocked. Jay came to the door. I don't think he was pleased to see me. I told him I had to talk to him and he said okay, he had five minutes. He let me in. He sat on the sofa and I sat in a brown leather chair. I told him I'd heard he'd picked Deirdre. He looked kind of surprised—"

I had a feeling that Harry Toomey was accurately describing his exchange with Jay. Now it was my turn to be surprised. I'd arrived prepared for denials, lies, evasions. Was I naïve? Certainly a murderer would be well prepared to spin a clever tale.

"—and I thought maybe what I'd heard was wrong, but he turned his hands over, said he'd had a visit with Randall, and Randall made it clear that he wanted Deirdre."

So Jay had planned all along to announce Deirdre's selection. If she'd succumbed to his wishes, she would always have thought she'd been chosen because of a tawdry quid pro quo. I wondered if Jay had any inkling how degrading that would have been for her. Had he been oblivious to how his acts affected others or had he simply not cared? How much emotional damage had he willfully or carelessly inflicted on those around him?

Harry's face was forlorn. "Jay said he sure wished he could have picked me but Dr. Randall wanted Deirdre. Jay said the old boy was sanctimonious about never interfering with faculty discretion, then he gave me this meaningful stare and said he was looking forward to the announcement that he hoped would be a pleasant surprise, an announcement that underscored the professional accomplishments of the faculty. Randall's big on faculty publications. I didn't need a fortune-teller to understand what he was telling me.' Jay said he hoped I understood that he had to go with the flow." The memory of what he'd learned last night was clear in his drooping face. His book was all that mattered to him. He wanted his book to be read and admired, loved.

I stepped closer, made my voice stern. "How angry were you?"

Harry's head jerked up. It was as if last night's misery had never been. He looked shocked and uneasy, but there was no trace of defeat or despair. "I was upset but I knew it wasn't really Jay's fault. She"—his tone was resentful—"was published by a New York house. I just got up and said I was sorry it hadn't worked out and left."

I pictured eyes hot with tears and a quick departure, Harry clutching at dignity.

"That's what you claim." My tone was skeptical. "But you wanted that job. Maybe you saw red. Maybe you walked to the coffee table, picked up the champagne bottle, and struck him down."

"Not me." A touch of malice glinted in his eyes. "Hitting a guy with a bottle sounds like a woman on a tear. You might check with Deirdre. Jay liked women. She has a good body. I'll bet he was hoping to score. Maybe she didn't want the job that bad."

The police would soon pick up on Jay's arrival at Deirdre's door last night and his angry departure. Harry's scenario would add to their suspicion.

"Do you know of anyone else who might have been upset or angry with him?"

"I heard he and Maureen Matthews had a thing going but he dumped her." Harry clearly enjoyed airing gossip. "That was about the time we were interviewed. Deirdre probably had something to do with that. Maybe she was playing up to Jay."

"Was Jay involved with Liz Baker?" The girl's thin face was clear in my memory—young, miserable, distraught.

Harry looked blank. "Not anybody I know. If she's a looker, I wouldn't be surprised."

I described Liz. "Young. Early twenties. Delicate features. Slender. Dark brown hair. Last night she was wearing a sleeveless white cotton shirtdress."

Harry's face changed. It was as if he drew a line from one dot to another. He gave a tiny nod.

I was certain he recognized the description. "You know who she is?"

Harry was suddenly bland. "Maybe I've seen her around." He was casual. "Does she have a guy with her, sandy-haired, maybe mid-twenties?"

"Yes." I waited and watched.

"Yeah," Harry was expansive. "I guess I've seen them around. I think she may be one of the writers Jay worked with. You'd have to ask her. I've never met the lady."

"Do you know anyone with reason to want Jay dead?"

His moon face was suddenly malicious. "I'd heard his

editor wasn't happy with his latest book. You could ask her. Jessica Forbes."

I rather doubted editors resorted to murder to rid themselves of lousy books. A simple rejection would suffice. "Did Jay say whether he was expecting anybody?"

Harry's lips pursed into a knowing smile. "I guess he was. He said he'd give me five minutes. Why else the champagne? Sounds like a woman to me."

"Did you see anyone when you left?"

He looked down at the floor. "I left real quick. I went down to the lake and walked out on the pier."

I could see him stumbling blindly down the steps, seeking a place to deal with his despair.

"You stayed there how long?"

"A while. Then I went up to my room." He looked up at me.

Any high school teacher knows that look. *I don't know what happened. I wasn't there. Had to be somebody else.*

I studied that round, smooth face. Some fact was hidden behind that bland gaze, that fatuously earnest expression. There was something more to his actions than withdrawal to the lake. "You passed cabin five on the way to your room. Did you talk to Jay again?"

"No." A quick, firm reply. The earnest look redoubled.

I gave him a hard stare. "If you know anything about the circumstances of the crime, it is your duty to inform the police."

"If I can help the police in any way, I want to do so. It's dreadful, what happened." But the words were glib.

I still found that earnest expression suspicious. There was

something there, knowledge or a guess or a glimpse. "Who did you see when you passed cabin five on the way to the lodge?"

His eyes widened. "I just hurried past. I couldn't say if anyone was there."

Couldn't say or wouldn't say?

I nodded. "We'll be in touch to take your statement."

I walked to the door, turned at the last instant. "Did you stop near the cabin?"

He looked shocked, then blinked as if puzzled. "Excuse me. I don't know what you're talking about."

His bland expression—*The dog ate my homework. The hard drive was destroyed*—told me he knew exactly what I was talking about. When he walked back from the pier, he had stopped outside the cabin. He either went into the cabin again or perhaps he saw someone go in or come out of the cabin.

"The person who killed Jay"—my voice was grave—"won't hesitate to kill again. Don't be a fool. Tell what you know." Was he a killer laughing inside at my suggestion?

He shook his head again. "I don't have anything for the police."

I stepped into the hall. As the door closed, I had a sense I had missed something more. I absolutely didn't believe his claim that he went straight to his room. So that wasn't making me uneasy. Something else . . .

I was almost to the stairs when I understood what puzzled me. Last night Harry had been in despair, seen his dreams destroyed. This morning he appeared cheerful when he opened the door to me. He'd looked out at me with no aura of depression or sadness. He was in a good humor, almost buoyant, until I introduced myself. Perhaps he was simply mercurial, an optimist who always recast circumstances to see a win instead of a loss. Maybe hope sprang eternal and he was sure that right around the corner the unicorn of success awaited him. If so, good for him. But I didn't have time to ponder Harry's publishing future.

∽

I knocked on the door to room 311. I was interested to see if anyone answered. I didn't know Liz Baker's relationship with Jay Knox, but she was a recent graduate of the college and had been involved in the writing program. Maureen Matthews indicated Liz spent quite a bit of time with Jay. I assumed she was attending the conference because she had a book to sell. If so, she might now be at one of the sessions. If she was in her room, it might indicate distress over Jay's death or—

The door swung open.

The young man who'd sat next to Liz at the small table near the bar looked out. He was not tall, perhaps five foot eight, slender, with sandy hair that swept back in a wave from his face. His features were clear-cut. There was an air of sensitivity about him. He would, I thought, be a good son—kind to animals, easy to like.

If you don't think faces reveal that much, look harder next time when you encounter a stranger. Or a friend. Or a lover.

I introduced myself, flipped open the black leather folder. "I'm looking for Liz Baker."

He shook his head. "She isn't here." He started to close the door.

I moved forward, blocked the door with my elbow. "I'll start with you. Let me see your ID."

"Why?" His young jaw jutted.

"To establish your identity." Was I dealing with a boyfriend or a husband?

"You knock on my door, want my ID. You got no right." The door slammed in my face.

I wondered if he had firsthand experience with police or if he was savvy from years of watching *Law & Order.* But his response wasn't the norm for the average citizen.

I glanced up and down the hall, disappeared.

Inside the small hotel room, he stood a few feet from the unmade bed, cell phone in hand. "A cop's been here." There was an edge of panic in his voice. "We got to talk. I'll meet you at the end of the pier. Now."

Chapter 5

From a distance, the couple at the end of the pier made an attractive picture, she quite slender and young in a blue knit dress that the breeze molded against her, he in a tight-fitting yellow polo, khaki shorts, and sneakers. The breeze stirred her short brown hair, tugged at his polo. An observer could be forgiven a pang of envy, for remembering when all things were possible, when bodies were lithe and spirits carefree, remembering youth.

Perched on a piling, I saw young faces ravaged by fear, despair, guilt, and anger.

"What happened, Tom?" She laced her fingers tightly together.

"This detective came." He slid a glance back toward the shore, but they were alone with the slap of water and the caw of ebullient crows. Three empty rowboats provided by the lodge were pulled up on shore. There was no one near to hear them.

She hooked thin fingers on the neck of her dress. "What did you tell him?"

"Her. Frumpy old gal. Flipped open her black folder, showed me her ID."

I would have taken offense, but decided instead to be pleased at the effect of my costume.

"She wanted to see my ID. I told her no way, shut the door. She was hunting for you. Liz, you set out looking for him last night. Does anyone else know that?"

She hunched thin shoulders, stared out at the water and the ripple of little whitecaps from the ever-present Oklahoma wind.

"Liz." There was desperation in his high voice.

She spoke in jerks. "I went out on the terrace. His agent was standing by the fountain, looking out at the gardens. I asked him if he knew where Jay was. He said he was probably in his cabin. I guess he could tell I was upset. He's a nice man. His name's Cliff Granger. He asked me if anything was wrong and I thought maybe he could help. I told him I'd given money to Jay, and Jay promised Mr. Granger would look at my book. I told him I had to get the money back and would he please not look at my book and tell Jay he wasn't interested and ask Jay to give me the money back. He said he'd be glad to do that and he'd tell Jay, but he didn't think it would help."

Tom reached out, pulled her to face him. "Did you tell him why you wanted the money back? Did you tell him how mad I was? Did you tell him Jay took money that belonged to me, money I'd worked two years to save—" His voice shook.

Those who have a comfortable bank account can't ever really understand scrimping and saving, the welling of panic when a tire blows out, the scramble when any unexpected expense arises and there's not enough money in the bank to buy the tire, unplug a toilet, pay the vet.

I looked more closely at Liz and Tom. They had the fine flush of youth and health but their clothes were from a strip-mall store. The wedding ring on her left hand held a very small stone, likely a zircon instead of a diamond.

"—that you took the money out of the bank and gave it to him." His drawn face reflected the anguish of loss, the loss of money he couldn't replace, the loss of trust in Liz.

"I did it for us. If my book sold it would be more money—"

"Not for us. For you. You took what was ours and threw it away for a bunch of stupid words." He dropped her arm.

"Stupid words?" Tears spilled down her cheeks.

"I'm sorry." His mouth wobbled. "But you took the money. I got to buy a new transmission for the car. I got to get to work. I can't pay for it." He turned, head down, walked away, and didn't slow when she called his name.

Liz stared after him, tears streaming down her face.

∽

In conference room A, Sam listened impassively to a petite woman with unnaturally black hair in a jagged, uneven cut. She was all sharp edges, her birdlike features animated, her thin hands fluttering. "I just happened to open the door to my room. And coming out of her room right that minute was Deirdre Davenport." A tone of astonishment at the wondrous workings of fate. "Well, it seemed like such a fortunate coincidence." Bright unabashed look. She trilled, "And, you know, carpe diem." She looked at Sam doubtfully. "That means—"

Sam nodded his big head. "I know what that means."

Detective Weitz stared stolidly ahead.

Detective Sergeant Hal Price's lips flickered and he gave the chief a quick glance.

Sam cleared his throat. "You came out of your room. What time was that?"

"Four minutes to eleven." Her eyes were bright, her tone precise.

I saw trouble ahead. This woman might act giddy and prattle, but she was nobody's fool.

Sam made a note. "You saw Ms. Davenport."

A wriggle of eagerness. "There I was and there she was, so, as I said, I thought, *Carpe diem*, and rushed over to her and introduced myself. 'Ms. Davenport, I'm Gladys Samson and if you can give me just a minute, I want to show you my book. I have it in my room. Six hundred and seventy-nine pages. The title is *Galactic Glory*. I love to share my first paragraph. It sets the tone.'" She took a deep breath, dropped her voice an octave. "'Colors whirled like a merry-go-round in the sky, that moment between waking and sleeping when all the world for an instant seems bright and clear and you see everything as if from a star looking down, down—'"

Sam broke in. "Yes, ma'am. That's very good. Did Ms. Davenport go in your room?"

The eagerness faded. "She said Professor Knox was expecting her and so she didn't have time." There was an edge of resentment. She'd offered to share her book and been turned away.

"Can you describe Ms. Davenport's demeanor?"

Hal stood by the window and the sun turned his hair as golden as wheat. For an unguarded instant, Hal's handsome face, set in tight lines, revealed tension. He was not a police detective dispassionately listening to a witness. He was a man who cared on an intensely personal level about Deirdre Davenport.

Sam didn't look toward Hal, but I'm sure he was aware that Hal abruptly leaned forward, muscles taut.

Drawn out of her self-absorption, there was a gleam of intelligence in Gladys's dark, beady eyes, a realization that the police would not be inquiring about Deirdre Davenport unless they considered her a person of interest to their investigation. "Her demeanor." She spoke slowly, as if considering what she had seen and what it might have meant. "Now that's interesting. Very interesting." She preened. "I pride myself on my power of observation—so necessary for a novelist, you know. Now that I think about last night, I realize that her aura was dark. Very dark. An aura," she explained, "is the emotional cloud that envelops each of us. Why, you"—she pointed a bony finger at Sam—"have a Viking aura, Nordic blue, stalwart, commanding."

I pictured Sam in a Viking helmet.

Gladys pointed at Detective Weitz. "Your aura is softer— mauve with streaks of saffron." Her gaze swung to Hal. "Golden. Gold as the morning sun." Another preen. "Such incredible good looks. I imagine women flock to you." She waited a beat to let everyone conjure a picture of women streaming toward Hal. "If you don't mind my saying so. But I am always frank."

And, I felt sure, a pain in the ass to everyone around her.

Sam cleared his throat. "Did Ms. Davenport appear happy?"

I wasn't sure where Sam was heading. But I never underestimate him.

"Happy? Certainly not." Gladys's tone was waspish. "She looked upset. I would definitely say she was preoccupied and uneasy."

I was aware of utterly different reactions.

Sam's heavy face was as intent as a bloodhound with a scent.

Detective Weitz looked satisfied, as if this statement confirmed her thoughts.

Hal's eyes shone.

Oh, of course Hal wouldn't want this woman who'd captured his imagination to eagerly rush off to a late night tête-à-tête with a man. Much better that she seemed distracted and unenthusiastic.

Sam pressed her. "Would you say Ms. Davenport looked like a woman on her way to a pleasant meeting?"

"Definitely not." An emphatic nod and the uneven strands of dark hair quivered. "Quite the contrary. She left behind her a definite sense of strife, perhaps even anger, certainly despondency. She was not a happy woman. I wouldn't think any man would have been pleased to see her in that state."

Hal glared at her. If looks could transport speakers to an

unpleasant destination, Gladys Samson would have been in the far reaches of a desert wasteland.

"In any event," Sam said quietly, "Ms. Davenport indicated she had an appointment with Professor Knox and walked down the hall. Did you see her again that evening?"

"No. I don't know when"—a suggestive pause—"she came back to her room."

Sam nodded. "Thank you for your assistance, Ms. Samson."

She chirped, "I'm delighted to help. Call on me anytime."

Hal gazed at her with obvious distaste as she crossed the room with a flounce.

The moment the door closed, Sam leaned back in his chair. "Not the same tone we got from Davenport. According to her, all was sweetness and light when she talked to Knox."

"Davenport was spinning a tale"—Judy Weitz was decisive—"when she claimed he invited her for a drink to celebrate her selection. I thought that sounded fishy. Pretty late at night for a champagne toast, unless he expected it to lead to something better."

Hal was brusque. "That's a poisonous witness. She was mad because Deirdre wouldn't look at her book. Deir—Ms. Davenport probably looked unhappy because she didn't want to be trapped by a writer, especially not one who quotes the opening paragraph."

I wondered if Sam and Detective Weitz noticed Hal's initial use of Deirdre's first name.

Judy Weitz was blunt. "Davenport's fingerprints are on the murder weapon."

So that fact had been established. I saw the box score now: 2 to 1, Sam and Weitz over Hal.

Hal leaned forward, spoke quickly. "Deirdre explained how that happened. Knox brought the champagne—"

Sam held up a broad hand. "I heard her. But it adds up: Davenport's fingerprints on the murder weapon, and she was on the scene around the time of death. Now we know she appeared upset on her way to see him." He gazed at Hal. "Davenport's session ends in ten minutes."

I wasn't surprised that Sam had a handle on the day's schedule.

Sam tapped a pen on his legal pad, looked at Hal. "Bring her here. Tell her we have a few more questions."

Hal gave an abrupt nod, kept his face wooden as he moved toward the door.

Sam turned to Weitz. "I want more about Davenport, about Knox, about last night. Get some officers going cabin to cabin."

The net was closing around Deirdre.

❧

". . . and the best way to start is always with action. Readers are smart. They don't need explanations. If your character— call him Paul—if Paul's moving in the shadows down an alley, the reader will come with him, knowing something big's going to happen and perfectly content to find out the reason for Paul's presence there through his actions. Don't tell. Show." Deirdre's enthusiasm made her voice warm. "Remember Ken Follett's beginning to *The Key to Rebecca*:

'The last camel died at noon.' The reader is plunged into a desperate moment. Put your reader in a desperate moment."

The applause was enthusiastic. Deirdre gave a shy smile. "Thank you. And now, we have a few minutes left. Does anyone have any questions?"

At the back of the auditorium, a conference staffer held up a card with a large numeral five, indicating five minutes left in the session.

Hands poked skyward. "The lady in the purple hat." Deirdre bent forward to listen, nodded, then spoke into the mic. "Her question is: Is it important to have a romantic interest in a mystery?"

Was it simply coincidence that a door opened as she spoke, her resonant voice carrying to the far reaches of the auditorium, and Hal Price walked into the room? Is it coincidence to look across a room and see someone you have to know? I rather believed serendipity was at work.

As Hal walked up the far aisle, I felt that I heard a faraway sweep of violins—haunting, lovely, delicate.

Deirdre took a quick breath when she saw him. She paused, repeated slowly, "A romantic interest?" Her eyes were soft. Pink touched her cheeks.

Hal gazed up at the stage, blue eyes wide and admiring.

Deirdre watched Hal as he came nearer, spoke haltingly. "Love . . . Everyone needs love. . . . Sometimes two people look at each other and somehow they know . . . It's like walking in a garden just after dawn. . . . Everything is fresh and good. . . ."

Hal was at the side of the stage now.

A bell rang.

Neither of them heard the clang.

The audience was up and moving, voices rising, feet shuffling as the exodus began.

Hal strode up the steps. He walked to her, looked down. "I'm Hal Price."

"I saw you." She gazed up at him as if they were alone in a wooded glen, a private, perfect place. She said breathlessly, "I was talking about characters—"

Hal's eyes never left her face. "I heard what you said. About love."

"Of course"—her voice was almost a whisper—"that's in a book."

"I like books." Three words, but the tone spoke volumes, said, *You're beautiful. . . . I want to know you. . . . Take my hand. . . .*

I felt that I was part of their enchanted moment. Love can't be explained in a diagram or illustrated by a formula. Love isn't dependent on logic. Love turns a day golden, dispels the night. Love shares glory, nurtures broken spirits. Love is there, day in and day out, in good times or bad, up or down, touched by sun or tossed by storm.

Finally, reluctantly, Hal spoke. "I'm afraid they have more questions." He didn't have to explain.

The light died out of her face.

∽

Sam Cobb didn't rise when Deirdre and Hal walked in. Sam gestured to the same chair where she had sat earlier.

Deirdre, still clasping her notes and a purse and book bag,

took her seat. She shot a quick glance at Hal, who remained standing near the wall. He gave her a reassuring nod.

Detective Weitz flicked on the recorder. There was nothing warm or reassuring in her gaze. Sam looked cool, measuring, intent. Detective Sergeant Hal Price looked like a man listening to faraway violins.

I bent close to Deirdre. She couldn't see me, but she could hear my murmur. "Try not to look scared."

The result was an immediate stiffening and the taut facial tension of a patient awaiting a root canal.

I whispered urgently. "Witness saw you in the hall on your way to Jay's cabin, said you looked harried. Tell them you had a headache."

Deirdre jerked toward the sound of my voice.

Sam Cobb frowned. "You uncomfortable, Ms. Davenport?"

She took a breath and stared at him with huge eyes.

With a glazed expression and wan complexion, she truly didn't look well. Her voice was thin and shaky. "I've been struggling with a headache ever since last night. I'd had it all evening, but when Jay called and was so pleased about my appointment, I felt I had to go. But I told him I couldn't drink champagne—"

Sam cut in. "There is no record of a call from cabin five to your room."

For an instant, her face was blank.

I bent low, said in the faintest of whispers, "Cell."

"No record . . . Oh, no. He called me on my cell."

"May I see your phone?" Sam held out his hand.

Deirdre picked up her purse, started to pull out her cell.

Then with an exaggerated shake of her head—she was no competition for Meryl Streep—she stopped, exclaimed, "What am I thinking? I guess so much has happened, I can't keep everything straight. My kids called me on my cell. Now I remember." Her tone did not ring true. "He called me on the hotel phone."

Sam simply looked at her. There was a long, uncomfortable pause. He knew there would have been a record of the call on her cell phone if it hadn't been erased, and in any event the phone company records would list all calls. He knew she'd thought fast, realized she was boxed in, and changed her story.

She knew he knew she was lying. She stared back.

"There's no record of a call from cabin five to this room," he repeated stolidly.

"Then," she managed in a bright tone, "he must have used a house phone. Maybe he was in the lobby and on his way to the cabin."

"Maybe." The word dropped like a stone sinking into a deep, deep pond.

"Anyway," she forged ahead, "I had a terrible headache last night and it came back this morning."

Sam glanced at Judy Weitz. She gave a small shrug.

Score one for Deirdre. Her apparently unprompted revelation about a headache lessened the impact of Gladys Samson's statement.

I gave her an approving pat on the shoulder.

She jerked again.

Sam looked concerned. "Can we get you some water or coffee?"

Deirdre sagged back in the chair. "Yes. Please." But her gaze flicked from side to side.

My whisper was feather soft. "Relax."

"Relax!" She bleated the word. "How can I—" She broke off, looked from face to face. "Sorry. My head."

Sam stared at her, puzzled. Weitz raised an eyebrow.

Hal gave her a worried stare, then scrambled toward the door. "I'll get some water."

Hal would bring water. I didn't need to be present to know that, when he returned, their hands would touch and some of his strength would go out to her. Deirdre would handle the rest of the interrogation as well as could be expected, though protesting innocence wouldn't get her very far. Right now, Sam was focused on Deirdre. I could inform him about Liz and Tom Baker, but I needed to know more. I wanted to find out where Liz and Tom were last night. I only knew they weren't together after they left the bar.

∽

Making certain I was unobserved in the shadow of the honeysuckle arbor, I appeared in a French blue uniform. Since Tom Baker had met Detective M. Loy in a far different guise, I would now be Officer Judy Hope. I blinked several times. I must be sure of who I was at any given moment. Juggling aliases was a challenge.

Liz sat alone at a small table for two on the terrace. She'd opened a box lunch but simply sat there with one hand on the container. She never looked up as I approached her. There was a sea of movement, the rising hum of voices as the lunch crowd gathered, filling the tables.

I spoke quietly. "Mrs. Baker."

Her head jerked up. She saw the uniform. Her face went slack. She had the air of a small creature as an owl swoops down.

I placed a hand on the chair. "I have a few questions." I pulled out the chair, sat, opened the leather folder with my identification.

She scarcely glanced at the ID, remained frozen in place.

"What time did you arrive at cabin five last night?"

A pulse flickered in her thin throat.

"There's no point in denying that you spoke with Mr. Knox last night." I kept my voice pleasant. "We know that from information received." It was one way to characterize my eavesdropping on the pier and the conclusion I reached. I pulled out my small notebook, flipped it open, sat with pen poised. "The time?"

"I don't know exactly." The words were a faint whisper.

"You spoke to Cliff Granger on the terrace."

She lifted a shaky hand to smooth back a strand of dark hair. "Oh, he told you. I saw him and we talked—"

"About the money you'd given to Jay Knox."

That crumbled any defense that might have remained. She gazed at me with stricken eyes. "He told you?"

"All communications to police are confidential. We simply work on information received."

"You know what I told him." She sounded stricken.

I presented a blank, by-the-book expression. "I want to hear your version."

She stared down at the table. "I thought if my book got to an agent, then it would sell and we'd have money. I paid Professor Knox five thousand dollars—"

If Jay managed to get that much money from ten writers, that was fifty thousand dollars. Surely there was some record of Jay's clients. It would be interesting to know how many of them were attending the conference.

"—and he sent my book to Mr. Granger. But you see, that money was in our savings account and my husband needed it. So I asked Mr. Granger to give my book back to Mr. Knox and tell him I'd changed my mind and would he please give me my money back."

"After you spoke to Mr. Granger, what did you do?"

"I knew Jay was in cabin five. Mr. Granger was nice but I could tell he didn't think Jay would agree. But I had to try. Tom . . ." She squeezed her eyes shut for an instant, opened them.

I knew her vision shimmered from unshed tears.

Her voice was high, strained. "I walked real fast before I lost my nerve. I got there and knocked." She lifted her gaze, but she wasn't looking at me. She was remembering. "When he opened the door, I told him I was in big trouble with my husband, that I had to get the money back and wouldn't he please give it to me. He said he'd set me up with the agent and if I didn't take advantage of it, that was up to me, but he'd done his part, earned his fee, and he didn't owe me anything. He shut the door in my face."

"Did you see anyone near the cabin when you came down the steps?"

Now there was more than worry in her eyes—there was fear. "It was too dark to see anyone." But she didn't look at me.

"Did you hear anything?"

"Some shouts from the pool." Her thin hands clenched.

I was sure she saw something in the shadows and heard more than faraway revelry. She glimpsed a movement or perhaps sensed a presence. She heard something that now terrified her.

I nodded as if accepting her reply. "You went up the path. And then?"

Her tension didn't ease. Her stricken look was stark and revealing. "I went up to the room."

"Was your husband there?"

She huddled in the chair, didn't look at me. "He came in a little later. I'd already gone to bed."

Had she lain still and quiet, pretending sleep? I thought so. I was only sure of one fact. She didn't know where Tom had been. Or what he had done.

∽

I was ravenous. A box lunch would be wonderful. But first I wanted to check on conference room A, then talk to Cliff Granger before he started seeing writers at one o'clock. I stepped into the midst of the willow fronds, disappeared.

In conference room A, Sam and Detective Weitz huddled over a list of attendees.

I surreptitiously used a marker to neatly print on the dry-erase board:

> *Knox charged authors big dollars to connect them with agents and editors. Check to see if any of his clients are attending conference. Any authors bitter over payoff?*

I could imagine authors filled with resentment if they paid for contacts that didn't result in publication. I put the marker in the tray. The sound was slight, only a click, but Detective Weitz's head turned.

Detective Weitz blinked. No doubt she'd noticed the board was unmarked when they'd set to work. "Chief"—her voice was studiously calm—"it appears someone's trying to be helpful."

Chief Cobb swung around to look. His gaze swept the area.

I resisted the impulse to draw a happy face. It would have been such fun. But I was mindful of Precepts One and Six. I felt exceedingly virtuous.

"Interesting." He looked down at the list of conference attendees. "Make an announcement over the hotel intercom. All authors who were clients of Knox are asked to report here."

I left in good spirits.

Cliff Granger wasn't in the cafe area, on the terrace, or in the lobby. I found him in cabin 6. He sprawled on the sofa, his face somber, arms lying on the back, legs outstretched, a man deep in thought.

In an arbor draped in honeysuckle, I reappeared as Officer Hope. In a few steps, I stood at the door to cabin 6, knocked firmly. "Police."

Cliff opened the door, looked at me politely. He was impeccably groomed, brown hair smooth against his head, freshly shaven. He appeared equable, relaxed, with no remnant of the somber expression I'd seen a moment ago.

"Mr. Granger, if you have a moment, I have a few questions." I held out my leather folder.

He gave it a perfunctory glance as he opened the door, stood aside for me to enter. He was natty in a Tommy Bahama shirt, palm fronds against a blue background, slate blue trousers, and expensive black loafers. Now his long face was suitably grave. "Jay's death is a great loss to the college and a shock to me personally."

I stepped inside. The living area was identical to that of cabin 5 except there was no body lying near the coffee table. I gestured toward the sofa.

He sat down, nodded. "What can I do for you, Officer?"

I sat opposite him in a straight chair. "When did you last see Jay Knox?" I had my trusty notebook in one hand, pen in the other.

His answer was prompt. "Early in the evening. We happened to be walking to our cabins about the same time. Around seven or so."

"What was his demeanor?"

He looked a bit surprised, shrugged. "Usual Jay. He was a motormouth. I wasn't paying too much attention. He said something about tomorrow being a full day, but he was looking forward to it."

"Did he mention his plans for the evening?"

"No."

I raised an eyebrow. "You and Jessica Forbes are from out of town. Did you expect to be taken to dinner?"

Cliff was relaxed. "That came up earlier. I'd already decided to order room service and look over some manuscripts."

"Do you carry them with you or were these manuscripts submitted to you here?"

"Carry them?" He was appalled. "Nobody reads paper anymore. I look at e-files on my iPad."

"So you spent the evening in your cabin?"

He flashed a wry smile. "Pretty awful stuff I was looking at. I went up to the bar for a drink."

"What time did you return to your cabin?"

He looked uncertain. "Hard to say. Maybe ten thirty. Maybe eleven. I wasn't paying any attention. It was a nice night. I strolled around the gardens for a little while."

"Did you see anyone?"

He turned his hands over in a gesture of dismissal. "I wasn't paying attention. I probably passed some people but I was planning a contact I need to make for one of my clients. I think I know a Hollywood agent who will go nuts for his book."

"Tell me about Jay."

"Ours was a business relationship. I represented him." Cliff's smooth voice rolled on, describing how he'd acquired Jay as a client, the two books that he'd sold, the movie deal that was handled by a California agent. "I don't know much about his personal life."

"Did you know authors paid him to get their books to agents and editors?"

His long face crinkled in indecision. He seemed to pick his words carefully. "I had heard that he offered a consulting service to authors."

"Is that ethical?"

He shrugged. "Some authors are willing to pay substantial sums to people they think can get them an entrée to being published. I can tell you"—he was emphatic—"that reputable agents never take money to represent a book.

That's against the canon of ethics. We take on an author and if we sell the book we receive a percentage of the royalties. No up-front money."

"Do you think it was acceptable for Jay to take money from authors?"

A dismissive shrug. "He wasn't an agent. He was a consultant. What he did was up to him. Savvy writers don't go that route."

"You didn't answer my question."

He rubbed the back of his neck. "I don't like to criticize Jay when he isn't here to defend himself. His attitude was hard-nosed. He said if somebody wanted to pay him for making a connection, that was their choice."

"Did he recommend authors to you?"

"Sure. He and a lot of other people. We get more queries than we can handle. Sometimes I look at the books; usually I decline."

"Did you take on any authors he recommended?"

"Occasionally." He smoothed back a lock of hair, looked weary, as if contemplating a tsunami of manuscripts.

"Are any of those authors attending the conference?"

"A couple. There's a woman from Dallas. And a guy from Tuscaloosa."

"Did you find a publisher for their books?"

"Not yet. I'm still trying."

"If you don't find a publisher, how do those authors react?"

He looked surprised. "Look, I do my best. I send the books around. When there's a rejection letter, I send it to the author.

If I get three or four passes, that's pretty much the end of the story." He was thoughtful. "Nobody's ever complained. I do what I promise to do. If it doesn't work out, it isn't because I don't try. They can read the rejection letters."

"Do you know any authors who were unhappy with Jay?"

Cliff shook his head. "We never talked about that."

I waited. But he was done, regarding me with patient forbearance. This was his opportunity to inform the police about Liz Baker and her angry husband. But he said nothing. I was intrigued. Did he feel sorry for Liz? I wouldn't have expected him to be kindly, but perhaps I did him an injustice. His silence about Liz and her angry husband suggested he felt no personal danger from the police investigation and therefore saw no need to set the hounds in motion after a possible suspect.

༄

I found a table in the main lobby where a conference staffer was handing out box lunches to attendees. My mantra in life—one of them—is that it never hurts to ask. Others? You must be willing to fail to succeed. Smile, and, if the world doesn't smile back, smile again. When you draw a lousy hand, remember the game isn't over. Laughter should always be kind.

I walked up to the table. "Hello."

The staffer was stout, perspiring, and faintly hostile. She had opened one of the box lunches and was munching on a sandwich. "I'm Officer L—" Oops. "Hope." I held out my leather folder.

She gave it a perfunctory glance.

"I wanted to tell you how much we"—I was expansive, waving one hand to encompass all the surroundings—"appreciate the cooperation and support of the English Department for our investigation. You have excelled."

The woman neatly wrapped the remainder of her sandwich in waxed paper. She brushed back an untidy loop of graying hair, looked less stressed. "We want to help."

I noted her name tag: *Sheila Devon, Administrative Assistant.* "Ms. Devon, are you part of the English Department staff?"

Her fairly heavy face was suddenly less formidable. She looked at me with pride, her light blue eyes attentive. "I am Dr. Randall's secretary."

"That's splendid. I know you can be a big help. It's important for us to explore Professor Knox's relationships. Obviously, you occupy an important post in the department. I'm hoping you can share knowledge only you might have about Professor Knox." My tone was inviting, encouraging.

Sheila's entire demeanor changed. Instead of an overworked woman, resentful at giving up her Friday, she blossomed. "I know a lot about the department. Dr. Randall is wonderful. I'm sure he didn't have much choice about hiring Jay Knox. The family, you know. Everyone remembers his grandfather." She looked troubled, hesitated, remained silent.

"You can be frank. Any information received during an investigation remains confidential, sources never revealed." I doubted this was accurate, but it sounded persuasive to me.

Sheila leaned forward, dropped her voice. "To tell the truth, Jay Knox was"—a pause—"well, he was from a fine family and very good-looking, but he was a real womanizer. Last year there was some talk about a party he had at his house; some of the men attending the conference were there, and women were brought in, and you know what that means. His grandfather would have been very upset. Why, the conference is supported by the college, and to have that kind of thing going on is very distressing. And all the while he was acting sweet as pie to Professor Matthews. I should have told her, because I don't think she had any idea, but some things you don't feel comfortable talking about. I heard him one time when I started to open the door to her office, telling her how crazy he was about her, how gorgeous she was, and everybody can tell you, she really is beautiful, but getting older now. Well"—an angry sniff—"this past week she went in his office and the door wasn't quite closed. She asked why he hadn't called and he—oh, it was awful—he wasn't nice at all, he told her he needed some space and to stop calling him, they'd had some fun together but that train had left the station. When she came out, I could have cried. She looked shocked. I'm surprised she's here at the conference, but I guess she had no choice."

We parted with smiles. I was almost to the terrace door when she called after me. "Would you like a box lunch?"

"I'm not free for lunch. Yet." I suppose I looked wistful.

"I'll save a box for you."

I smiled my thanks. I looked about and was pleased to see Deirdre having lunch with Hal. I wondered how Sam

Cobb would feel about this tête-à-tête. They sat at a table near the weeping willow, out of the main traffic flow on the terrace.

I walked briskly to the honeysuckle arbor, stepped inside. After a quick glance, I disappeared.

I slipped into the chair opposite Deirdre.

Deirdre was still wan but her long face was open and unguarded. Her gaze was fastened on Hal as if absorbing his presence, the kindness and reassurance in his face, the warmth of his voice, his solid muscularity.

Hal was being earnest. ". . . have to ask all kinds of questions. You've been very patient."

She pushed back her sandwich box. "Chief Cobb looks at me like I'm"—she took a quick breath—"a criminal."

Hal reached across the table, took her hand. "No one can look at you and not see how good you are."

"Oh, that's lovely." I placed my fingers over my lips. I'd been touched by the depth of feeling in his voice but that was no excuse for speaking aloud. No one could confuse my voice with Deirdre's—a definite difference in tone, her voice light and clear, mine husky.

Hal looked startled.

Deirdre blurted out, "That wasn't me."

"I didn't think it was." He spoke slowly. His face was interesting—uncertainty, concern, a sudden attentiveness. "Who was it?"

"I don't know"—her voice was scarcely above a whisper—"if I can make you understand." Deirdre brushed back a frizzy lock of hair, and finally, reluctantly, said, "I think she's there but we can't see her."

Hal slowly nodded, his eyes skewing around the table.

Deirdre took a shaky breath. "This is going to sound kind of crazy." She stopped, shook her head. "What do I mean, *kind of crazy*? But maybe I can make you understand. I really need to get a book written and sell it, but no matter how hard I try, I can't seem to get started. So I kept thinking, if I could just get some inspiration, I would be all right. And I thought and thought and thought about inspiration and then out of nowhere this really gorgeous redhead—"

Ooh, what a lovely thing to say.

"—showed up and said she was there to help me. She's the one who came last night when Jay was there and said her name was Judy Hope."

Hal's eyes narrowed. "Red hair? About five foot five? Green eyes?"

Deirdre nodded.

"Judy Hope." His face was thoughtful, and I had no doubt he was filing *Judy Hope* as an alias for Officer Loy. "Good to know. Well, I wouldn't worry about her. Sometimes it's swell to have an unseen champion."

"I'm going to need all the champions I can get." Deirdre's voice was thin. "I'm afraid I'll end up in jail unless they find out who killed Jay. I don't know that much about Jay, but I think I'd better start finding out. Maybe I can help look for the murderer."

Hal reached across the table, grabbed her hands. "You can relax. I'll find out what happened. I promise. And now, you get busy with breakfast. You need to keep up your strength. As for the redhead who's sometimes here and sometimes not, we know she's on your side. Like Bill

Shakespeare said, 'There are more things in heaven and earth, Horatio, than are dreamt of in our philosophy.'"

They looked at each other in understanding, an acceptance that more existed in their lives and in the lives of many than they would ever understand or be able to explain.

∽

This time I reappeared in an old phone booth near the door to the ladies' room. I felt confident as I stepped out that no one in the busy lobby was paying attention to this twentieth-century relic. As promised, a box lunch and ginger ale awaited me at the check-in table. I thanked Sheila. As I crossed the lobby, I glanced down the hall to my left and saw a row of occupied seats outside conference room B.

Cliff Granger, relaxed and smiling, strolled toward the door, nodded at the occupants of the chairs, the hopeful authors waiting to see him. Harry Toomey was in the third chair holding several copies of his book. One knee jounced as he fidgeted.

I strode outside and down the winding path, all the way to the end of the pier. I leaned against the railing as I ate a ham-and-cheese sandwich, enjoyed salty potato chips, sipped crisply cold ginger ale. I finished with a sugar cookie iced with a happy face. I'd hoped for more information from Cliff Granger, such as a handy list of authors attending the conference who were Jay's clients. There might be others as disappointed and angry as Liz and Tom Baker. That was the problem of being on the outside of an investigation. If only I could take a look at Jay's cell phone. He was young, hip, very likely to keep notes and schedules on his iPhone. But there was another possibility.

I deposited the box and soda can in a waste receptacle, strolled to the honeysuckle arbor, stepped inside, relished the sweet scent. I made sure no one was passing, and disappeared. Transport was no problem. I simply thought, *Jay Knox's house*, and I was there.

Chapter 6

Jay's house was in an older part of town, not far from the campus. One-story homes, mostly brick, were shaded by oaks and elms. Jay's house was among the oldest, a mellow stucco bungalow. Mail was jammed in the black iron mailbox on the porch. Two newspapers in plastic bags were halfway up the lawn. There was no sign of life or movement, no car in the drive.

Inside, the air-conditioner hummed. Air-conditioners run 24–7 during an Oklahoma summer and Jay Knox had fully expected to return to his house. I was grateful for the coolness. There was no other sound. I was sure no living creature was in the house. Even though I was invisible, a dog or cat would have found me, known I was there, perhaps been friendly, perhaps not. But nothing broke the silence.

I stood in the center of a long living room, a rather well-appointed room for a bachelor—angular modern furniture with brightly colored cushions, two sofas, three chairs, a long, low, glass-topped coffee table. A painting with huge splashes of crimson and turquoise hung above the fireplace mantel. I gave the room a cursory glance, noting what was likely an expensive black metal sculpture of geometric shapes in one corner. I wondered if the artist harked back to the assurance of mathematical precision or was illustrating the complexity of modern life.

I walked down a hallway, checked several rooms, found a large office at the back of the house. The door was open. I stepped inside. Everything appeared to be in order. The top of a brown wooden desk was bare except for in/out boxes and a small legal pad with a pen lying across it. A computer monitor glowed on a side table. The swivel chair was turned toward the monitor, away from the desk.

I was thoughtful when I stood by the desk. I looked from the monitor to the desk. The pad contained a list in large, looping handwriting. All of the notes were unremarkable reminders of tasks to be done—get a birthday card for Aunt Helen, attend dinner next week at Dr. Randall's, renew driver's license, make out bills. Each number had a check mark by it.

I glanced at the in/out boxes. The bottom tray was empty. Several stamped envelopes were stacked in the top tray. I picked them up, noted the addresses—utilities, a cable company, a car dealership.

Obviously, Jay paid some bills the old-fashioned way, rather than authorizing withdrawals from his checking account or making purchases with a debit card. What mattered to me at the moment was whether Jay's last action at the desk had been paying bills or working at his computer.

If he paid the bills, checked the last number, pushed back the chair, and stood, it would seem more natural to slide the chair forward against the desk. Instead, the chair faced the computer.

Had someone other than Jay slipped into the house, come to the computer, looked for and possibly found a particular file or photo, and deleted it? It was quite possible. If a shadowy figure came to the house late last night, it could have been the murderer. Or it was possible, after Jay's death was made public, that someone else hurried here today to access a particular file or photo.

I still held the envelopes Jay had placed in the out-box. As I returned them to the top tray, I was struck by an idea. I pulled open the center desk drawer. His checkbook was lying next to an ornate fountain pen with an eagle crest serving as the clip. I opened the checkbook, read the stubs. The recent checks had been written the day before. I skimmed back over the month and found a deposit of five thousand dollars marked *Baker Consulting Fee*. I closed the checkbook, shut the drawer.

I slipped into the chair facing the computer and had a sudden shivery feeling. I wondered if I'd spooked myself with my conjectures. Was I was sitting in a chair last occupied by a murderer?

I pushed away that shrinking feeling and focused on my task. Thankfully, Jay kept his computer on, so I wasn't stymied by lack of a password. I didn't bother to look at files or photos. That kind of search would take far more time and expertise than I possessed to discover if anything had been deleted after his death.

I went to e-mail.

I've learned my computer skills on the fly, so to speak, but they are adequate. It took only a few minutes to find a series of e-mails Jay sent to authors confirming the submission of manuscripts to Cliff Granger. Three responses indicated excitement over seeing Cliff at the conference and were effusive in their thanks. I memorized their names and would make sure Sam Cobb spoke to them, although it didn't seem likely any were involved in Jay's death, since they were apparently satisfied in their arrangement with Jay.

The e-mail string from Liz Baker was an entirely different matter. In five e-mails, the first late last week, she begged him to return the money. ". . . I took it out of our joint checking account. . . . Tom didn't know. . . . He left paying the bills to me . . . then his car went out. . . . He needs the money. . . . The money wasn't mine. . . . I should have asked him before I wrote the check but you said I had to pay now or I couldn't see Mr. Granger. . . . I'm afraid of what he might do." An e-mail sent Thursday was stark. "I've never seen him like this. . . ."

Two other e-mails Jay received Thursday, and his answers, needed to be explained.

The first, from Maureen Matthews, was cryptic:

I have an appointment with Gilbert on Monday.

Jay's reply was brutal:

122

Cancel it. Or I'll do a collection of love letters, self-
pubbed, a pink cover with a red hot arrow pointing
at your name.

The second, from Professor Ashton Lewis, was apoplectic:

You have a week. I've warned you.

Jay:

Your word against mine.

A faint creak sounded, then the click of a door shutting.
I turned my head, listened.

Quick footsteps sounded in the hall. There was no hesitation, no uncertainty. Maureen Matthews walked past the
open doorway to the office. She would have been a lovely
figure in a swirling silk dress with splashes of violet against
gray, except for the anguish in her face, her beauty shadowed
by memory and fear.

I immediately followed her.

At the end of the hall, she turned to a closed door,
stopped, one slender hand gripping the knob. Now her face
carried an imprint of sadness. She remained with her hand
in that tight grip, her shoulders tensed for one minute, two,
then shook her head, turned the knob. She stepped into a
masculine bedroom—dark furniture, a king-sized bed with
an Indian blanket in a red and black, diamond-and-star pattern used as a spread. A brown chest of drawers sat against
one wall next to a bookcase.

I watched from the open doorway.

Maureen walked to the chest, pulled out the top drawer, moved the contents about. In a moment, she lifted out a packet of letters, blue envelopes held together by a double-looped red rubber band.

She expelled her breath in a slow sigh. Tension drained from her body. The presence of the letters appeared to provide her with enormous relief.

I made a quick decision. Detective M. Loy appeared with her blond pageboy, purple-framed harlequin sunglasses, and shapeless gray dress. I cleared my throat. "I'll take those." I spoke quietly, but with confidence, and moved toward her.

She stood frozen for a moment, then jerked around, the packet of letters clutched to her chest. Her face was stark white, the red of her lipstick garish in contrast.

I pulled out the black leather folder, opened it. My steps sounded loud on the hardwood floor. "Detective M. Loy." I held out my other hand for the letters.

She stared at me intently, then gave me a cool smile and opened her purse, dropped the letters inside, zipped it shut. "I think not."

"Detective M. Loy," I repeated stolidly. "You are removing material from a murder victim's home. The house and its contents cannot be disturbed—"

She shook her head. Her lustrous black hair, fine as silk, rippled. "Pretty good job. Not good enough. You can't hide bone structure."

I suppose my astonishment was evident.

She studied me with a sharp gaze. "I admired your bone structure when you talked to me in the bar last night—high

cheekbones, a slightly pointed chin. Judy Hope, as I recall."
Maureen took a step forward, reached up, pulled. The blond
wig dangled from her hand. "And your voice is rather distinctive."

I'd forgotten to alter my tone.

She tossed the wig to me, tucked her purse under her
arm, started for the door. "Perhaps it would be better for
both of us if we pretend this moment never occurred. I doubt
your employer would be impressed by your behavior. Only
the most scandalous online tabloids go in for disguises."

Ah, yes, she thought I was Judy Hope, reporter extraor-
dinaire for the *Rabbit's Foot*. I blocked her path. "I can tell
Sam Cobb about the letters and that Jay Knox threatened to
publish them."

She was shocked. Her hands tightened on the purse as
she tried to figure out how this stranger, this woman who
worked for an entertainment site, not only knew about the
existence of the letters but was aware of Jay's threat. "Did
you talk to Jay?"

"Let's leave it that I am well aware of all of Jay Knox's
activities."

"Are you planning on writing a titillating tell-all story?
You'd better think twice." Her voice was harsh. "It's a
serious offense to impersonate a police officer. I don't think
the police chief would approve."

She was unaware that I wasn't worried about the chief
being told of my actions. But perhaps, if I were adroit, I
could take advantage of her perception.

I fluffed my hair. I knew it was squashed from the wig,
and it never hurts to appear at one's best. I wished I could

also be rid of the ill-fitting gray dress. "I suggest we see if we can reach an understanding. I have no wish to cause you any concern about your letters." If later evidence pointed to Maureen as the killer, the e-mails existed for the police to find. "However, it is imperative you tell me what you intended to report to Dr. Randall."

She brushed back a strand of that incredibly fine, soft hair. She was puzzled. "I don't understand how you know about that." Her brows drew down in a tight frown. "Did Jay show you his e-mail? I would think he would have kept quiet about that night. But I have no reason not to tell you or anyone else who is interested. Jay and his agent and a few more men from the conference were here at Jay's house on the Thursday night before the conference last year. Jay arranged for some 'entertainment.' I have no idea how he chose the girls involved but they were students. I have photos and some names. At least one girl was underage at the time. I was told it was a bang-up party with whiskey and plenty of sex. I intended to inform Dr. Randall. Jay was pretty much off-limits to criticism because of his family, but Gilbert wouldn't ignore that kind of behavior, even though it was a year ago."

"How did you know about the party?"

For the first time she looked uncomfortable. "A student told me."

"When?" I watched her closely.

Her gaze dropped. "That doesn't matter." She moved around me, walking fast. She was in the hall. Hurried footsteps clicked on the hall floor. A door slammed.

I rather thought that when she became aware of the facts

about the party mattered a great deal. Did she confront Jay at the time? Did Jay express remorse, promise never to take advantage of students again? Even though a year had passed, if one of the coeds had been underage at the time, somebody could be in big trouble. Had Jay—handsome, appealing Jay—set out to ensnare Maureen? Had he engineered an affair to ensure her silence? When he discarded her and she made her threat to report the evening to Randall, he taunted her with a threat to publish her love letters to him. That's why she had been so relieved to find the packet of letters in the chest.

I understood her desire to protect her reputation, but the letters would be critical evidence if it was she who snatched up the champagne bottle and crashed the base against his temple.

That left me with a dilemma.

I disappeared.

Maureen was in the drive, hurrying to a red Corvette Stingray. She opened the driver door, slid into the seat, tossed her purse on the passenger seat.

Not even the most preoccupied driver would remain unaware if a purse in the next seat opened and an item appeared to depart of its own volition.

The motor roared.

I never had a sports car but the sound of the engine made me adjust my view of Maureen. Mid-forties and fiery.

I rapped five times on the trunk as the car started.

The Corvette jolted to a stop. Maureen put the car in park and climbed out, her face furrowed.

As she moved toward the trunk, I was in the passenger

seat. I opened the purse, grabbed the letters, closed the purse. I lowered the window a couple of inches, pushed the packet through. By the time she slid behind the wheel, I was outside the car, picking up the letters from the drive. Would she notice the open window? Possibly. But she was likely preoccupied by her thoughts about our encounter. She would be interested in getting away as soon as possible with the letters safely in her purse.

As the Corvette roared down the drive, I settled on a sturdy limb of an oak tree. I surveyed the roof of Jay's bungalow, shook my head. The likelihood of someone wandering about on the shingles was remote, but I didn't want the letters to be found.

A deep-throated growl rose from behind the next-door neighbor's fence. I looked down at one of the largest German shepherds I have ever seen. His hackles rose. He lifted his thin face and howled.

"Hey, boy." I dropped down beside him, made soft cooing sounds.

He looked right at me. His taut shoulders relaxed.

A large doghouse, elevated on cinder blocks, sat in the shade of a sycamore. In an instant, I was there. I thrust the packet of letters deep beneath the house. The German shepherd had followed and stood watching. "Thanks, buddy."

No one would get those letters now.

ᔕ

There is something reassuring in finding a pluperfect example of type in a world where often nothing is what it seems to be. Although there are many kinds of academics—the intellectual, the blowhard, the conniver, the dreamer, the overachiever, the floater—there are also plenty of piercing-glanced, goateed, lanky, tweedy (in season), dramatic iconoclasts.

Ashton Lewis jabbed a stubby forefinger, glared out at his listeners over heavy-rimmed glasses as he concluded the session on journalism. "Don't play the big-time-news corporate game. Those reporters are shills. They don't report. They interpret. How do they interpret?" His voice dripped sarcasm. "With insight." His voice reverberated with disgust. "Insight. Hmm, it couldn't be they're crafty, could it, using words that demean one side, elevate the other? Grab a highlighter the next time you read a news story. Pick out words that nudge opinion one way or the other. You'll find them. But"—he leaned forward, gripped the edges of the lectern—"you can do better. Go out there, ask questions, delve to the bottom of each side's claims, report the damn facts that you find, don't embellish. Don't interpret. If you give readers unembellished facts, they'll draw conclusions, make judgments. Write the truth, and then, to paraphrase Kipling, then you'll be a reporter, my son." A sudden, charming smile lit his face. "And daughter."

He bowed to resounding applause.

Behind the curtains, I appeared as Officer Loy, a redhead who felt quite comfortable in the French blue uniform. I rather thought Professor Lewis liked young women. I hurried across the stage.

He was almost to the steps when I caught up with him. "Professor Lewis."

He turned, gave me an appreciative—I hew to truth—glance.

I opened the black leather folder. "If you'd be so kind, sir, we are seeking information about Professor Knox."

His face transformed into a glower. "I don't have anything good to say about the man. Being dead doesn't grant a halo. If you want a testimonial, find a simpering woman." He started to turn away.

"Sir." I lifted my voice. "You e-mailed Jay that he had one week. Please explain the circumstances."

He hunched his head down until his neck disappeared beneath the point of his white goatee, stared at me out of light blue eyes. "I suppose I have to. I always instruct students to tell it straight. But I won't give you a name. There's no point in hurting the girl's reputation. I knocked on Jay's office door Wednesday. I turned the knob and walked in. This was during faculty office hours. There was a girl in his arms. They jerked apart. Her hair was mussed, makeup smeared. He—well, no point in graphic details. I checked. She's a student. She's only nineteen. She ran out. I told Jay in no uncertain terms—" A bark of laughter. "I'm not given to uncertain terms. Ask anyone who knows me. I told him he'd crossed the line. I almost went to Randall then, but I thought it over. I wanted to save the girl embarrassment, but Jay had to go. I told Jay he had a week to resign. If he didn't, I was going to Randall. If necessary, I intended to tell the world." As he talked, his face turned an ever-deeper shade of red.

"Jay e-mailed you saying it would be your word against his."

Lewis glowered. "He was an absolute cur. I don't think anyone would ever accuse me of lying."

I was touched. Very Kiplingesque. But I wasn't deterred. "When did you talk to him last night?"

His shaggy gray brows knotted. "Least said, soonest mended. I didn't kill him. But I'm not surprised someone did. As I said, he was an absolute cur. And now I've said all I'm going to say." He turned and, head down, walked away, stomped down the steps. I watched his determined march away from me. The back of his neck was still red. Here was a man who was easily angered, the kind of man who might in a haze of fury pick up a champagne bottle and strike.

The auditorium was empty. As I recalled, no more main talks were scheduled. The afternoon was devoted to appointments. I moved behind dusty curtains, smothered a sneeze, and disappeared.

∽

Conference room A was empty. That meant Sam Cobb had concluded interviews, but he would be at work, scanning reports at the police station.

I felt an uncertain lurch within. I hadn't checked on Deirdre since lunch. I assumed she was still here at the lodge. I remembered the gloom of the interrogation room at the police station. Surely she wasn't being questioned there, wasn't close to arrest. But the evidence had been mounting against her.

Sunshine streamed through the windows in Deirdre's room, adding light and cheer. She sat on the sofa, a soft smile on her face, hands loose in her lap.

I was so excited to see her, I gave a glad whoop.

She gasped and looked wildly about.

I was standing by the desk. "I'm over here." I was cheery. I chose a navy tee with a V-neck and ankle pants in a matching navy with a silver fish pattern. Silver sandals completed my outfit.

Deirdre watched colors swirl and settle with a familiar look of disbelief and shock.

I would have thought she'd be more comfortable with me at this point.

Deirdre gazed at me with wide, strained eyes. "I wish you wouldn't come and go, here one minute, gone the next. Maybe I'm really nuts. Hal says—" She looked at me questioningly.

"I know Hal."

"Good." She didn't sound overjoyed. "You won't mess things up with him, will you? Today at lunch, he knew that voice wasn't mine. I don't want him to think crazy things happen around me."

"Sweetie"—I was reassuring—"nothing will come between you and Hal. Especially not if we can figure out what happened and satisfy the police that you had nothing to do with Jay's death."

"'We can figure out what happened'?" Her voice rose. "Somehow I don't like the sound of that. I'm not a detective. You're not a detective." A pause. "Are you?"

I was vague. "I do this and that. I'm here to help you, and right now we need to show the world that you are innocent. You know"—I tried to break it to her gently—"everyone here is fascinated by what's happened, and I imagine there is a great deal of discussion. I think it's likely that you've been mentioned as a suspect." With waspish Gladys Samson on the loose, I was sure of it.

Deirdre said happily, "Hal promised he'd find out the truth."

I was touched by her confidence in him. "Hal will certainly do his best. But you have a reputation to defend. You need to show the flag."

She looked at me blankly.

Sometimes I wonder at the education young people receive now. I explained gently, "'Show the flag' means to make your presence known no matter what the circumstances."

"Do you have any idea how quaint that sounds?" For an instant, she looked young and amused.

"Quaint or hip, I'm positive you have to be on the scene to make your case. The afternoon is winding down. Go mix and mingle. Show everyone you aren't afraid."

Deirdre gave a resigned shrug. "Okay. Have it your way. I might as well go downstairs. Maybe if I talk to people, I can forget about you."

෴

The afternoon sessions over, guests streamed from the hallways. The lobby was full. Some headed for the bar, others strolled out onto the terrace, blinking in the sunlight like moles awakening from a stupor. So many ways to write, so many notes to take.

Scraps of conversation floated past me. "Clichés are clichés because they're true. . . . cardboard characters . . . If prologues are passé, how can the reader know the background? . . . I like using the present tense. . . . vampires in da Vinci's studio . . ."

The speakers were also among the exodus from the meetings. Cliff Granger avoided looking directly at anyone, clearly hoping to escape yet another author ready to make the inevitable pitch. Long face preoccupied, obviously a man with a destination, he glanced at his watch, walked swiftly onto the terrace. He strode past a clump of writers and stopped at a table near the weeping willow and bent forward to speak to Jessica Forbes. She wore her silver hair in coronet braids today. A heavy-link gold necklace glittered in the sunlight. Granger made a gesture toward a chair. She nodded and he pulled out a chair and joined her. Her expression was pleasant, perhaps to indicate she wasn't dwelling on their exchange last night at the bar. Once seated, he appeared to be making an effort to be charming.

Sidelong glances followed Deirdre as she crossed the terrace. When she approached a table, most faces reflected a mixture of embarrassment and uneasiness.

At a table in the center of the terrace, Gladys Samson tossed her head, a defiant gesture. It didn't take a mind reader to know that she'd spent the afternoon regaling anyone who would listen with her version of Deirdre stalking down the hall on her way to see Jay Knox in his cabin late at night.

Deirdre noted gazes shifting away from her, slight pauses in conversations as she passed.

I dropped down beside her, whispered softly, "Last night in the hall, you talked to Gladys Samson, the woman with short dark hair and a thin face and jangly bracelets. She told police she saw you and you admitted you were going to see Jay and she described you as distraught and upset."

Deirdre looked around the terrace, spotted Gladys. Deirdre walked straight to Gladys's table, gazed down at her. "To think"—her clear voice was easily audible to everyone in a sudden fraught silence—"that I spoke with you when I was on my way to see Jay last night. It's shocking to remember that the last time I saw him he was full of life, eager to celebrate my happiness at joining the faculty. That's how I will remember him. I'm so glad I hurried on my way there. If I'd stopped to look at your manuscript, I might have missed seeing him. It still seems unbelievable that someone killed him. I know we are all feeling sad today."

At a nearby table, Maureen Matthews gave a nod of approval. Very likely she'd heard the rumors about Deirdre, didn't believe them, was glad to have reassurance. Although Maureen still looked weary, she was quite lovely, her soft dark hair in a cloud around her elegant, memorable features. Her expression gave no hint of worry, so I assumed she had yet to discover that the packet of letters was no longer in her purse.

Jessica Forbes was a dominating presence, the coronet braids emphasizing the strength of her features—deep-set eyes, long nose, sharp chin. She watched Deirdre with interest. Likely she, too, was aware of the rumors swirling around Deirdre. She leaned toward Cliff Granger and spoke with one hand shielding her lips. He listened with an intrigued expression, his gaze riveted on Deirdre. He'd spent the afternoon meeting with authors and was likely just now learning from Jessica that Deirdre had been a subject of speculation by the conference attendees and gossip had fingered her as a suspect in Jay's murder.

I imagined whispers in the hallways, around the tables, at the bar. *They say she looked mad. Why did she go to his cabin late at night? They say he slept around. They say he was killed with a champagne bottle. They say . . . They say . . . They say . . .*

Last night Liz Baker was alone in the bar after her husband left. She was alone now, late in the afternoon on the terrace. She, too, watched Deirdre, but there was no relief from tension in her young face. Where was her husband? Did she know where he was last night when she ran away from Jay's cabin, tears streaming down her face?

Harry Toomey stood at the edge of a group of writers. There was a slight smile on his plump face. No doubt he was enjoying Deirdre's effort to salvage her reputation.

Deirdre stared at Gladys until the older woman's gaze fell. Deirdre waited an instant longer, then turned away from the table.

The silence still held.

Deirdre stood tall and thin and alone on the terrace. The breeze stirred her long frizzy brown hair and molded her patterned silk dress against her. "I hope everyone here is cooperating with the investigation." She looked from table to table, her gaze touching every face. The silence was absolute. "I told the police everything I know. I believe I was helpful. Anyone with information about Jay from ten forty-five to midnight is asked to contact the police. If you saw Jay or know of anyone who intended to speak to him last night, please tell the police. The police assure me they are making progress in finding out what happened."

I scanned faces. I don't know what I was seeking. A fleeting look of worry, uncertainty, fear?

Maureen Matthews was pensive. She might have known that Jay had been in full pursuit of Deirdre, but there was a sensitivity in her eyes, an understanding of Deirdre's isolation.

Jessica Forbes's gaze was appraising. Did she find Deirdre gallant? Or suspect?

Cliff Granger leaned back in his chair, a portion of his face in shadow. The uneven lighting emphasized the jut of his jaw, gave him a predatory aura. But he seemed to be looking beyond Deirdre.

I followed his gaze, but the crowd eddied and shifted.

Liz Baker no longer stood at the edge of the terrace. The crowd shifted again and I had a clear view of Harry Toomey, his round face pleased, then a heavy woman blocked him from view. I suspected Harry was taking pleasure in Deirdre's efforts to discredit the ugly gossip and hoping the gossip was true.

Maureen Matthews pushed back her chair, came to her feet. "Deirdre is speaking for all of us at the college." Her clear voice could be heard throughout the terrace. "Please contact the police if you can help with the investigation."

Deirdre flashed her a look of gratitude, then brushed back a tangle of wiry curls. "Please come forward if you feel you know *anything* about last night. It's up to everyone here to help." Deirdre forged ahead, a light flush in her cheeks. "If anyone feels shy about talking to the police, I'll be glad to pass along information to them. I have them on speed dial."

With that, Deirdre lifted her chin and walked swiftly to the path. With her back to those watching her depart, her long face drooped and she pressed trembling lips tightly together.

I walked beside her. "Good job."

Her stride checked momentarily. She gulped in a breath. "Are you always next to me?"

"Oh no. I'm here and there."

"Maybe you might go there for a while."

"Where would that be?"

She turned her hands over. "Somewhere where you can find out what really happened."

It was excellent advice. I decided to follow it.

Chapter 7

W hen the hallway was empty outside the door to Liz and Tom Baker's room, I reappeared in the blond pageboy, sunglasses, and frumpy gray dress. I would be delighted when the gray dress was only a memory. I knocked firmly on the door.

Tom Baker opened the door, looked apprehensive.

I flashed the black leather folder. "It's time we talked, Mr. Baker."

His young face was pale and set. He jerked his head, stood aside for me to enter.

I moved confidently forward, waited until the door was closed.

He paced to the window, stared out at tree leaves fluttering in the breeze. "Yeah?"

I looked at his back. "Face me, Mr. Baker."

Slowly he turned. The muscles in his throat moved convulsively. "Look, I don't know anything about—"

"I'll ask. You answer." I'd watched a few interrogations at the police station. I snapped, "You stood in the bushes outside cabin five. We have casts of footprints. They'll match yours." I pointed at his faded black running shoes, old shoes. The right one had a decided list from a worn front sole. "What did you do after Liz left?"

A muscle jumped again in his throat. His eyes were wide and staring. "I didn't do anything."

"You saw Jay slam the door in her face."

He realized that I knew what had happened between Liz and Jay.

He licked dry lips. "All right. I was there. I heard. But he was fine when Liz left. You got to know that." His tone was urgent. "Liz wouldn't hurt anybody. She was crying." His voice was shaky. "She did her best to get the money back. He—" Tom broke off, as if realizing he was saying more than he should. "Yeah. I stood there a minute." His face was hard and set, reflecting remembered rage. His eyes flickered from side to side as he tried to decide what to say.

I knew he was going to lie.

"Yeah. She left." His gaze was open and guileless, but a slight tic pulled at the side of one eye. "I almost went after her but my mind was all messed up. I kept thinking about the money and my car, and I ran down to the lake. I went to the end of the pier and stood there for a long time. Too long." A bitter twist to his mouth. "Some big damn bird crapped on me. Damn bird. I went back to the shore and slopped lake water on my shirt. That's when I went up to the lodge. Liz was asleep. I took off my shirt and washed off the stuff and went to bed."

But I didn't think he'd slept for a long time. And I didn't believe he watched Jay slam the door in Liz's face and went meekly down to the lake.

∽

Only a few tables on the terrace were still occupied. I imagined most guests had gone to their rooms, the industrious perhaps looking over notes from the sessions, others resting in anticipation of this evening's barbecue. I didn't see any familiar faces. Lodge staff bustled about, setting up the outdoor buffet. Paper tablecloths covered a couple of Ping-Pong tables on the left side of the terrace. Rackets were neatly stowed in shelving on one wall that also held pool cues, badminton racquets, and horseshoes.

I took my time following the walk that wound among the trees and the cabins. Privacy was enhanced by trees and shrubs. In effect, each cabin was tucked into its own wooded area. I stopped outside cabin 5. Police tape remained in place around the cabin. At this particular point, a portion of the front porch to cabin 6 was visible.

A blooming crape myrtle with reddish violet blossoms cast a thick shadow by the steps to cabin 5. Was that where Tom Baker hid as Liz hurried onto the porch? I dropped down for a closer look and was pleased to see separate crime-scene tape that marked off two footprints. I was sure a mold had been made. And yes, the right one had an uneven depth. So my fictional threat was a reality.

On the other side of the cabin, a bamboo thicket could also have afforded a hiding place. I studied the ground there, saw no footprints, but there was a layer of grass clippings carelessly left by a gardener, so no footprints were likely.

I returned to the path. At cabin 6, two wicker chairs sat on the porch. They were unoccupied. Anyone seated there would have a good view of Jay's porch.

I followed the path around a curve. The remaining cabins were also half-hidden among thick woods. I reached the shore and walked out on the pier. A few energetic guests were on the lake in rowboats. A huffing fiftyish rower jerked past. On shore, a long-haired man in a cowboy hat and a scrawny woman with a too-red face occupied a seat in a beached boat. Scraps of conversation rose over the slap of water on the pilings. ". . . so I started with action. 'At the third blow, the door exploded in a shower of wood. Three masked men catapulted into the room. She turned to run, but a loose shoelace brought her down. The snub nose of a rifle pressed against her throat.' You know what that editor said? She said rifles don't have snub noses. She missed the whole point!" The man picked up an oar from the boat. "That's not as bad as what that guy told me." He tilted the oar over the side of the rowboat, thumped the ground. "Wish I'd had this with me. I would have whopped him one. See, I had this great segue to the next chapter. 'The door creaked behind him. That was the last thing he heard.' What reader's not going to turn the page, find out what happened? He gave me this snide look, and said, 'Man, that's about as subtle as elephant tracks.'" The two of them were united in mutual outrage.

I shut out their impassioned defenses of their creative

efforts and imagined the pier as it was last night. Silent. Possibly dark. There were occasional lights, but they were high on poles and far apart. Both Harry Toomey and Tom Baker claimed they'd visited the pier, yet neither mentioned seeing anyone else.

I started with one fact known to me: Jay Knox was dead by a few minutes before eleven, when Deirdre Davenport came to cabin 5.

Liz Baker and Harry Toomey also claimed they spoke to Jay. Tom Baker confirmed Liz's claim. I rather thought they were both telling the truth that Jay was alive when Liz left the cabin.

I wasn't at all certain about the rest of Tom's story.

As for Harry, I thought he also told the truth about his talk with Jay.

But either Harry or Tom was lying about a sojourn on the pier.

Had Tom knocked on Jay's door, pushed his way in, quarreled? Maybe Jay shoved him, knocked him down. Jay was a much bigger man. Could Tom have struggled to his feet and moved backward toward the coffee table, snatched up the bottle, and attacked Jay? But if he committed a murder in haste, almost a blow in self defense, his fingerprints should be on the neck of the bottle. But once Jay lay motionless on the floor, Tom might have realized his danger, wiped the bottle with a washcloth from the bathroom. I doubted Tom usually tucked a handkerchief in his pocket. Possibly then, upset and scared, Tom slipped out of the cabin, seeking the shadows, and ran to the pier, trying to escape the reality of what he had done.

Yet that left the contradiction of Tom and Harry, both claiming they'd stood alone on the pier with their thoughts.

The evasion I sensed with Tom might be much more innocent. Perhaps he had confronted Jay, but Jay, bigger and stronger, manhandled him out the door. Furious and thwarted, Tom ran to the pier and, as he gazed out at the dark water, a bird had flown above him and soiled his shirt.

What if Harry didn't go to the pier? What if instead he'd started down the path toward the pier, then—still upset, desperate to restore his dream—he swung around, returned to the cabin?

Why would Jay have admitted him to the cabin? Perhaps Harry was charming. *Just want to tell you how much I appreciate you. . . . How about a drink to show no hard feelings? Call room service. . . . Can I introduce Deirdre tomorrow at her morning session? . . .* Something, anything to get back inside. Then perhaps a return to a plea, Jay responding rudely, and Harry snatching up the bottle.

Tom or Harry. They were on the scene. But there was the possibility that someone else arrived just before Deirdre came. Maureen Matthews was bitter about Jay's rejection and desperate to prevent publication of her love letters to him. Professor Ashton Lewis angered easily and he despised Jay because he was messing around with coeds. Cliff Granger looked grim after Jessica Forbes warned him he was submitting too many rubbish-heap manuscripts. Perhaps Cliff went to the cabin to tell Jay he wasn't willing to represent any more of Jay's clients.

I shook my head. All Cliff had to do was say no. The anger

would be on Jay's part. Still, Cliff was a possibility. Maureen was likelier. I thought it was clear Harry spoke to Jay after his quarrel with Liz, so I discounted Liz as a suspect.

I couldn't be sure of the timetable, but I thought it likely that Jay's visitors arrived in this order: Liz, Harry, Tom, the murderer, Deirdre. Maureen Matthews, Professor Lewis, or Cliff Granger might have preceded Deirdre. If I had to put money on the wheel, I'd have gone for Tom or Harry.

I walked briskly up the path, stopping only long enough in the deep shade of a honeysuckle shrub to once again change into a French blue uniform. It was a relief to be rid of the blond wig, sunglasses, and shapeless dress. I fluffed my hair. I do like being myself.

I concentrated to recall how I'd appeared to each person. My various personae were beginning to confuse me. Ah, yes. I was Officer Judy Hope when I spoke with Cliff Granger. I'd also been Officer Hope with Liz Baker. I was Officer Loy with Ashton Lewis. I promoted myself to Detective Loy in the wig and gray dress with Tom Baker, Harry Toomey, and Maureen Matthews. Maureen had seen right through the disguise, recognizing me as Judy Hope, reporter for the *Rabbit's Foot*. It was enough to make my head spin.

I came around the curve and ran lightly up the steps to cabin 6.

Once again, Cliff Granger opened the door. His sandy hair was slicked back. He had a fresh look as if he'd just stepped from a shower. His blue oxford cloth shirt was crisp, his pleated tan trousers unwrinkled. He neither welcomed nor rebuffed me, simply nodded. "Yes?"

"I have a few more questions, Mr. Granger."

There was a slight tightening of his lips, but he stepped back, held the door for me.

I followed him into the living room, noted he was barefoot. I remained standing when he slumped onto the sofa, thrust out long legs, looked up at me with a resigned expression. "I'm counting the hours until I get out of here. I signed up for a conference, not for a murder investigation. This evening I'm supposed to charm the locals at the barbecue. Part of the job. There are sessions tomorrow, but Sunday afternoon I'm off to Dallas for a flight home. I'll be glad to get back to New York." He was suddenly apologetic. "Sorry to complain. I guess Jay would like to have something to complain about right now."

I understood. Little discomforts always seem petty when they butted up against a harsh reality like death.

He locked his hands behind his head, looked apologetic. "What can I do for you?"

I was brisk, matter-of-fact. "You spoke to Mrs. Baker on the terrace after you left the bar. What time did you see Mr. Knox?"

His face crinkled in a puzzled frown. "I didn't see Jay."

"We were informed you spoke to Mr. Knox around eleven o'clock—"

"Hey, hold up." He sat up straight, his hands dropped to his knees as he leaned forward, looked at me intently. "Somebody told you wrong. I didn't talk to Jay last night. If anyone saw me on the path, I was on my way here. I suppose"—now he sounded comfortable—"that it would be an easy mistake to make; the cabins are right next to each other."

"You didn't make an effort to see him last night?" My tone was skeptical. "Perhaps to talk about his clients and the manuscripts you've been offering?"

His green eyes were wary. "No."

"Did you plan to tell him you weren't going to offer those manuscripts?"

He looked surprised, then shrugged. "I guess you've talked to Jessica. Yeah, I realized I had to make some changes. I was being a sap. I wanted to help Jay out, but she brought it home to me that I had to turn down the kind of stuff she called rubbish. As you can imagine"—his tone was rueful—"that wasn't a talk I wanted to have with him. He was a good client, but I was going to tell him when he dropped me off at the airport—" He paused, frowned. "That reminds me. I'll have to see if somebody'll give me a ride down to Dallas. Anyway, I intended to tell him then that I'd done all I could do for the writers he was pushing. Enough was enough. He was my client and a friend, but I had to draw the line." His big shoulders lifted and fell. "Too bad."

I didn't know if the latter comment referred to the task of informing Jay or the disappointment of the authors sent to him by Jay.

"When you left the terrace, you went straight to your cabin?"

He shook his head. "I took a walk in the garden. It was a nice night."

"Did you go down to the lake?"

He was definite. "Not that far. Perhaps halfway, then I came back."

"Did you see anyone near cabin five?"

His eyes narrowed. "I'm not sure. I glanced that way. There might have been someone coming down the steps, but it was just a quick glimpse. It's shadowy there. Sorry I can't be more definite. I didn't go as far as cabin five. I turned in, fixed myself a drink, relaxed. I went to bed around midnight."

I was reminded of an eel slipping through water, moving too quickly to be caught.

"Anything else?" He glanced at his watch. His tone was slightly peremptory, that of a busy man who'd indulged an inquisitor but was nearing the end of his patience.

"What can you tell me about the party at Jay Knox's house last year during the conference?"

"Party?" He looked blank.

"I understand there was plenty of whiskey and sex."

"Oh." He brushed a large hand through his damp hair. "A year's a long time. Frankly, I just went to be polite."

"No whiskey or sex for you?"

"Officer, some matters a gentleman doesn't discuss."

I resisted the impulse to ask how gentlemanly it was to attend a party with students where alcohol was served and apparently consumed in quantity. "This is a murder investigation."

He was irritated. "What does a stupid party a year ago have to do with anything?"

The party and its circumstances had a lot to do with Maureen Matthews's plan to get Jay in trouble. But Jay was dead. "Did you know the girls attending were from the college?"

"I didn't know or care." Now he was clearly impatient. "Like I said, the party was a year ago. Everybody was on a first-name basis. The lights were dim. I wasn't taking an inventory of the guests."

"Do you remember the name of the girl you were with?"

"I wasn't with a particular girl. Some trouble I'm smart enough to avoid. I stayed at the bar until a couple of the guys were ready to go back to the lodge. I hitched a ride. So, I don't know much that would interest anybody."

Except, perhaps, Dr. Randall.

I thanked him for his time. I had a feeling he was delighted to see me go.

∽

Sam Cobb's office was familiar, a long, wide room with an old brown leather sofa facing the windows. He sat with his back to the sofa at a battered oak desk littered with files. His wrinkled suit coat hung from a wooden coat tree near the door. Two framed Matisse prints added a spot of color to one dingy beige wall. Between the prints were a bulletin board and an old-fashioned blackboard. A stub of white chalk lay in the tray. A street map of Adelaide hung to the left of the hall door, a map of Pontotoc County to the right.

Sam's right arm moved as he wrote on a legal pad. His left arm dropped as if without volition, pulled out a side drawer, fished out a sack of M&M'S, his sustenance when thinking. He put down his pen and a stream of gaily colored candies flowed onto a broad palm. He swiveled around to face the windows.

At the blackboard, I eased the chalk into my hand, checked to be sure Sam still faced the windows, squeezed my eyes in remembrance, and began to print:

*1. Four authors attending the conference paid
Jay Knox to place manuscripts with an agent or
editor: Liz Baker, Joseph Burns, Wanda
Hamilton, Ellen Ben—*

"Want some M&M'S?" Sam's deep voice was amused. I swung around.

Sam had turned and was gazing at the blackboard. "You're still holding the chalk. Looks funny hanging there in the air. Lots of trouble to write everything on the chalkboard. How about we sit on the sofa." He waggled the M&M'S sack as he heaved himself to his feet.

I replaced the chalk and walked toward the couch.

"Kind of wonder who's visiting me today." He was deadpan except for a slight twitch of his lips. "Officer Judy Hope spoke to Liz Baker and Cliff Granger. She's a redhead. Cute, they said. Then there's Officer M. Loy. Redheaded, too. It's pretty clear Professor Lewis thought she was a knockout. Like the old joke about a younger man's surprise at an elderly gentleman leaning on a cane as he eyes a good-looking woman. The old codger says he may be old but he isn't dead yet. Then there's Detective M. Loy in a blond wig and a baggy gray dress. She checked out Tom Baker and Harry Toomey."

He didn't know about my interesting encounter with Maureen Matthews.

"An officer does what an officer has to do." My tone was demure.

Sam laughed, turned a thumbs-up. "Your cover is still

good. I figured I'd be getting some celestial pointers and I wouldn't interfere."

A faraway clack sounded, wheels rolling on rails. A faint scent of coal smoke alerted me, a warning that the Rescue Express was en route for me. "Sam"—my words were rushed—"there's a hitch." Wiggins knew more than I. Perhaps my work was done. "Before I talk to you, I need to know something ASAP."

Sam was a big, heavy man but he thought fast. He heard the change in my tone from ease to tension. His reply was immediate. "Sure."

"Is Deirdre Davenport still a suspect?"

Sam raised a grizzled dark brow. "Is she your charge? You've got a tough job. Davenport's at the top of the list. The mayor wants to know why I haven't picked her up already. The mayor wants to have a press conference and tag her as a person of interest. I said no way, not yet. But Davenport doesn't have any clout in town. No money. No connections. She came here fresh out of a Texas college to work on the *Gazette*. She married a guy who taught for a couple of years at Goddard, then went to work at the Chamber of Commerce in public relations. The mayor doesn't like reporters. Not even ex-reporters, and that includes Davenport."

Mayor Neva Lumpkin was living proof of the adage that there's a fly in every ointment. In her case, more like a big black splotch of selfishness, greed, ambition, and backstabbing. Sam loved his job, was well respected round town, but the mayor would happily replace him with a political supporter.

Sam was thoughtful. "The mayor has a point. Davenport's the only person linked to the crime scene physically. Plus she had motive. Plus a witness describes her as looking angry and vengeful when she set out to see Knox."

The smell of coal smoke was acrid now and the rumble of the wheels loud as thunder. Sam continued to placidly munch M&M'S, obviously unaware of the imminent arrival of the Rescue Express. I had only a moment. "Officer Loy's report can definitely expand the field." I enunciated clearly for Wiggins's benefit. "I will return shortly"—I hoped—"but I've been summoned to consult for a moment with a higher authority."

Sam spoke quickly. "I sure hope you can help us. Right now we're stuck." His eyes skittered around the room, perhaps wondering if the higher authority was lurking near. "It looks bad for Davenport."

I could have given him a hug. He sensed that I needed all the help I could get for my upcoming interview. "Back in a flash." If Wiggins could be persuaded to let me remain.

I'd conferred at other times with Wiggins atop City Hall. I was sure he remembered with clarity. Those encounters were on fall days, a brisk wind scudding leaves across the roof. This evening the blacktop roof radiated heat. The smell of coal smoke burned my nose. The only shade was a patch on the east side of the small shedlike structure that gave access to the roof.

If Wiggins was wearing his long-sleeved, heavy white cotton shirt and black flannel trousers and black shoes, he must be melting.

I popped into the shade. "Wiggins." My voice lifted as if this were the very nicest surprise the day could offer.

"Precept. One. Three, and Four. Especially Four." Wiggins's tone was doleful. "My patience is at an end. I've lost track"—now his tone was stentorian—"of just how many times and ways you've appeared. As yourself, as Judy Hope, as—"

I was facing the shed that provided access to the roof. The door eased open a crack.

I was delighted. Sam had guessed where I would be. I was hartened that he came up to see if I succeeded in continuing my mission, but I kept an expression of remorse on my face. I've never been sure whether Wiggins sees his emissaries when we aren't visible, but I wasn't taking any chances.

"—Officer Loy, as Detective Loy. Perhaps next time you'll be Inspector Loy?"

I wouldn't have expected irony from Wiggins. I couldn't resist an exclamation. "Heavens, no, Wiggins. I would never be so presumptuous."

"You wouldn't be . . ." A pause and then a rumble of laughter.

I grinned.

"Did anyone"—his deep voice was both chiding and admiring—"ever tell you that you're a minx?"

A pert, saucy girl—how sweet! Perhaps while Wiggins was bemused by my charm—and, of course, my excellent intentions—I would plead my case. "Wiggins, I am thrilled to bring you up to date, but"—a pause for dramatic emphasis— "the situation is perilous." If he envisioned a heroine tied to

153

tracks and an oncoming locomotive looming, that would be all to the good. "Mayor Lumpkin wants Deirdre Davenport arrested. ASAP. Deirdre is innocent. I am trying hard to be an exemplary emissary. I appeared only out of dire necessity in order to find out information that will help save poor, innocent Deirdre." I was earnest. "You know I would never appear unless I had no other choice. However, I have collected information that will help Chief Cobb. You don't want him to arrest Deirdre, a young mother whose reputation would always be besmirched." If I sounded like a Victorian novel, I knew my audience. "A young mother struggling to put food on the table, provide for her children, abandoned by her former husband."

"Poor child." He harumphed. "Very well. One more day. Not a moment more. And see if there is some way to make your report to Chief Cobb without blatantly revealing your presence."

He didn't have to mention Precept Four again.

The door to the structure eased shut.

I was suddenly alone, the clack of wheels on rails fading in the distance, the scent of coal smoke dissipating.

I reached the chief's office before he returned from the roof. He closed the door, walked to his desk, clicked on his intercom. "No calls or visitors for half an hour." He clicked it off. "Sometimes when I think, I hear voices." His expression was musing. "I kind of have a picture in my mind of an ideal police officer. Redhead. About five five. Green eyes. One of those interesting faces. Lots of freckles." His tone was cheerful. "This officer speaks out and it's like having a voice tell me stuff. She's got a good voice, kind of husky. I find that's a good way to think." He picked up the sack of

M&M'S, strolled to the couch, sat down. He held up the sack, ready to pour. "I can see her now. Though, of course, I know it is purely my imagination at work."

If Wiggins were still about, he surely wouldn't fault the chief for being so imaginative. I settled beside him.

Sam noted that the cushion gave a little.

I positioned my unseen hand at the lip of the sack. "M&M'S always give me a boost."

Red and yellow and brown candies poured into my out-stretched hand until there was a generous mound.

Sam moved the sack, filled his left hand, popped several in his mouth.

After a scrumptious M&M'S moment, I talked.

Sam listened.

At one point, his face intent, he retrieved a legal pad from his desk, dropped heavily onto the couch, made notes.

When I finished, Sam tapped his pen on the pad. "Any-time you want to join the force, you're on. This gives us a lot to work on. Harry Toomey and Tom Baker were on the scene. One of them went to the end of the pier, one of them didn't. Toomey could have quarreled with Knox about the job, lost control, knocked him down. Maybe Baker slammed in, threatened Knox, maybe Knox came for him. Baker's not big. He might have grabbed the bottle, swung. Or Liz Baker might have killed Knox and Tom's covering for her. Maybe she's the one who grabbed the champagne bottle. As for the bottle, there are fragments of Davenport's prints on the neck, but they're smudged. DA could claim she tried to wipe them off but was too stressed to do a good job. Or somebody else grabbed the bottle and then wiped it or maybe held it with a handkerchief or a washcloth from the bath. That's always a possibility. Say X is there, spots the bottle, decides to whack Knox, steps into the bathroom. Takes only a second to grab a cloth from a rack, walk out with a hand down to one side. Knox had no reason to suspect danger. X strolls over to the coffee table, comments on the champagne, picks up the bottle—holding it out of Knox's view—swings around, moves fast, strikes, and Knox is on the floor. It didn't take a paramedic for the killer to know he was dead. We'll take a look at Liz and Tom Baker and Harry Toomey. Professor Lewis might have lost his temper if he confronted Jay about the coed and Jay laughed it off, said he'd insist Lewis was a liar. Lewis sounds like he'd blow up if Knox smirked and said he'd claim Lewis was making up the accusation to cause trouble. Definitely Maureen Matthews is in the running. Women don't like to be dumped, especially if they figure out they've been used. She wants revenge, so she plans to tell the department chair about Knox's party with coeds and sex and whiskey. I'll have Weitz ask around, see what she can find out about that party. Maybe Granger was more involved than he let on. Anyway, Knox's threat to publish those letters might have been the last straw for Matthews." He frowned. "You said she came for the letters. What are the odds she's gotten rid of them by now?"

"She put the letters in her purse. They aren't there now. For the present, the letters are in a safe place." My tone was bland.

Sam looked uncomfortable. "Screwing around with evidence gets cops in trouble."

"Not to worry." My tone was soothing. "If you need to discover the letters, they will be found."

Sam rubbed knuckles against one cheek. "Yeah. I get it. I think. Untouched by human hand, so to speak." He leaned back on the leather sofa.

"It might be more accurate to say untouched by corporeal hand." I popped the last M&M in my mouth.

He held out the candy sack. "Want some more?"

"No, but thanks."

Sam put the legal pad on one knee. "The crime scene looked straightforward, but there are two twists you need to know about." Sam made a quick sketch on the pad of a prone stick figure. "Knox was lying on the floor. The champagne bottle was in the shadow of the TV. The living room light was on, the porch light off. We got pix, made notes, measurements. Got the prelim ME report: single blow to left temple, death by blunt trauma. No other apparent wounds. Hands showed no sign of injury. No bruises on his bare arms. He didn't put up a fight. Looks like he wasn't expecting trouble, that he was in the room with someone he knew. That means we didn't expect to find forced entry, and we didn't. There were no traces of a break-in. Then it got interesting. We emptied his pockets. His billfold contained three credit cards, two hundred and thirty dollars in cash. A handful of change in left trouser pocket. But"—and now Sam's dark eyes gleamed—"we didn't find a cell phone. That's anomaly number one. We didn't find car keys. That's anomaly number two. We checked out the entire cabin. No cell phone. No car keys. His car, a 2004 Thunderbird, was parked in the lodge lot adjacent to the auditorium. Guess what we found in the car?" Sam's tone was silky.

I had a quick vision of a black panther gliding low to the ground, intent upon prey.

He didn't wait for a reply. "The keys were in the ignition. We checked the steering wheel for prints. Shiny and clean as off the showroom floor. And still no cell phone."

I sat bolt upright. My words tumbled out. "That means someone else drove his car last night. Jay wouldn't leave the keys in his car. After he was killed, his murderer took the keys, drove Jay's car to his house. If anyone happened to notice lights, movement in the house, Jay's car was in the driveway. I may know why the murderer went there."

Sam leaned forward, pen poised above his legal pad. "Yeah?"

"I went to his house this afternoon." I described the swivel chair facing the computer. "I checked his desk. He'd been paying bills. The stamped envelopes are neatly stacked in the out-box tray. The natural thing would be to leave the chair facing the desk. I know that's slender evidence, but that chair didn't look right. The chair was facing the computer, pushed back a little as if someone sat there and, when finished, got up, shoved the chair back. I think someone checked out his computer, and that fits in with a missing cell phone."

Sam absently drew a swivel chair. "The position of the chair wouldn't speak to me except for the fact that his cell phone was taken." He muttered, as if to himself. "Sure. There was something in his cell phone and something in his computer that somebody wanted to hide. Likely, the murderer tossed that phone into the lake and we'll never find it." He pushed up from the couch, walked to his desk, perched on one edge. He picked up the phone, punched an extension. "Colleen, check the schedule. Is Smith off today?"

Don Smith was a tall, darkly handsome detective who'd worked with Detective Weitz when I was last in Adelaide.

As he waited, Sam said in an aside to me, "Don's nuts about computers. Compares computer programs to works of art. Yeah, I told him, just like Picasso in his Blue Period. A barrel of fun." He drummed impatient fingers on the desk-top as he waited, then began to speak. "Good. Thanks." He ended the call, punched a number, pressed Speaker.

"Hey, Don, you sitting poolside with a cool one?"

"Yo, Sam. My day off. Remember?"

"Sure. But you're the man with a happy hand when it comes to computers. Swill down some coffee, take a ther-mos with you." He looked at some notes, rattled off Jay Knox's address. "We've got his house keys here at the sta-tion. Take a fingerprint kit. Dust the mouse, the chair at his desk, the area around the computer for prints. We got a tip somebody deleted something from Knox's computer last night sometime after eleven p.m. Check e-mails, files, pho-tos. You're the computer genius. Find it."

Don was grumpy. "Thermos? Am I getting a vibe that I don't leave until I come up with something?"

I hadn't thought about what might be missing. But cell phones have become ubiquitous recorders of fleeting images, and those photos could be shared with the computer.

Sam was still talking. "The sooner you find what's miss-ing, the sooner you get to go home. Check with Weitz for full names, descriptions of Liz and Tom Baker, Harry Toomey, Ashton Lewis, Maureen Matthews, Cliff Granger. Pull their photos from Facebook pages, yearbooks, wherever. One of them was busy last night. You figure out which one."

Chapter 8

Deirdre sat at a small bench in front of a mirror, a makeup brush in one hand. She was a stylish mixture of dressy and casual, with an elegant creamy beige lace blazer over a lacy tank and beige cotton crops with a wide cuff. As she turned her head, shining gold hoop earrings glittered. More subdued was a double-strand necklace of small hoops.

"Are we going to a party?" I love parties, and there was reason to celebrate.

Her response was familiar by now: instant rigidity, seeking glance.

I took a moment to appear, considering my own wardrobe. I felt festive and chose a silvery polyester poncho, delicate as a wisp of smoke. A cloud design on either side was enhanced by a front panel with alternate rows of gold beads and tiny black crows. A necklace of gold and onyx beads repeated the colors of the central panel. Slim white trousers and silver high heels added a finishing touch.

I hurried across the room to stand behind Deirdre, made a pirouette. "I think we both look marvelous."

Deirdre faced me, reached out to touch the poncho. "That's beautiful."

"Thank you." Preparatory to an announcement, I cleared my throat. As I clapped my hands together for emphasis, I just happened to glance at the mirror again and saw how gracefully the silky material swished. Certainly this was no time to take pride in appearance, but I was buoyed. "My dear, I have conferred with Police Chief Sam Cobb."

Deirdre drew in a deep gulp of breath. The hand holding the brush dropped onto the vanity table.

I patted her reassuringly on the shoulder.

She tensed but didn't flinch. An improvement.

It took me several minutes, but I ended on a triumphant note. "The police now have suspects in addition to you." I ticked them off. "Liz Baker. Tom Baker. Harry Toomey. Ashton Lewis. Maureen Matthews. Cliff Granger. By tomorrow"—I had confidence in Detective Smith—"they'll know what was deleted from Jay's computer." I awaited applause and appreciation.

"The mayor wants me arrested?" Her fingers clutched at the chain around her neck.

"Sam knows you're innocent. I told him so."

Her eyes squeezed shut for an instant, blinked open. "That's good. Vouched for by a ghost. Don't get me wrong,

I appreciate you and I'm glad the police chief believes you, but it sounds to me like I'm still in deep trouble."

I hurried to the bath, found a plastic glass sheathed in a wrapper, tore it free, filled the glass with cold water, and returned to the bedroom.

Deirdre was standing at the window and looking down at the terrace and wooded area. "All the suspects will be at the barbecue. They don't have any choice. It's a command performance for staff. We exude charm and wisdom for the benefit of the fragile egos of a hundred-plus writers. It would be more fun to swim with piranhas."

I handed her the glass and she downed the contents in three gulps. Water wasn't whiskey, but it gave her a boost.

"Act just the way you did at lunch and—"

The phone rang.

Deirdre tossed the cup into a wastebasket and walked to the desk, picked up the receiver. "Deirdre Davenport." Her face changed. "Hi." Her voice was soft. She dropped into the desk chair.

I perched on the edge of the desk.

She cupped her hand over the receiver. "Go away." Then she said quickly, "Not you, Hal. She's here. . . . Oh. Okay." She looked at me. "Hal says hi."

I beamed. "Tell him I'm on the case."

Deirdre spoke to Hal. "She says she's on the case. . . . Oh. I'll try that." She again cupped her hand over the receiver. "Hal says to tell you he considers you a good-luck omen and that all assistance is welcome."

I nodded my thanks.

Then she turned away, listening. "Oh, Hal, I wish I could.

But I have to be here tonight. Staff attends a barbecue to mix and mingle." Her voice held all the thrill of a woman looking at a plate of dead worms. "But if this horrible weekend ever ends, if—" She stopped, thought for a moment, frowned. "Hal, tell me something."

I reached over to punch Speaker Phone.

Hal's voice filled the room. ". . . answer any question. How about asking me about my favorite things? I have a list of new favorite things: The way you look quizzical and amused and skeptical all at the same time. The way you laugh. The way your voice reminds me of Kate Smith singing during the seventh inning. I get shivers deep inside. What are your favorite things?"

Deirdre's face softened. "A man who says what he thinks, and what he thinks is honest and real. A man"—there was a slight catch in her voice—"who puts his job in jeopardy to ask a woman out to dinner. I saw the way your boss and the other detective looked at me, but you didn't care. If you took me out to dinner, wouldn't that be"—she paused, struggled for the right word—"seen as a conflict of interest? Isn't there some kind of police policy along those lines?"

There was silence.

Deirdre gave a small sigh. "Thank you for not lying to me. Somehow I know you won't ever do that, will you?"

"I won't ever lie. But I don't give—"

"I do. Next week we'll go out to dinner." Her voice was shaky. "If they haven't put me in jail. But thank you, Hal, thank you for calling. Thank you for being . . . Hal."

"Deirdre, listen—"

She replaced the receiver.

I clicked off Speaker Phone.

The phone rang. One peal, two . . .

Deirdre paced back to the window, stood with her back to me, shoulders bowed.

I came up beside her. "Deirdre, you're more important to Hal than what anyone thinks of him."

Deirdre swung around. Her smile was misty. "I want to believe that's true. But he's too important to me to let him do anything that will hurt him. In any way. I want to have dinner with him so much I could cry. I want to touch his hair. I want . . . But the only way that can happen is for me to figure out who killed Jay. There are things I can do. I'm here. I know these people. Or if I don't know them, I can find them, talk to them. Look, I write fiction. I know all about body language. I can write it in my sleep. 'The heroine saw Roderick out of the corner of her eye. Now his face was smooth, but for an instant he'd stared with cold eyes. She'd glimpsed a depth of anger that chilled her. The scrape of leather on the cement. Roderick was walking toward her. . . .' So I'm going to talk to a select list. You told me the ones the police are going to investigate. Maureen Matthews. Ashton Lewis. Liz Baker. Tom Baker. Harry Toomey. Cliff Granger. But the cops have to ask questions like 'Where were you at eleven o'clock?' and 'When did you see Jay Knox?' But I can do a lot more than that."

"What are you going to do?" I admired the combative jut of her chin, but I was worried. One of the six had snuffed out Jay Knox's life. Poking and prodding a murderer could put her in danger.

Deirdre gave me an almost whimsical smile. "For starters,

I'm shedding you. As much as I enjoy your company and appreciate your efforts, I'm handling this by myself. Tonight I'm on my own." She gave me a level glance. "Or if you do hang around, stay at least ten feet away from me whether you're there or not. Don't mess things up for me."

I understood her desperation, but I didn't like this plan. "What are you going to say to these people?"

She was at the door. She looked over her shoulder. "That's for me to know and for you to wonder about. Cheerio." The door slammed.

I took one last regretful glance in the mirror. Such a lovely outfit and perfect for a party, but duty called. I disappeared.

✧

Lanterns strung in the trees added to the party ambience. The barbecue was informal. Dress ranged from casual tops and jeans to an occasional T-shirt and shorts to a few dressier outfits. Revelers jammed the terrace, the crowd spilling out into the garden. Although it was only a quarter past seven, the noise level was intense, fueled by women's voices rising higher and higher. Men, greatly outnumbered, gathered in small clumps on the fringe of the terrace.

Deirdre, contrary to her plan, was at the center of a jostling group. A tall, thin man with a goatee, resplendent in a yellow cowboy shirt that no cowboy would ever have worn, corduroy trousers, and red cowboy boots leaned over her. ". . . imagine the tension. His prize bull stolen, a ransom note tucked into the visor of his pickup truck . . ." A white-haired woman in a silky top and patchwork skirt bobbed in between Yellow Shirt and Deirdre, stared rapturously up at Deirdre. "You touched my soul." A plump hand pressed against a generously endowed chest. "Your understanding of the human psyche, simply profound." She scrabbled in a huge pocket, pulled out a small tablet. "I know you will want to see how I begin the scene between Camille and Armand. Of course, you realize the significance"—a significant stare—"of their names? It sets the stage. The despair of a love affair ending in heartbreak." She thrust the tablet at Deirdre. "The working title is *The Despair of a Love Affair.*"

I whispered to Deirdre, "Perhaps you can slip away."

"Slip away?" Deirdre looked harried. "What am I supposed to do? Disappear?"

The white-haired woman was startled. "Do you think she should disappear? Or perhaps Armand . . ."

Yellow Shirt leaned nearer, said firmly, "You have to understand about the bull. . . ."

It was up to me to provide a diversion. I returned to the secluded spot in the honeysuckle arbor and appeared. Enjoying the ripple of the feathery poncho-style top—a nice outfit always makes me feel like high-stepping—I hurried up the path and crossed the terrace.

White Hair, animated and waving the tablet, remained between Deirdre and Yellow Shirt, who glowered at the interloper.

I took Deirdre's elbow. "I'm sorry to pull you away from these lovely people, but staff is assembling for final instructions." I smiled at White Hair and Yellow Shirt and propelled Deirdre toward the gardens. We didn't stop until we were at the end of the pier.

I looked over my shoulder. "I'm surprised that woman isn't right behind us. With that kind of persistence, she'll probably cow an editor."

Deirdre managed a smile. "I read the first couple of paragraphs. How could I not with that tablet shoved under my nose? Each paragraph was followed by a frowny face. Trust me, her book won't sell." She gave me an appreciative nod. "Thanks for getting me out of there. Piranhas. I've got to figure out a way to avoid the piranhas if I'm going to talk to anyone about Jay."

I had an idea. By this time I understood the staying power of aspiring writers. "I'll spot them one by one and tell you where they are. You can walk toward the terrace and pretend to talk on your cell. You know: intent face, very focused, obviously an important call. That should get you past any writers."

She looked at me suspiciously. "I want to talk to the people on my list one-on-one. Not you."

"I understand. I won't interfere." I would be present though unseen.

"Why are you suddenly cooperative?" She was wary. "You don't want me to do this."

She was right. I was afraid she was putting herself in danger. But I knew determination when I saw it. "What can happen in the middle of a party? Wait here. I'll be back in a moment."

As I disappeared, soft colors whirling and fading, Deirdre's eyes flared and her hands clenched. I regretted distressing her. I would have thought a writer might readily embrace new dimensions. Apparently not.

I skimmed above the path, slowed halfway to the terrace.

Maureen Matthews held a drink but she, too, was alone. She stood in deep shadow below the spreading branches of a white oak, remote, contained, aloof from the crowd surging on the terrace as lines formed for the buffet. Maureen's fashion choice was an excellent foil for her ebony dark hair and fair skin, a lime green cotton shirt with a stylish bow at the waist. Ankle-length white linen slacks and white sandals emphasized the brightness of the blouse. A multistranded necklace with brilliant stones was matched by a three-stranded bracelet. She was dressed for a party, but her face, in the privacy beneath the tree, drooped with worry and indecision. Likely she had discovered the packet of love letters was no longer in her purse. I imagined that discovery resulted in a thorough search of the car and a despairing realization she had no idea where the packet might be. Or who might have the letters. Or whether the letters would be revealed to the world at large.

I returned to the end of the pier. Deirdre stood with arms folded staring out at the water. I dropped down beside her. "Maureen Matthews is well off the path. She's standing near an old white oak, a huge tree."

Deirdre tensed on hearing words without an apparent source, then guardedly looked in the direction of my voice. She managed a faint "Thanks" and started for the shore.

I called after her. "Cell phone."

Deirdre glanced over her shoulder. "No kibitzing. Okay?" But she pulled the cell from her summery cotton bag, held it to one ear.

I followed her up the curving path. Just short of the white

oak, a plump woman in a cerise tank top and pumpkin-colored shorts gave an excited squeal. "Mrs. Davenport, your session—"

Deirdre covered the mouthpiece, looked apologetic. "Sorry. I have to take this call. We'll visit later." She picked up speed.

It wouldn't be Heavenly to whisper *I told you so*, so I didn't.

The white oak loomed to the left. Deirdre veered from the path, slipped the phone into her bag. Leaves crackled under her shoes as she plunged deeper into the shadows.

Maureen Matthews's eyes flared for an instant as she watched Deirdre approach. She brushed back a strand of silky hair, looked weary, her lovely face drawn and pale.

"Maureen, I've been looking for you." There was a tiny sound of uncertainty in Deirdre's voice. She stopped perhaps a foot from Maureen, clasped her hands together.

Lights strung in the tree offered enough illumination for me to see them clearly, like spots on a stage illuminating the actors.

Maureen waited. Was there wariness, possibly fear, in her stillness?

I wondered if Deirdre had been an actress at some point in her life. Everything in her expression and posture hinted at a momentous encounter, something known, something she was hesitant to share, something she felt compelled to pursue.

Maureen's haggard face was alert. Was she wondering if Deirdre had somehow come into possession of those revealing letters? "What can I do for you?"

Deirdre glanced about, as if making certain no one was near to overhear. She stepped closer, dropped her voice. "I don't know what to do. I haven't spoken to the police yet. You see, last night I caught a glimpse of someone hurrying through the trees near Jay's cabin. I thought it was you." Deirdre watched Maureen.

Now I understood Deirdre's objective: a provocative statement and the hope that a look, a breath, a physical tic would betray the listener.

Maureen's fine features remained immobile for an instant too long before she arched one dark brow, gave a husky laugh. "I'm flattered you can imagine me skulking in the shadows. Quite the romantic heroine." She lifted her wineglass, took a sip. "I'm afraid"—now her gaze was challenging—"your eyes were playing tricks." There was the slightest emphasis on the final word. With that and a cool stare, she stepped around Deirdre and walked swiftly away.

I was crisp. "That was an interesting response."

Deirdre looked toward the sound of my voice. "Why am I not surprised you're here? But you're right. A very interesting response. I think she went to the cabin."

"She never answered your question. I think you may be right." I appeared.

Deirdre stiffened, but she managed a tight smile. "Next time give me a little warning. There's something about wavy-colors-and-there-you-are that makes me just a teeny bit uncomfortable. In addition to having you around at all."

I gave Deirdre a reassuring pat, ignoring her quick intake of breath. "I'm here for a reason." I spoke firmly just in case Wiggins was checking on me. Certainly it wasn't the elegance of the swirly poncho that prompted me to appear, although one should never waste a beautiful outfit. "This is a good spot to talk to people. You stay here. I'll go out and lasso them one by one."

Deirdre homed in on the logical flaw. "You're going to tell each one to come and talk to me? Why would they pay any attention to you?"

"Not to worry. I always find a way." I turned toward the path.

The roar of loud voices and throb of amplified music increased as I neared the terrace. I surveyed the crowd. Two lines snaked toward the buffet table. Many tables were already filled. Guests carrying paper plates and drinks walked into the garden, some sitting on a low wall, others choosing chairs around the pool.

Liz and Tom Baker sat at a poolside table in a poorly lit area. There were no plates of food before them. He held a drink in one hand and slumped in his chair, his face morose. Liz stared down at the small glass-topped table.

I moved confidently toward them. Tom had seen me as blond Detective Loy. I had spoken to Liz as redheaded Officer Loy. Now I was a dimly seen figure in the dusk, and I knew what I told them would rivet their attention, not my appearance. I reached their table, stopped. I spoke quickly, forcefully. "I believe you're Liz and Tom Baker. A woman wants to see you about last night at cabin five." I pointed at the path. "She's waiting under a big oak tree just around the first curve." I turned and walked swiftly away.

A chair scraped. Quick footsteps sounded. Tom Baker

caught up with me. "How'd you know who we are? Who are you? What's—"

"Just passing on a message." I looked past him, lifted a hand to wave excitedly. "Maisie, I see you. I'm coming." I darted away, plunged into a milling crowd, slipped into deep shadow behind the lifeguard stand, disappeared.

Tom stood uncertainly near the edge of the pool. He nervously brushed back a strand of sandy hair and stared at the crowd. Of course, he didn't see me. His sensitive face looked stricken with an edge of panic. He swung around, hurried toward Liz.

I reached Deirdre. "Liz and Tom Baker are coming. All they know is that a woman is waiting here who wants to see them about cabin five last night." I knew Liz and Tom would soon arrive. Fear is a powerful motivator.

Deirdre gazed in the direction of my voice. "Thanks. I guess you always deliver."

"I try. They're coming because neither one is sure about the other." I felt sad for them, so young and so frightened.

Leaves crackled above the rasp of cicadas, the chitter of a startled squirrel. Two figures came nearer and nearer.

I perched on a low limb of the oak for an excellent view.

Deirdre looked imposing, a tall figure waiting with arms folded. Her face, clearly visible in light from a lantern in the tree, was composed with an underlying gravity.

Tom came first, Liz a step behind. Tom's face was young and vulnerable. A too-small polo shirt and tight jeans accentuated his slight build. He edged slowly nearer, stared at Deirdre, stopped, said uncertainly, "You want to see us?"

"Yes. I thought that was only fair. When I talked to the police, I didn't tell them everything I saw last night. I wanted to speak with you before I see them again. I know"—there was a ragged edge to Deirdre's voice—"how awful it is to have the police suspect you. It's like being in a dark dungeon and you don't see any way out and you know something horrible is waiting in the shadows."

Liz lifted a hand to her throat. She slid a terrified glance at Tom.

Deirdre noted that glance. She looked at Liz. "You ran down the steps of the cabin." Deirdre remembered what I had told her: Liz begging Jay for money, Liz leaving the cabin in tears, Tom claiming he'd gone down to the pier. Now Deirdre turned toward Tom. "You were furious. You stormed up the steps, pushed your way inside."

Tom's shoulders tightened. His hands balled into fists. He took a step toward Deirdre. "He shouldn't have made Liz cry."

I was ready to drop down, find a rock or a branch.

Liz thrust herself between Tom and Deirdre. "Leave him alone. Tom wouldn't hurt anyone." Tears coursed down her face. "He wouldn't. Leave us alone." She turned, grabbed her husband's arm. "Don't say anything. She's trying to save herself. That's all anyone was talking about this afternoon. Everybody thinks she killed him. Her fingerprints are on the champagne bottle. Don't say anything, Tom."

Tom's face was flat and hard, perhaps the look of an innocent man desperate to explain his presence in the cabin, perhaps the look of a man fearing testimony that might put him in prison.

"Tom." Liz was frantic, tugging at his arm. "We don't have to talk to her." She pulled again.

Tom gulped down breath, took a step backward. "Yeah. Liz's right. You can't make us say anything. Come on, Liz." He turned and they walked away, moving faster and faster.

Deirdre gave a forlorn sigh. "As they say in the kind of novels I don't write, not an auspicious beginning."

"You're doing splendidly. There's no reason to be discouraged. Chin up."

I'm sorry to say Deirdre didn't appear to find my response cheering.

Deirdre managed a wan smile. "Discouraged? Why should I be discouraged? Two kids blew me off like an annoying chaperone, but that's okay. My chin, what's left of it after a haymaker from little Liz, is definitely up. Go for it, Bailey Ruth/Judy Hope, bring them on. I'll be waiting."

Chapter 9

Ashton Lewis's cheeks were slightly pink, possibly from several glasses of wine.

An older woman with upswept gray hair and an intelligent face smiled up at him. "I appreciate your advice. Thank you very much." She turned and walked away.

I approached in my blond wig and baggy gray dress since he had seen me as redheaded Officer Loy. I would not present myself as a detective. I was simply an attendee at the conference.

There was not a hint of recognition in his kindly gaze.

I spoke in an eager, chatty tone. "I just talked to Deirdre Davenport, and she's hoping you will take a minute to visit with her."

He was professorially sporty tonight in a blue-and-white-striped seersucker suit. He made a courtly bow. "That would be my pleasure." He looked about, seeking Deirdre.

"It's rather frantic here on the terrace and you know how the writers like to monopolize the speakers. She's playing hooky from the crowd for a few minutes. If you go down the path, she's relaxing in the shade of a big tree." I pointed at the path, described the oak tree. "Oh, there's my husband, waving at me." Actually, Bobby Mac had been known at rowdier parties to let rip a vigorous *yee-hah!* when needing my attention. If you've never heard a *yee-hah*, you've never spent down-home time in the South or the West. I felt warm inside, thinking of Bobby Mac. "Glad I was able to pass along the message." And I turned and plunged into the thick of the crowd. On the other side of the terrace, I slipped into the shadows and disappeared.

~

"Ashton Lewis is on his way. He knows you want to talk to him. He has no idea why, but he's a gentleman of the old school responding to a lady's request. It's very endearing."

When I spoke, Deirdre stiffened only slightly, a marked improvement. "So you're back. Do you find it tiring to appear, disappear, appear?"

"That's an interesting question." At an appropriate time, I would consider my feelings. Did I have a sense of electricity as colors formed? Hmm.

Leaves crackled.

"Here he comes," I whispered. I regained my perch on the branch.

Ashton Lewis exuded dignity with every step, his spare face and perfectly shaped goatee aristocratic, his tall, stooped figure in the crisp seersucker suit evocative of long-ago town squares and gazebos and bands playing "In the Good Old Summertime."

He approached with a slightly questioning look, but his deep voice was cordial. "My dear, how nice of you to want to see me."

Deirdre was clearly not at ease. "I . . ." She took a deep breath. "I don't know how to say this."

He was close now. He gave her a sudden impish smile. "I usually follow Aristophanes's advice: 'If you strike upon a thought that baffles you, break off from that entanglement and try another. So shall your wits be fresh to start again.'"

Her face softened. Wariness eased from her face.

I found him incredibly charming. But the most ruthless intellect can affect disarming qualities. I tensed.

Deirdre met his curious gaze, gave him a quick smile. "That's good advice. I'll be blunt. I want to ask you about last night."

Lewis made no move, but his face was suddenly alert.

I leaned forward, watched him carefully. Ashton Lewis was highly intelligent, intuitive, empathetic. He was also a big man, tall and thin with long arms and large hands, and he stood between Deirdre and the path.

An owl whooed in the distance. The rasp of the cicadas pulsed. Leaves rustled in the evening breeze.

Deirdre looked at him gravely. "Last night when I left Jay's cabin, I thought there might have been someone standing in the shadows. Was it you?"

Lewis's eyes flickered around the shadowy area, darker now than when he'd arrived.

I dropped to the ground behind Lewis, moved fast, picked up a rough stick, two inches in diameter, a foot long.

Lewis's gaze slowly returned to Deirdre. "It's rather remote here, my dear. I suppose you chose this sequestered spot as an effective background for the heroine to confront suspects. Are you talking to several people in turn? If I put my mind to it, I, too, could assemble a credible list of suspects. But"—he took a step nearer—"I don't look for trouble." He reached out, touched her gently on one cheek. "Don't be foolish, Deirdre. Come back to the terrace with me. Let the police conduct the investigation."

Deirdre's voice was shaky. "They suspect me."

Slowly, he nodded. "So you are seeking an alternative. Be careful. Be very careful." He turned and strode away.

I breathed deeply, moved nearer. "Maybe it's too remote here."

Deirdre stared after Lewis. "For a moment, I was afraid."

"Perhaps you should be frightened. I think you need to be very careful."

She looked at the stick hanging in the air. "Thanks for being ready to defend me." She spoke in a strong, firm voice. "I run three miles every day. If you trip anybody up, I can get out of here. So, let's finish up."

I admired her. She was gallant, determined, and smart. She was smart enough, in fact, to be scared, very scared, despite her bravado.

◌

". . . she's waiting down the path in the shade of that big white oak tree."

Cliff Granger gave me a hard stare. He looked muscular and fit in a blue polo, khaki slacks, and brown loafers.

I hoped the blond wig was on straight, but I resisted the impulse to straighten it.

"Who are you?" He wasn't wasting any charm on a woman in a baggy gray dress.

When in need, think big. I drew myself up, looked haughty. I can do haughty, even in a blond wig and baggy dress. "I'm Evelyn Burlingame, the provost." I exuded the attitude that any fool at a college function would know the name of Evelyn Burlingame. "I am facilitating the effort Ms. Davenport is making to assist the authorities in their investigation of Jay Knox's death."

"What's that got to do with Deirdre Davenport? Or me?"

"There is a rumor you were seen at cabin five last night. The English Department has no desire to validate rumors. That's why it seemed more appropriate for Ms. Davenport to speak with you. Likely that will settle the matter and we need not bring any of this to the attention of the police. I'm sure that is your preference as well. We are doing our best to cooperate with the investigation and I know you will help us." I gave him a commanding nod, turned away.

∽

Deirdre paced back and forth beneath the low hanging limbs.

"Deirdre—"

She tensed, turned in my general direction. "Do you have any idea how weird it is to hear a voice and no one's there? Especially when it's darker than the shades of you-know-what, except for the lights in the tree. I keep picturing this dark figure swinging that champagne bottle. I'd like to run to my room and bolt the door and shove the dresser against it." She looked around. "It's so dark out there I can't tell if anyone's around." Her voice was shaky.

"You needn't worry. I'm right here."

"Somehow that assurance doesn't make me feel like the Marines have arrived. Anyway, don't talk to me when I can't see you."

I hoped to put Deirdre at ease. "There's no need for me to appear every time I return. After all, you know my voice."

"Oh, yes," she replied. "I know your voice." She spoke with a noticeable lack of enthusiasm.

I, of course, didn't take umbrage, but kept on point. "I don't know if Cliff Granger will come." I wasn't optimistic. The agent might ignore a directive from a Goddard administrator. "I told him I was the provost, Evelyn Burlingame, and we at Goddard were making every effort to dispel the rumor that he'd been seen at cabin five."

Deirdre's lips twitched. "Burlingame. How'd you come up—"

Leaves crackled.

She broke off, turned toward the path.

Cliff Granger strolled forward. He stopped a few feet away. "Hi, Deirdre. I'm not sure what's going on"—his tone was relaxed and casual—"but this rather forceful woman ordered me out here to talk to you. Is it true the English Department has you nosing around the conference, running down rumors about Jay's death?"

"True enough." Deirdre sounded embarrassed.

He looked amused. "Anything to hold a job, right?"

"Right. You're swell to come. Look, here's what's being said. Apparently someone"—Deirdre sounded vague—"saw you going in Jay's cabin last night."

Cliff shook his head. "Somebody's mistaken. I was in the vicinity. I'm staying in cabin six. I wandered around a bit, almost went down to the lake, but I changed my mind, came back to my place. I definitely did not—repeat *not*—go into Jay's cabin last night. Probably somebody saw me going into my cabin and got confused."

Deirdre took a step nearer, her face crinkling in inquiry. "Since you are staying nearby, did you happen to see anyone at Jay's cabin?"

He was silent for a moment. His long face folded in a frown.

Deirdre was suddenly sharp. "Please, Cliff, if you know anything, saw anyone, tell me."

He gazed at her soberly. "You sound desperate."

She hesitated, then said unsteadily, "Look, we can put a good face on my situation, pretend I'm talking to people to help the department. But I have to find out what happened to Jay, who killed him, for my own sake. The police are this close"—she held up her right hand with thumb and forefinger scarcely apart—"to arresting me. I went to the cabin. My fingerprints are on the champagne bottle someone used to kill him."

Cliff looked surprised. "Your fingerprints are on the bottle?" He looked at her searchingly. "That's not good."

"You're telling me. It's a long story. He came to my room earlier with the bottle and some glasses and we talked, but

I had to look at this writer's manuscript and I handed the bottle and glasses back to him. He took them to his cabin. Somebody came there to see him and used the bottle to bash him over the head." She was grim. "Plus, I'm sure everyone's rushing to tell the police how Jay hassled women for sex. They'll assume that was true for me—"

"Was it?" Cliff looked shocked.

Deirdre shrugged. "What else is new? It happens all the time. Once I had a city editor— Oh well, you learn to handle it. I would've handled Jay. But you can see why I'm scraping around trying to find out something that points away from me. When I asked you if you saw anyone, you didn't say anything. Cliff, if you know anything at all, it might make a difference."

He rubbed knuckles against one cheek, finally said, "I see what you're saying. Well, I don't know when Jay was killed. But when I was walking on the way to my cabin—"

Deirdre scarcely breathed.

Cliff's face was partially in shadow, partially illuminated by a lantern on a limb far above.

I tried to decipher what I could see of his expression. Uncertainty? Reluctance? Indecision?

"—I kind of noticed out of the corner of my eye that the door to cabin five was opening. The door stopped as if someone stood on the other side, one hand gripping the jamb. It was a tiny instant in time. That's all I saw, then I was past the cabin."

Deirdre reached out, touched his arm. "You saw a hand. A man's hand or a woman's?"

His uncertainty was apparent—uncertainty and a reluctance to speak. "It was just a glimpse. I can't swear to anything."

"Please think back. Try to remember." Deirdre was imploring. "You saw a hand on the jamb. Your mind has a memory of that moment. You must have some impression of the size, the shape."

"It was too quick. I can't be sure." He started to swing away, stopped, looked back with an expression of regret, commiseration. "If I thought anything at all, I thought a woman was standing there, that a woman was coming out on the porch."

As soon as he was gone, I said softly, "Perhaps he saw you."

Deirdre shook her head. "I didn't stop and hold the door. I got out of there as fast as I could. I came flying down the steps and bolted into the darkest shadow I could find and stood there and tried to breathe."

I cautioned, "He didn't sound certain. But if he thought it might have been you, that would suggest the hand belonged to a woman."

Deirdre was thoughtful. "If he saw a woman's hand, it was either Maureen Matthews or Liz Baker at the door."

I wasn't so sure. "Ashton Lewis is a big man with big hands. Cliff couldn't mistake his hand for that of a woman. But Tom Baker is slender with thin hands. In a quick glimpse, his hand could possibly appear to be a woman's. And then there's Harry Toomey." As I recalled, his hands were small and plump.

"Speaking of Harry"—Deirdre looked discouraged—"I see no way even *you* can persuade Harry to come here"— she waved a hand at the increasing gloom beneath the oak—"and talk to me. If there's anyone at the conference he wants to avoid, it's me."

I was sure she was right in that judgment. Moreover, I'd talked with Harry as Judy Hope, that scintillating reporter from the new online magazine, and as Detective M. Loy in a blond wig and gray dress.

I appeared in the softly swirling polyester poncho and white trousers. I looked down and admired the silvery heels.

Deirdre was plaintive. "There you go again. Colors whirling, swirling. Whistle next time."

"I'll try to remember. But I need to be here now. Let's go to the terrace together. If you're talking to me, writers won't interrupt. When we reach Harry, here's what we'll do. . . ."

వ

Harry Toomey sat on the low wall between the terrace and the garden. Next to him was a bottle of beer and a cardboard bowl with strawberry shortcake topped with a mound of whipped cream. He licked a smear of barbecue sauce from one finger. He was almost finished with a rack of baby back ribs. His plate still held coleslaw and baked beans. His moon face was amiable.

He looked up as we approached. Of course he recognized me as Judy Hope, the reporter from the soon-to-be-launched online magazine. Thursday night he'd been eager to cultivate me. Tonight there was a slight flicker of unease in his eyes.

I beamed at him. "Harry, I'm glad I found you. You're just the man I need to see."

He dropped a stripped baby back rib onto his paper plate

and scrambled to his feet. "You were looking for me?" Eagerness lifted his voice.

If I hadn't been hunting for a murderer, I would have felt a pang of guilt. He hoped, dared, prayed I was looking for Harry Toomey, author of that gripping novel *Grabbed*.

I gestured toward Deirdre. "You know Deirdre Davenport." I didn't wait for an answer. "She's given me some insights and I know you can do the same."

He looked at Deirdre, forced a smile. "I know Deirdre."

"Hello, Harry." Deirdre spoke diffidently.

I bent toward Harry. "May we join you? I want to get your take on the crime. I can quote you: Harry Toomey, suspense author."

He fumbled to pick up the beer and dessert.

When the space was clear, I nodded at Deirdre. "You go ahead and sit down. I'll get us some food. You two can visit while I'm gone." I turned and slipped into the fluid mix of those now finished with their meals and standing on the terrace talking. I started in the direction of the buffet, put a half dozen people between the wall and me, then slipped into the shadows of a willow. It took only a moment to reach the honeysuckle arbor, disappear, and return to Deirdre and Harry.

Deirdre gave Harry an apologetic look. "I'm sorry it couldn't have worked out for both of us. I was desperately hoping I'd get the job, so I understand how disappointed you are."

"Nice of you to say so." He didn't look at her. His round face was defensive.

"I really am sorry, Harry." There was genuine distress in her voice.

There's a special glow in Heaven when kind hearts offer solace.

"Yeah." He tried to sound upbeat.

"Well, I hope it all turns out for the best. I know you'll write a lot more books, Harry."

Some of the unhappiness seeped from his face. "I've got a new one started. It's set in a coal mine." Obviously ready to stand up, escape into the crowd, he shifted a little on the wall.

She said quickly, "I'll bet you've made some great contacts this weekend."

There was a return of his old bluster. "You better believe I have." His watery brown eyes gleamed. "Cliff Granger's going to take on my book." He spoke with pride. "He's a big-time agent. He'll land a deal for me. Maybe sell *Grabbed* to TV, too."

Deirdre hid a quick flicker of surprise behind wide-eyed admiration. "That's wonderful. So you're going to be all right."

"I'm going to be fine." He was suddenly puffed with self-satisfaction. "He said my book should've been snapped up by somebody and he can take it all the way to the top."

"Jay would have been pleased for you." Deirdre's face changed, as if recalling the grim reality of murder. "Speaking of Jay"—she looked both anxious and hesitant—"there's something I need to ask you. Before I talk to the police again."

His moon face was suddenly intent, and there was nothing soft or agreeable in his expression. "Again?"

"Yes. I told them about seeing Jay. But I didn't tell them what I saw when I left the cabin. I don't want to make a mistake."

He waited. The silence held a sense of menace. Harry's brown eyes never wavered as he stared at her.

I was glad Deirdre was at the edge of a terrace filled with people, with noise, movement, chatter, not in the deep shadows beneath the white oak.

Perhaps Deirdre sensed danger. She drew back a fraction. "Last night when I left cabin five, I was in a hurry. I had a headache and wanted to get back to my room, but I kind of half noticed someone was standing near a shrub, that big one about ten feet from the cabin steps. I just caught a glimpse. I don't know why, but I had the idea it was you. Were you there?"

"You saw someone?" His voice was soft.

"I wasn't sure." She squeezed her eyes shut for an instant, opened them. "When I concentrate, that's what I feel. Someone was there."

His gaze was hard and hostile. "Why did you think it was me?"

"I don't know. There was something about the shape of a shadow. I think that was it. I just had this little idea—*Why, Harry's waiting to see Jay*—and hoping Jay would explain why he picked me. He said he selected me because Dr. Randall preferred I be the one. I don't know why, Harry. It may be Dr. Randall wanted another woman faculty member. You never know what makes a difference in these kinds of decisions. Anyway, I was sure you were waiting there for a word with Jay, and I walked even faster because I thought it would be better if I was gone. I knew you'd be upset that Jay hadn't picked you."

"And you thought maybe I was the one who killed Jay?" His voice was cold.

She met his stare directly. "Somebody killed Jay."

Harry said shortly, "Yeah. Somebody did. But why pick me?" His gaze shifted slowly around the terrace. "I see a lot of people Jay pissed off." He looked at Maureen Matthews. "There's the prof he was sleeping with." He glanced at Liz and Tom Baker. "And how about that kid writer and her husband?" Then he gave an abrupt laugh, nodded toward Ashton Lewis. "Somebody told me that old guy was livid with Jay." He flicked a glance at Cliff Granger. "Or maybe Cliff was mad because Jay's last book stunk. But I guess all he had to do was tell Jay to take a hike. Anyway, I don't care who you pick on, but I hope it's not him. He really likes my book. Anyway, if there was somebody in the shadows, I can tell you it wasn't me."

As if aware of Harry's scrutiny, Maureen's head turned and she gave him a thoughtful look. Ashton Lewis faced our way. He stood alone, his face somber, arms folded; imposing and dignified in his seersucker suit. Liz and Tom were a few feet away, and there was no joy in either face. Once again they appeared tense, worried, fearful. Cliff Granger held a drink, appeared to be watching Deirdre.

I wondered if each of them noticed Harry's passing gaze. Possibly.

Harry turned back to Deirdre. "Maybe you saw one of them." The suggestion seemed to amuse him. He came to his feet. He wasn't physically impressive, but he was taller than Deirdre, heavier. He looked down. "Maybe you better worry about what someone saw you do." He put his plate, dessert bowl, and beer bottle on the wall, where he'd been seated. "I heard your fingerprints are on the champagne bottle. So smearing other people probably isn't going to get you anywhere. But you can take it to the bank: You didn't see me near that cabin." He had his old cocky look as he turned away.

I waited until he was out of earshot. "He was ready to unload on a lot of people."

Deirdre's face had a hollow, strained look. "I don't blame him. I know how it is to have people look at you and wonder. It's horrible. Now I'm looking at all of them and wondering."

"Stay here. I'll be back in a jiffy," I said softly. It took a moment to reach the arbor and appear. When I returned to the terrace, Deirdre, nose wrinkling in distaste, was gathering up Harry's plate. She picked up the beer bottle, carried the refuse to a nearby receptacle, nudged the flap, wedged the trash into the nearly full barrel.

She looked up as I approached. "I'm actually glad to see you. I never thought I'd say that. But"—she gave a sign of relief—"I never thought I'd be half-scared of Harry Toomey." Her voice held surprise.

"There might be good reason to be afraid of him." I spoke softly. "Harry claimed he talked to Jay, then walked down to the pier. But Tom Baker also said he went to the pier. One of them is lying. My money's on Harry. Maybe Harry saw something at the cabin. Or maybe he killed Jay and came out the door and heard footsteps and hurried into the shadows."

She gave me a quick, anxious look. "You've forgotten. I made it up about seeing someone in the shadows."

"That doesn't mean," I said gently, "someone wasn't in the shadows."

Deirdre shivered. "That's scary." She looked across the terrace, but she wasn't seeing lights and people and hearing loud voices and louder laughter. She was remembering that moment of cold horror when she opened the door, stepped into Jay's cabin, and saw him lying there, a purplish bruise on his temple, his body slumped in death. She shivered. "I've had all I can handle. I'm going to go wash my hands, then grab some food from the buffet and take it up to my room."

I watched her go. I understood her stress. She'd been scared and now she probably couldn't help feeling that her efforts wouldn't lead anywhere. We needed something specific, something concrete. I remembered the chair turned toward the computer in Jay's office. . . .

∽

Detective Don Smith's handsome face was impassive. He sat at Jay's computer, brows drawn in concentration. His index finger clicked, clicked, clicked. Abruptly, he leaned closer to the screen. "Got it. Got it. Sam's right." His tone was smug. "I can find deleted files better than anybody. No wonder somebody tried to get rid of these."

I liked his satisfied tone. I looked over his shoulder, and my eyes widened.

The photos were explicit, revealing, damning. Cliff Granger had been casual in his dismissal of a year-ago party as irrelevant, casual and dishonest. I didn't doubt the date corresponded with the night at Jay's house before last year's conference. I also felt sure Cliff had been unaware a camera had filmed his sexual encounter with a girl. Both were— But I don't need to describe them. The pictures revealed everything.

Why had Jay Knox filmed what Cliff must have assumed at the time was private? The filming could easily have been done, a camera cleverly concealed in a clock, lamp, or book, set to turn on and film whatever occurred for a period of several hours. Certainly the host—Jay—directed which bedrooms were available to those at a licentious party.

Don Smith was thorough. He not only sent e-files to Chief Cobb, he took advantage of Jay Knox's color printer and printed out a copy of every photograph that contained Cliff Granger and the young woman, including those in the bedroom and others taken at earlier points during the evening.

I waited until he was almost done, then popped to the front porch and rang the bell. As I expected, Don walked down the hall and to the door. Back in the office, I selected a print of a photo of Cliff's companion that had been taken earlier in the evening. Shoulder-length blond hair shimmered. I admired her sleeveless sundress with huge peonies splashed against a white background. She stood with an out-flung hand as if gesturing in excitement. I rose to the ceiling with the photo. Don never looked up. His face creased in irritation, he strode back into Jay's office.

The photo I'd filched could be shown to anyone. That wasn't true of many of the others. What had Jay done with those photos? He'd made them and kept them for a purpose.

I remembered Jessica Forbes's unconcealed contempt at the bar Thursday night. *More dreck?* she'd asked. Had Jay used the photos to blackmail Cliff into accepting manuscripts from Jay's clients? Did the pictures matter that much? Did Cliff have a jealous wife? Or was there a more dangerous outcome from a public revelation?

Cliff claimed last year's party didn't matter. Perhaps the party and what happened that night mattered immensely. Had Cliff seen a woman's hand at the door of cabin 5? Or was that an invention to suggest a woman killed Jay?

∽

As soon as I settled into the shadows of the honeysuckle arbor near the terrace, I appeared as Judy Hope, my redhaired, freckled self. I was evening casual in a pale yellow pullover cotton shirt; paisley print pants with a yellow, green, and light blue pattern; and calfskin thongs in lime leather with bamboo trim. I strolled through the garden to the terrace and around to a side entrance. In the dimness, no one paid any attention to the photograph I now held down to one side. I hurried up the stairs. At Maureen's door, I knocked firmly. If she wasn't there, I'd have to look for her. But the peephole opened.

I spoke quickly, holding up the photograph. "You will want to help."

The peephole closed. The door opened. She stared at me, her quite remarkably lovely face tight with anger, her violet eyes scornful. "You took my letters."

"They are quite safe. Please let me explain."

She remained in the doorway, blocking my entrance. "I

don't know who you are or what you want." Her voice was low and angry. "Maybe you're a blackmailer. Maybe worse. A person is dead. Why should I let you in my room?" Her gaze slid up the hall as a couple came off the elevator. She was ready to push past me, ready to cry out.

"I need your help to find out who killed Jay." I thrust out the photo. "Take this. Find out who she is. She was at the party last year. I want every fact you can scrape up. I'll contact you in the morning." I started to turn away, paused. I remembered her wariness, her looking to see if help might be near, fearful I might be Jay's killer. Was that an excellent actress at work or the caution of an innocent woman? I rather thought the latter. I made a quick decision. "I believe you are innocent. Your letters will be returned to you."

∽

In the honeysuckle arbor, I changed from my evening casual clothes to the French blue uniform, walked swiftly up the path. I knocked and the porch light came on in cabin 7. Jessica Forbes opened the door. "It's rather late—" She broke off and gazed at the uniform. "Yes?" There was polite inquiry and, as might be expected from a guest staying not far from the site of a murder, a flash of alarm. She was her usual commanding figure, silver hair drawn back, strong features, and wearing a long-sleeved green silk blouse and cream trousers.

"Officer Judy Hope, ma'am." I held out the black leather folder. "I'm sorry to bother you, but I have a few questions about last night." I flashed what I hoped was an ingratiating smile. "I know it's late, but I'll be very appreciative if you can spare a moment."

"Of course." Her agreement was quick. "I want to help if I can." She held the door for me.

After we settled on the sofa, Jessica crossed her ankles and looked at me inquiringly.

I admired the saucy cream bow on the instep of her attractive heels.

She waited for me to speak. I imagined she often used silence to her advantage and rarely offered impulsive comments.

I took a small notebook from my pocket, opened it, held a pen poised to write. "Could you tell me your whereabouts last night between ten and eleven?"

Her dark eyes were thoughtful. "Between ten and eleven . . . Let me think. I left the bar a few minutes after ten and walked directly here. I noticed Jay's lights were on as I passed. I did not see him. I sat here"—she gestured at the couch—"and talked to one of my authors in Hawaii until shortly after eleven. Then I read a manuscript until almost midnight. I did not leave this cabin until I went to the terrace for breakfast at half past seven."

The call to Hawaii could easily be checked. If Jessica was on the telephone from ten thirty to eleven p.m., she could not have killed Jay.

"That's very helpful. May I have the name of the author with whom you spoke and the telephone number?"

Her smile was cool. "Of course." She turned on her cell, went to Contacts, provided the information. "Would you like to call her?"

In only a moment, the call was placed and Jessica's alibi

confirmed. I'd not thought her a likely suspect, but certainty of her innocence added credibility to her responses.

"What was your relationship with Jay Knox?"

She was formal. "I was his editor. He had recently turned in a manuscript. Frankly, it was third rate. I sent it back, asked him to revise, but I told him there would have to be a huge improvement." Full stop.

This gave a different picture of Jay Knox as an author. Perhaps he wasn't as successful as he tried to appear. "Was he upset?"

"He knew"—another cool smile—"that histrionics wouldn't matter to me. I offered to drop out of the conference. He insisted I come. Of course, that was for the prestige of the conference. Having a New York editor is a huge draw." She shrugged. "We maintained a pleasant relationship. I suppose he intended to try to fix the book. I'm not sure that was possible. It would have required a huge rewrite, and I never thought Jay was unduly burdened with a work ethic. I didn't expect it to work out. I thought he was one of those writers who manage two or three passable books, then fizzle."

"It wouldn't bother you to drop an author?"

Her eyes were unsmiling. "My job is to publish good books." She spoke with finality.

"Is that why you warned Cliff Granger to stop sending you lousy manuscripts?"

There was a flicker of surprise in her dark eyes. "On what do you base your question?"

"You were overheard."

She slowly nodded. "I suppose you talked to someone who was at the bar." Another shrug. "I don't deny our conversation."

"Will you really decline to look at manuscripts he offers?"

"I meant what I said. I always mean what I say." Her tone was crisp. "I don't have the luxury of spending time on unpublishable manuscripts. No editor does."

"Are you going to give Cliff Granger one more chance?"

"One more chance." Now her face was formidable.

⌒

One light shone in the backyard of the house next to Jay's. The doghouse was in deep shadows near the back fence. I reached past the cinder block, swept the ground with seeking fingers. *Ah, there.* I pulled out the small packet of letters.

The dog poked out his head, growled. He was beautiful in the moonlight, the creamy glow turning his ruff silver.

"Good boy." I reached out and stroked his fur, felt taut muscles relax. "Just a quick visit. Thank you for taking good care of these letters."

It was late now and easy to pass unseen high in the sky to Silver Lake Lodge.

The hallway outside Maureen's door was dim and empty. I made sure no one was about, then placed the letters on the floor. I passed inside the room, waited and listened. In a sliver of light from the cracked bathroom door, I could make out the bed and a sleeping form.

Maureen's breathing was light and relaxed.

It took only a moment to carefully loosen the chain, ease

open the door, bring the letters inside. With the door closed, I put the chain in place, let my eyes adjust to the dimness. I crossed to the suitcase sitting on a rack against the wall. She'd emptied out the contents. I slipped the packet of letters into a zippered compartment. She was unlikely to open that compartment until she was ready to check out. If tomorrow proved her to be among the innocent, the letters would be there for her to find. If not, Sam would easily discover them.

∽

Sam Cobb's office was dark. I'd known him to stretch out on his long, comfortable brown leather couch when working on a case, but he now had a wife waiting at home and I imagined she always had a hot meal ready. Sam and Claire Arnold met when I was in Adelaide on a mission that almost saw me stranded here. I still felt a little breathless when I recalled being visible and, no matter how hard I tried, not being able to disappear. A shocking development. But all had ended well. When I was most recently in town, and could happily appear and disappear at will, Sam and Claire had been on their honeymoon. However, Sam had hurried home when I called him for help.

"Sam?" I kept my voice soft.

When there was no answer, I turned on his desk lamp, aimed the light at the blackboard. I worked diligently for several minutes, then stepped back to check what I'd written:

Deirdre Davenport told the following people she saw a figure near cabin 5 in order to observe their reactions:

Maureen Matthews hesitated an instant too long before she answered. She may have gone to see Jay

Liz and Tom Baker refused to talk to Deirdre. Liz may think her husband killed Jay.

Ashton Lewis warned Deirdre Davenport to be careful.

Cliff Granger claimed he saw the door to cabin 5 open, a woman's hand on the jamb. (Deirdre didn't hold the jamb when she left.) Cliff Granger claimed the party at Jay Knox's house a year ago didn't matter. However, Detective Smith found that explicit photos of Granger and a college girl were deleted Thursday night from Jay's computer.

Staring at the blackboard, I stood with the chalk in my hand. I couldn't decide what to write about Harry Toomey. His threat as he left Deirdre held a ring of truth. He could know something about Deirdre, something she might not want the police to know. He could know that Deirdre found Jay dead, that she lied to the police. I tried to figure out the implications. If Harry knew Jay was dead before Deirdre came, either Harry killed him or found him dead. If he killed Jay, then he'd been leaving as Deirdre arrived and ducked into the shadows to avoid being seen. Or he could have found Jay dead and hurried to get away, just as Deirdre had done, but Deirdre arrived before he could escape. Finally, I wrote:

*Harry Toomey lied about going to the pier. Find
out what he was doing during the period
between his talk with Jay and his return to his
room in the hotel.*

I returned to Silver Lake Lodge. Instead of a comfortable
sense of satisfaction at what I'd learned today, I felt unsettled, uneasy. I didn't know what accounted for my discomfort. Had I half noticed an expression that puzzled me? Had
someone said something that lodged in my subconscious?
But people could be evasive, have something to hide, without being guilty of murder. Deirdre was a prime example.
Also, there was Maureen and her missing packet of love
letters. The danger those letters posed to her could account
for her wary behavior.

I hovered above the lodge. A fat-bodied moon spilled
creamy light over the building and onto the now almost-
deserted terrace. The moon had climbed high enough that
I judged it was likely near eleven. The pool was closed and
only a few guests lingered on the terrace, which held no
traces of the evening's barbecue.

Most guests were probably settling in for the night.

I decided to survey the grounds. No lights shone from
cabin 5. The shadows were deep on either side of the cabin
near the stand of bamboo and the crape myrtle, just as they
would have been on Thursday night. Certainly anyone wishing to remain unobserved could have stood near the bamboo
or crape myrtle and not been noticed.

Although I could have gone from here to the end of the

pier in one quick thought, I dropped to the path and walked. I paused for an instant outside cabin 6. Light shone around the edges of the drawn blinds. I moved inside. The lights were on, but Cliff Granger was not in the living room. I checked the bedroom. It, too, was empty.

Back on the path, I followed winding curves to a final straight stretch. A lamppost stood at the edge of the pier. A walkway and steps led up to the pier, which jutted out over the water. Trestles supported the wooden deck. I walked up the steps and out onto the pier. The only other light was at the far end. Of course, I made no sound as I walked on the boards. The pier was about twelve feet wide, thirty feet long, and rose approximately twenty feet above the dark water.

Although the temperature had reached the high nineties during the day, the breeze off the dark water was cool and refreshing. It would be pleasant to linger, smell the richness of an Oklahoma night, listen to cicadas and crickets and rustling tree leaves.

Was Deirdre all right?

Burgeoning unease crystallized.

In an instant, I was in her room. I took in everything in a hurried glance.

Deirdre, as on the evening we met, sat cross-legged on the lumpy sofa, her pink sateen shirt tunic hiked up over her legs. She gazed down intently at her laptop, began to type.

I was thrilled to see that not only was she obviously in no peril but possibly had broken through her writer's block. I peered over Deirdre's shoulder.

". . . know you'll be excited, too. I called Joey and told

him and he said, 'Hey, Mom, when Katie and I are home we'll celebrate!' I told him we'd do fireworks and have chocolate sundaes. I would have called you but I looked at the schedule and you're supposed to start out tomorrow on a big hike so I wanted you to get a good night's sleep. Then you spend tomorrow afternoon at the pool. That sounds wonderful. Anyway, now that I have the job, you don't have to worry at all about money and how much camp costs. It means a lot to me that you are able to be at the camp and now you can relax and have a wonderful time. Remember to be careful and use sunscreen. Be sure and take your vitamins every morning. . . ."

I sighed. "When I saw you concentrating—"

Her head jerked up. She twisted to look behind the sofa, gave the old familiar *I wish you would go away* expression.

I am not thin-skinned. I continued pleasantly, "—so deeply, I hoped you were beginning a chapter."

Deirdre sighed. "Not yet. Just a sec, let me send this to Katie." She finished with three happy faces, clicked send. She leaned back on the sofa. "Yeah. Everything's perfect— if I don't go to jail."

"You won't go to jail."

She pushed up from the sofa. "I want to get out and do something. But the only thing I can think of is seriously stupid."

I looked at her quizzically.

"It crossed my mind that I could go down to the lobby and use a house phone, call everybody in turn." She pretended to hold a phone to her face. "Hello, X, how *are* you tonight? I hope you're having a jolly conference. Oh, by the way, we have to talk. I saw *you* in the shadows." She dropped her voice to a husky whisper. "Meet me by—"

The phone rang.

I looked at the clock. A quarter past eleven.

Deirdre froze.

Every mother knows the feeling. Both kids off somewhere. A call late at night . . .

She flew across the room, snatched up the receiver. "Hello." Her voice was breathless, strained. She listened, her expressive face changing from fear to disbelief. "Are you—" She stopped. "Hello? Hello?" She shook her head, put down the receiver, snatched it up, touched *0* for operator. "Connect me with Harry Toomey."

I was right beside her. I reached around her, touched Speaker.

We listened as the rings sounded, one, two, three. . . . Finally: "The party you are seeking does not answer. You may leave a message after—"

Deirdre slammed down the phone, looked at me. "I don't like it. Harry called me. He was talking fast, almost in a whisper, said I need to come to the pier, he knows who was in the shadows but he needs help to prove it. He wants me to be a witness. He'll tell me everything if I'll meet him there in twenty minutes. Well, I may think seriously stupid thoughts, but I'm not crazy." She clapped her hands on her hips. "I can tell him what to do. Call nine-one-one. Call Dr. Randall. Call the Marines. Call anybody. Don't call me."

"Twenty minutes." I was puzzled. "Why twenty minutes?"

"Twenty minutes, twenty hours, twenty days, makes no difference to me." Deirdre's lips closed in a determined line.

"It does sound like a trap."

"Duh." Deirdre shot me a scathing glance.

I had no idea what prompted Harry's call. I didn't trust him. But we had to find out what was happening. "We can't ignore his call."

Deirdre snapped, "Maybe you can't. Be my guest. Whiff off to the pier. You come and go like lightning. You can go see what Harry's up to, give me a report. As for me, I've written this scene. The heroine finds a note pinned to her pillow: *Meet me in the cemetery at midnight.* The idiot grabs her parasol and dashes off. Readers are chanting: *Don't go, don't go.* But, of course, this was before cell phones. Now she gets there, the ax murderer pops out from behind a headstone, she screams, runs like hell, gets out her cell, calls nine-one-one. But I'm no midnight heroine. You'd better remember, if I stir out of this room and something goes wrong, I'm the only one anybody sees." She gave me a meaningful glare.

"Agreed." I was crisp. "Do you have Hal Price's cell phone number?"

She slowly nodded.

"Call him."

Chapter 10

Deirdre held the cell, looked at it as if seeking a portent. She wanted to call. She didn't want to call. Her head jerked up. "What if he comes and we go to the pier and nobody's there? He'll think I'm a hysterical idiot."

I was firm. "He'll think you're doing the right thing to ask for help when you get a call from a man who may have committed murder."

Her expressive face was suddenly relieved. "I'll call nine-one-one."

I looked at the clock. "We have eighteen minutes before Harry will be looking for you. As much as I admire the Adelaide Police Department, it's late and a nine-one-one call will likely be answered by someone who wouldn't know anything about Jay Knox's murder and Silver Lake Lodge

and the pier. By the time you explained everything and
police cars came roaring up—"

"Okay, okay. I got it." She tapped. "Hal, this is Deirdre.
I didn't want to call but she insisted. . . . The redhead . . .
Here's what happened. . . ." She listened. "You'll come here?
Thank you." Her face was soft as she ended the call, then
she whirled, moving fast. She changed into a white tee and
light blue slacks, stepped into white sandals, added a dash
of makeup, hurriedly brushed her hair. She glanced in the
mirror. Her face was appealing, hopeful, hesitant, eager. Hal
was coming.

Deirdre fastened her wristwatch. She walked to the door,
opened it, moved the metal latch to serve as a wedge, prop-
ping the door ajar. She settled on the sofa.

I joined her, pointed at her laptop. "You might consider
making some notes. Re-create as exactly as possible your
conversation with Harry."

She shrugged but set to work.

I stretched a bit to read as she typed.

> *Phone Call from Harry Toomey*
> *Deirdre: Hello.*
> *Harry (breathless, whispery): This is Harry. I
> need to talk to you. I'll meet you at the pier. I've
> figured out who was in the shadows but I don't
> think the cops'll believe me. I need a witness. I'll
> explain everything and you can help me. Twenty
> minutes. At the pier.*

A light tap sounded and the door swung in.

I disappeared.

Deirdre came to her feet, turned. She held the laptop in one hand.

Hal stepped inside. He was blond and muscular in a blue polo, faded jeans, and sneakers. He carried a flashlight tucked under one arm. I needn't have worried that he might catch a glimpse of swirling colors. He saw only Deirdre.

There was a tiny moment of magic when Hal and Deirdre looked at each other, her angular, too-long face lovely and vulnerable, Hal's blue eyes soft and admiring.

Deirdre held out the laptop. "I wrote down everything Harry said."

Hal came across the room. They stood close together, shoulders touching. Hal's hand closed over hers on the side of the laptop. He glanced down. "Right." Then he was intent, crisp. "When did Harry call?"

Deirdre took the laptop, closed it, dropped it on the sofa. "Almost precisely twenty minutes ago."

Hal's eyes narrowed. "If we had more time, I'd call for backup. But we'll take a look. He had something in mind or he wouldn't have called you. I don't get his wanting you to come to the pier. Why not meet downstairs in the bar? He claims he knows who killed Knox but needs your help to prove it. That sounds fishy. If he's there, I'll have a little talk with him." His tone was grim.

∾

Pinpoints of light from lanterns strung in the trees offered little illumination. The path curved through dark shadows, an occasional lamppost along the way offering brief patches of light. Hal used his Maglite. As they came to the sweep of open ground in front of the pier, he turned off the beam, said softly, "Let's stop here, see if we spot anyone."

Straining to see, they stood at the edge of the woods. Across a clearing of perhaps twenty feet, the pier was in darkness except for small lights at the top of the steps and at the end. In the moonlight, the trestle beams that supported the pier looked like black bars. No figure was visible near the steps or on the wooden platform or on the ground in the shadows on either side.

Deirdre gently touched his arm. "I'm sorry I dragged you out. Maybe he was playing a joke."

Hal spoke equally softly. "He may come. We'll wait awhile. Or he may be waiting in the darkness underneath the pier."

Deirdre's voice was thin, but firm. "I'll walk out there. He's probably watching for me."

Hal instantly stiffened, gripped her arm. "You'd be exposed on the pier."

Deirdre shook her head at Hal. "I can't see Harry Toomey with a gun, and I know, not from personal experience but from research, it is notoriously hard to hit a target with a handgun unless you're a superb shot and even then you'd better be close. I won't get near enough to him that he could hit me with a weapon."

"I don't like it. He looks like a puffball, but if he's the killer, he's dangerous as hell."

"You're here." Her voice was lighter. "I'm not worried. We came to see if we could find out what Harry's up to and I'm the one to go out there."

"Yeah." He wouldn't disagree. He knew she was right. That didn't mean he wanted Deirdre to march out on the pier, a clear target. He stared out into the night, head jutting forward. He was gauging distance. If Deirdre needed help, how soon could he reach her side?

She gently unclasped his hand from her arm, stood on tiptoe, brushed his cheek with her lips. "That's for luck. I'll be fine." She walked toward the pier. In the moonlight, she looked insubstantial.

Hal moved nearer the edge of darkness, poised to run, ready to shout, prepared to protect her.

I imagine every step away from him was painful to Hal.

I walked beside Deirdre, alert for any movement. If I sensed a threat, I could push her down to safety or interrupt an attack. But I didn't have any sense of danger. The moon looked fat and placid midway up the sky. The water was dark. There were no lights from boats, no solitary figure standing near the steps to the pier. The only sounds were the rasp of cicadas and the chirp of crickets. Far overhead a jet plane moved among the stars, the roar faraway.

Deirdre reached the base of the stairs, started up, one hand on the railing. Midway, she jerked to a stop, gazed over the side. She leaned perilously far out, looking down. "Hal, Hal!" She turned and started down the steps.

I was already on the bank, staring down.

Hal ran, feet pounding on the grass, Maglite beam blazing through the darkness.

Deirdre clattered down the steps. "Somebody's down there in the water."

Hal's bright white light swung out, illuminated a half-submerged body facedown in crumpled reeds a foot or so from the bank.

Hal thrust the Maglite into her hands. "Call nine-one-one." He took three long strides, splashed into the water, fighting his way through the reeds. As he pulled and tugged, Deirdre's words ran together, her voice uneven. ". . . Silver Lake . . . behind the lodge. A man's in the water near the pier. . . . think he's dead . . ."

Grunting with effort, water spraying around them, Hal tugged the limp body of Harry Toomey, head lolling, to the bank, pulled him out of the water. Hal turned Harry over, straddled him, began CPR, trying, trying. . . .

Deirdre was still on her cell phone. ". . . here with Hal Price, Detective Sergeant Price."

I said urgently, "Ask for a resuscitator, EMSA. Tell the officer to alert Chief Cobb that there's trouble at Silver Lake Lodge."

Hal worked and worked. Deirdre remained on the phone.

I stared at Harry's body. Obviously, he had not come to the pier alone. But why had he called Deirdre?

Within minutes, sirens squalled. EMSA techs arrived first, a burly middle-aged man and a whip-thin young woman. The man took over from Hal. Lights flashed on, illuminating the terrace and grounds. More lights dotted the lodge facade as guests woke to sirens and noise. Guests in various stages of dress poked out of cabins. By the time uniformed officers set up police tape at the edge of the woods, the techs were standing to one side. Harry was past saving.

A muscular officer boomed through a megaphone. "Everything's under control. There has been an accident at the lake. Only emergency personnel and police are permitted beyond this point. Everything's under control. There has been an accident. . . ."

Two searchlights mounted on tripods illuminated the body, the trampled area around it, crushed reeds and dark water.

Hal and a trembling Deirdre waited at the base of the steps to the pier. Hal's arm was tight around her shoulders. She kept her face averted from the sight of Harry's wet, bedraggled, unmoving body.

I was shaken as well. It hadn't occurred to me when Deirdre received the call from Harry that the contact was anything more than an effort by him either to honestly enlist Deirdre's help or a lure to take her into danger. Instead, the pier was a trap for Harry. Someone was with him when he made the call, told him to set the meeting for twenty minutes later. As soon as the call was made, Harry and his companion came down to the pier. That's why Harry didn't answer when Deirdre immediately called his room. Harry and Jay Knox's killer came to the pier, but only the killer walked away, leaving Harry's body for Deirdre to find. The killer didn't care whether she ran away or called the police. There would always be the record of Harry's call to Deirdre's room.

The medical examiner pushed up from the ground. Jacob Brandt had obviously dressed hastily into a ratty T-shirt with cut-off sleeves, paint-stained khaki shorts, and flip-flops, but his eyes were bright and intent as he faced Chief Cobb. "Classic case of drowning, aided and abetted by a couple of whacks to the back of the head. I can be definitive after the autopsy, but I can tell you that somebody knocked him out, lugged him to the water, plopped him in face-first. It wouldn't take long for him to drown. And, now"—he made a casual gesture "you can set your bloodhounds loose." Police could not search or move a body until the ME determined death had occurred.

As he spoke, a uniformed officer took a series of photographs, another sketched the scene, a third began a careful search of the ground.

Sam pointed at the body. "Any idea of the weapon?"

Jacob Brandt looked judicious. "Something rounded. A depression similar to the one on Knox's temple." He gazed at the bank and the reeds. In the brilliance of the searchlights, each bent and crushed reed was distinct, and the dampness of the ground around Harry's body evident. "Rounded," he muttered. His gaze stopped on a beer bottle lying perhaps a foot from the water. He jerked a thumb. "Something like a pop bottle or a beer bottle. The depression had that kind of curve."

Sam nodded at a balding, stocky officer. "Photos. Measurements. Take the bottle into evidence, just in case. Check for hair, blood, prints. Pick up everything lying on the ground along the bank and between here and the terrace. Get somebody in waders. I want any piece of debris found in the water, bottles, rocks, anything with a rounded surface. Check anything that could make a rounded head wound."

A careful search of the lakefront began.

Sam turned and walked toward Hal and Deirdre. In the glare of the searchlights, Sam looked disheveled, his grizzled hair hastily combed, a growth of beard on his heavy face, dress shirt rolled to the elbows, brown suit pants wrinkled, but he was focused, intent. "You're here." This was directed at Hal. There was a faint undertone of disapproval. "She"—he jerked his head toward Deirdre—"finds a body." Sam knew I was Deirdre's champion, but her presence at a murder scene was too suspicious to ignore.

Detective Weitz stood a few feet away. She was looking at a clipboard, but I didn't doubt she listened to every word. She lifted her eyes to give Hal and Deirdre a brief, searching glance, then once again gazed at the clipboard.

Detective Howie Harris was watching, too. His eyes were bright and curious as he stared at Hal and Deirdre.

I didn't like the expression on Howie's pudgy face, a mixture of pleasure and suspicion. Howie had been in charge of the department when I was last in Adelaide, subbing for Sam while he and Claire honeymooned. Howie was a favorite of the mayor's and he liked to cause trouble for Sam.

Sam folded his arms. "Let's have it. You first, Hal." He listened with a frown. When Hal finished, the chief's gaze turned to Deirdre. "Ms. Davenport."

Deirdre, her voice shaky, kept her gaze determinedly away from Harry's body. "Harry called me. He said he knew who killed Jay and he wanted my help to prove it. He asked me to meet him at the pier in twenty minutes. I was afraid to go by myself. I called Hal—Detective Sergeant Price. He came to my room and we went together."

Sam was brisk. "Anybody hear your conversation with Toomey?"

Deirdre's voice quivered. "Only me and my imagination." She gave a brief glance about, knowing I was likely near. "Who else would be there?" There was the slightest edge of hysteria in her tone. "It was late when the phone rang. I don't have any witnesses to prove anything. I talked to Harry just like I told you, I started to tell him no way but he'd already hung up. I called his room. No answer. I almost ignored the whole thing, but I decided I should do something. I thought I did the right thing to call Hal."

Even if she hadn't called Hal, she would have been caught up in an investigation, which must have been the plan—that, when his body was found, calls from Harry's room would be checked and there would be a record of his call to Deirdre's room and a record of the call from her room to his. I could hear a DA now: "And the defendant offers a fanciful explanation of the victim's call. But, ladies and gentlemen of the jury, she called Mr. Toomey's room. Now why would she do that? To confirm an appointment to meet at the pier? That seems obvious."

Sam studied her, and I knew he thought Deirdre was well aware calls between rooms would be traced. If she met Harry and killed him, she had to scramble to find a way to explain those calls. A possible solution—call Hal Price, give him a fictional version of Harry's call, go with him to the pier. Sam clearly realized Deirdre might have called Hal to create an aura of innocence. "You could have called nine-one-one."

Deirdre was grim. "I wish I had."

It was as though Sam and Deirdre and Hal formed a triangle of intensity apart from the activity around them, the sound of voices, footsteps, flashes from cameras. Sam bulked large and demanding, Deirdre stood stiff and defensive, Hal struggled to remain silent.

Sam pressed her. "Why didn't you?"

Deirdre turned over her hands—long, thin, expressive hands—in a gesture of hopelessness. "I knew"—she hesitated, spoke formally—"Detective Sergeant Price was involved in the investigation. I called him. I wish I hadn't. Oh, how I wish I hadn't." Her look at Hal was sad and worried, regretful; she knew he was compromised by her call.

Sam's brows drew down. "How'd you have his cell number?"

Hal spoke quickly, defiantly. "I gave it to her."

Sam studied Hal for a long moment, gave an almost imperceptible head shake. "You and Davenport wait over there." He pointed at a bench near the steps to the pier.

Hal looked at the chief's face, almost spoke, then nodded. "Yes, sir." The words were clipped and formal.

Sam swung around, moved closer to the lake, watched as the stocky officer, hands in plastic gloves, carefully used pincers to pick up the beer bottle.

Deirdre put her hand on Hal's arm. "He doesn't believe me." She pulled her hand back. "He thinks"—her eyes were huge with despair—"I called you to—"

Hal cut in, his voice brusque. "I don't give a damn what he thinks." His face was serious, intent, determined. "I know better."

Deirdre lifted her chin. She spoke steadily, even though her lips quivered. "Until all of this is over, you need to stay away from me."

Hal shook his head. "That I won't do." His face quirked in a half smile. "The chief said for us to wait on the bench. You won't be getting away from me." His hand closed over her arm.

Detectives Weitz and Harris watched them walk away, Weitz with a considering look, Harris with malicious pleasure.

As they walked, Deirdre pulled away from his touch, kept a distance between them. They settled on the bench.

Hal moved closer, put a hand on her arm, bent near to speak.

Sam walked to the edge of the bank, asked an officer kneeling on the ground, "What's in his pockets?"

The officer pointed at a collection lying on a plastic sheet—a billfold, coins, several soggy pieces of paper, car keys, a room key.

Sam nodded at Judy Weitz. "Go to his room, see if there's a cell phone there."

As the careful survey of the area continued, I hoped to find a moment when I could drop near and whisper to Sam, but he was occupied every instant—directing, inquiring, conferring. I hovered near. I considered appearing but knew I wouldn't get past the young policeman charged with barring entry to the crime scene.

Detective Weitz returned in a few minutes. "No cell phone. No sign of disarray in his room."

Sam glanced toward the lake. He likely felt sure that both Jay's cell phone and Harry's had been flung out into the water to plummet to the bottom. Harry's killer had made sure police never saw any incriminating phone messages or texts.

After the gurney with Harry's body rolled away, Sam turned to Weitz. "Bring Price and Davenport to that conference room and get us some coffee."

He walked briskly up the path and across the terrace.

Guests had gathered in clumps. Voices called out, "What's happened?" "Who was on the stretcher?" "Is there a killer loose here?"

Sam paused, held up a big hand. "We are investigating a drowning that occurred near the pier this evening. Everything is under control. Please return to your rooms." Ignoring shouted queries, he walked briskly toward the lobby.

Chapter 11

I waited inside conference room A. The dry-erase board had been wiped clean.

The door opened and Sam stepped inside.

"Officer Loy reporting."

Sam froze for an instant, then closed the door, stood with his back against it. Despite the stubble on his face and evident weariness, his gaze was alert. "Weitz is bringing Davenport and Hal here. What have you got?"

"Deirdre's telling the truth about the call from Harry Toomey. She never left her room tonight until she went to the pier with Hal."

"You're—" He broke off. He didn't ask if I was sure. He knew I was sure. "That changes everything."

The door opened and Weitz stood aside for Hal and

Deirdre to enter. Weitz carried a tray with a coffee server and cups in one hand, held the door with the other while managing an attaché case wedged between her arm and side.

Once again Deirdre sat in a hard, straight chair facing a table. This time Hal Price occupied a straight chair beside her. Deirdre sagged in fatigue, her long face pale and worn. Perhaps more accustomed to late-night, stress-filled encounters, Hal didn't appear tired, but his expression was somber.

Detective Weitz put the tray on a stand near the door, then moved to the table to unpack a recorder from the attaché case. She placed the recorder in front of the chair she'd occupied earlier in the day. She returned to the stand, poured coffee into four cups. She deposited a cup at her place and Sam's, carried a cup in each hand around the table, offered them to Deirdre and Hal.

Deirdre softly said, "Thank you." Hal managed a slight smile as he took the cup.

Weitz nodded, turned away. She took her seat next to Sam. Responding to the late-night call, she'd obviously also dressed hurriedly in a magenta blouse and tan slacks—definitely unfortunate. She kept her gaze studiously away from Hal, her friend and co-worker but now a witness to be interviewed.

Steam rose in wreaths above the cups in front of her and Sam.

Deirdre took a cautious sip.

I yearned for a cup of coffee. I eyed the stand with the tray. Several extra cups were stacked by the server.

Sam cleared his throat. He was brisk. "It's late. I won't keep you long."

222

Judy Weitz's eyes widened a little. The chief's business-like tone surprised her. She slid a swift glance at him.

Sam gazed at Deirdre. "Ms. Davenport"—Weitz turned on the recorder—"as I understand how the evening unfolded, you were in your room preparing for bed. Were you in pajamas?"

Deirdre was clearly surprised at the question. She nodded. "Yes."

"You did not expect a call from Mr. Toomey?"

"I did not." Deirdre was emphatic. "I didn't expect the call and my first instinct was to ignore it. I wish that's what I'd done."

Sam nodded. "That's understandable, but bear with me"—Judy Weitz's eyes rounded—"while I establish the background. Why do you think he called you instead of someone else who knew Mr. Knox?"

I reached the side table, turned the top of the server, held the cup on the far side, tipped just enough to pour.

Hal watched Deirdre, whose attention was focused on the chief. Sam and Judy had their backs to me. So far, so good. I eased the cup—my, that was really hot coffee— below the level of the table, moved until I was behind Sam and Judy. I crouched behind Sam and took a generous swallow, felt the instant magic of caffeine. It may come as a surprise, but a ghost—excuse me, Wiggins: an *emissary*— is subject to earthly fatigue when engaged on a mission. I savored several more sips.

Deirdre brushed back a tangle of frizzy curls. "I was stupid. Tonight I was all over the barbecue looking for information about Thursday night. I talked to Harry and others

I thought might be upset with Jay." She held up a finger for each. "Maureen Matthews. The kids, Liz and Tom Baker. Ashton Lewis. Cliff Granger. Harry Toomey, I thought maybe I could find out something to help figure out who killed him. I was afraid you'd arrest me since my fingerprints were on the champagne bottle. That's why Harry knew I was looking for the killer. Now it doesn't seem like it was such a good idea."

Hal gave her an encouraging look. "It's understandable that you wanted to try to help the police." He faced Sam. "Rumors are all over the conference that Deirdre's the chief suspect."

Judy Weitz gave him a quick, sympathetic, almost pitying glance. She thought Hal had lost all objectivity, that he was enchanted, that he was being played for a fool by Deirdre.

Sam repeated the names. "Maureen Matthews, Liz and Tom Baker, Ashton Lewis, Cliff Granger. Harry Toomey. You set out to talk to them. Why did you expect one of them to admit to anything incriminating?"

Deirdre leaned forward, her face both eager and anxious. "I hope I can make you understand. I didn't expect any of them to *tell* me anything." There was emphasis on the verb. "Writers use body language to reveal how characters feel or think. Their reactions tell you a lot. I was counting on watching each person's reaction when I claimed I saw someone in the shadows last night near cabin five."

Sam cleared his throat, said mildly, "Policemen look at body language, too. Would you like to know what your body language tells me?"

Judy Weitz quickly hid an expression of shock at Sam's genial tone.

Hal's face brightened. He was surprised, but encouraged.

Deirdre met Sam's gaze directly. "Yes. I'd like to know what you see." Her voice was tremulous, but hope shone in her eyes.

Sam leaned back, his expression thoughtful. "I see a woman under great stress who's doing her best to be helpful. You do not exhibit either the shifting glances or the steady, straight stare of a liar. The fact that you contacted a police detective after you received the call from Harry Toomey indicates either great guile or good common sense. At this point, common sense seems more likely to me."

Judy Weitz stared at Deirdre, then slowly nodded in agreement. Hal was scarcely able to contain his delight.

Sam continued to look at Deirdre. "I may be wrong, but right now I see you as a willing witness, and I'm interested to know if you feel that you learned anything that can help us."

Deirdre laced her fingers together. "I felt"—her tone was reluctant—"that Maureen Matthews knows something she isn't telling. I think she may have gone to Jay's cabin. Liz and Tom Baker were panicked. They didn't admit anything but they ran away from me. Ashton Lewis warned me I was putting myself in danger. Cliff Granger said he saw a woman's hand on the doorjamb at the cabin. As for Harry—"

The door burst open, slammed back against the wall.

Startled, I dropped my coffee cup.

Turning toward the door, Judy Weitz and Sam saw the

cup, which to them had no place of origin, plummet onto the floor.

A weedy twentysomething in a grubby singlet and ragged jeans thudded through the doorway, stopped, watched the paper cup's downward arc. He watched as coffee splashed on the floor. "You guys tossing coffee cups? A new kind of game? A little bit of fun at taxpayers' expense? Too bad I didn't get a shot. But right now, I got bigger fish to play. This is great." He held the camera, panned from Judy and Sam to Deirdre and Hal. "Yeah, yeah, yeah. Good stuff. Cops interrogate suspects in lake kill. Renegade cop and chief suspect. Perfect for the early morning news shows, courtesy of Special Correspondent Deke Carson."

Sam stood so quickly that he knocked over his chair. He started toward the cameraman, held out his hand. "Give that to me." He stepped around the spilled coffee, slid a sideways warning glance where he thought I might be standing.

Backing up, Carson wrapped an arm protectively around the video camera. His thin face was excited. "Public place. Freedom of the press. I got sources. Dead man's Harry Toomey. Signs of trauma, suspected homicide. Body found by"—a quick look at Hal and Deirdre—"Detective Sergeant Hal Price and conference speaker Deirdre Davenport. I have the facts on deep background. Davenport's fingerprints were on the weapon that killed Jay Knox. Any word yet about the beer bottle found down at the lake by Toomey's body?"

"Get out of here, Carson. Or you'll go to jail."

One arm still hugging the video camera, Carson scrabbled in a pocket, pulled out a stub of pencil and a scrap of paper. "Got your name, Chief. And Price. And Davenport."

He peered across the room. "Yeah, yeah. Detective Judy Weitz. Your comment on the investigation, Chief?"

"No comment." Sam jerked a thumb toward the hall.

"Any explanation for a detective hanging out with the chief suspect in the first kill who just happened to be on the scene for the second homicide?"

Hal Price rose, his face hard. "Ms. Davenport reported a phone call from Mr. Toomey that needed to be investigated. She contacted me and together we discovered the body in the lake. Those are the facts, Carson."

Carson's smile was malicious. "Maybe. Maybe not. But she called you on your cell, right? Not a call to nine one one or the police tip line. And you and the lady were parked on a bench by the pier for a couple of hours. Now you're both in here and it looks like the chief and Detective Weitz had some questions for you. Now, how come you're being questioned?" He whipped the camera around, flicked on the recorder.

Hal was quick. "Department policy prohibits discussion about an ongoing investigation."

Carson smirked. "Are you and the lady an item?"

Sam started toward the tall, skinny inquisitor, who turned the camera on the chief as he moved into the hall.

Sam stood in the doorway. "You are interfering with a police investigation. There will be a formal news conference at eleven a.m. tomorrow." Sam turned, slammed the door.

I worried at the choleric red of his face.

Sam took a deep breath. "That little—" He looked at Deirdre, stopped. He turned to Judy Weitz. "Find out who's been talking. Carson will spread it all over the state that we're engaged in a cover-up."

"Who is he?" Deirdre was puzzled.

Sam was grim. "If he lived in New York or LA, he'd be paparazzi. Around here, he's a flake with a camera but he manages to sell stuff. He has a police scanner, shows up like iron to a magnet. He takes anything that can be blown up for a news bite. He strings for one of the Oklahoma City TV channels."

Deirdre looked at Hal. "This is terrible. I'm sorry. I'm so—"

Hal interrupted. "No apologies. You did the right thing. You called for help. Maybe I should have alerted Sam." He turned toward the chief. "I didn't want to scare Toomey off. I intended to be in the shadows when Deirdre talked to him. There wasn't enough time to set up surveillance. I thought we could find out what he knew. So maybe I made a bad call."

Sam was unperturbed. "It's always easy to look back and see how we could have done things differently. You did what you thought would work. We'll keep after it." But there was weary knowledge in his eyes. Truth didn't always win. Lies were like graffiti; you could do your best to eradicate it but sometimes the stain remained.

Sam rubbed his face. "All hell's going to break loose. We'd better call it a night. Get ready for tomorrow."

∽

Hal stood in the doorway to Deirdre's room looking obdurate. He pointed at the sofa. "I don't snore. I won't talk. But I'm not going to leave you alone. Somebody went to a lot of trouble to set you up as Harry's killer. You need an alibi 24–7."

Deirdre looked up at him, her eyes soft but her face equally determined. "How will it sound if anybody finds out you spent the night in my room? How will that look for a member of the police department?"

"It will be more evidence that the Adelaide Police Department protects the citizens." He stepped inside, closed the door.

∽

Chief Cobb's office was dark. I cautiously approached the old leather sofa, leaned over, lightly swept my hand down. The sofa was unoccupied. I settled comfortably and drifted off to sleep, secure in the knowledge that Deirdre was in no danger of arrest. Since I'd vouched for her, Sam knew he had to keep looking.

I was up at first light. I was sure Sam would be at his desk shortly, but I had time for breakfast. In an instant I was on Main Street. I looked through the plate-glass window of Lulu's, a fine cafe when I lived in Adelaide and still thriving. In Lulu's ladies' room, I checked to be sure I was alone. I knew Wiggins resisted emissaries appearing unnecessarily, but I would point out that being on earth demanded huge reserves of energy. Surely he wouldn't begrudge me a quick breakfast. I pondered for a moment. I wanted to start my day in the very best way. I watched in the mirror as I appeared, and I admired the white crocheted tunic with a V-neck. The fringe reminded me of froth on a breaking wave, so I chose aquamarine soft slacks that narrowed at the ankle above white leather stiletto heels with aquamarine beads across the instep. A multistranded blue necklace was the coup de grâce. I smoothed back red curls, added a touch of lipstick. I felt young and buoyant, ready to take on the world.

I stepped into the narrow corridor not much changed from the days when Bobby Mac and I brought the kids for chicken-fried steaks and played rock 'n' roll on the jukebox. The old jukebox was still wedged in an alcove between the restrooms along with a wall pay phone. I wondered if either still worked. I paused to look at the list of tunes, knew them all. Oh, yes—Les Paul and Mary Ford's "Vaya con Dios" and Tony Bennett's "Rags to Riches." Those were the days. . . .

I strolled into the dining area. There were four booths to my left, several tables straight ahead, and the counter to my right. Despite the early hour, three booths and four tables were occupied. I was halfway to the counter when my stride checked.

Sam Cobb sat on a red leather stool second from the door. He was watching me in the mirror behind the counter. He gestured at the empty stool to his left. Instead of his wrinkled brown suit, he wore a crisp navy suit with a white shirt and red tie.

I slid onto the round vinyl-covered seat. "Morning, Sam."

A plate with a partially eaten cake doughnut and a mug of coffee sat in front of him.

He was freshly shaven, but dark shadows under his eyes indicated fatigue. "I thought you might show up."

Was I that predictable?

"I didn't see you come in." For an instant, there was a gleam of humor in his brown eyes. "I guess that's no surprise. What'll you have?"

I ordered country bacon, scrambled eggs, grits, coffee, and orange juice. "Have you seen the photos that were deleted from Jay's computer?"

"Don called me last night. I went over after I left the lodge."

I wasn't surprised that Sam already knew. "Cliff Granger acted as though the party last year was no big deal. You may be able to find out more about the coeds who were there from Maureen Matthews. A student told her about the party."

Sam nodded. "I'll check with her." His gaze flicked up at the TV screen mounted above the mirror. The sound was muted. Below the picture of an arm-waving politician ran the continuous news ticker. His heavy face rock hard, Sam said, "I don't suppose you've seen the news. That's one reason I came over here this morning. Claire fixed me a big breakfast. We have a little TV set on the kitchen table. That's when I first found out. So I came over here to show everybody that the Adelaide Police Department is fine." He jerked his head toward the tables and booths, mostly filled with Adelaide movers and shakers. "I stopped at each booth and every table, made it clear that it's business as usual at the department. Look up now. Here's the feed."

I gazed at the screen:

Adelaide police face cover-up questions. Chief suspect in prof's murder has detective on speed dial.

Above the feed was a shot of Sam Cobb and Detective Weitz, Deirdre Davenport and Hal Price. Deirdre looked pale and anxious, Hal startled.

So last night's image taken by the scruffy young man with a video camera was now showing on TV around the state, and viewers could enjoy a taste of scandal with breakfast.

The waitress, a buoyant blonde with a ready smile, brought my order. "Here y'are, hon."

Sam picked up his coffee cup, drank. "Deke Carson didn't waste any time."

I could see reverberations from many directions, none of them good. I buttered a biscuit. "What are you going to do?"

He managed a half smile. "Speak to anybody I missed earlier on the way out. Laugh off the TV stuff as sensational junk. Go hell for leather the rest of the day."

Hell for leather—that's Oklahoma speak for ride hard, do what has to be done, no matter the cost.

Chapter 12

At the station, worried glances followed Sam as he walked down the hall to his office. Good-mornings were subdued. There was an air of gloom, except for Howie Harris.

Howie stood next to the watercooler, a plastic cup in hand. No doubt he'd been ready to talk about the morning news with anyone who stopped. *Gee, what do you think? . . . Sure looks bad for the department. . . . What was Hal thinking? . . .* Perhaps to compensate for his height, about five foot six, Howie pulled his shoulders back and poked out his chest.

The smirk on his face reminded me of our last encounter, when he'd done his best to sabotage Sam while he and Claire were on their honeymoon. A pet of Mayor Lumpkin's, Howie hungered to replace Sam. I wondered if he was responsible for the leak to Deke Carson. From his satisfied expression, I thought so. Howie was ready for golf in a polo shirt and shorts, so he obviously had the day off, but the inflammatory news flash brought him like a crow to road kill.

Howie's thin voice called out, "Hey, Chief, looks like Hal Price has his hands in the cookie jar."

Sam didn't slow down, looked like a lumbering bear. He didn't turn his head to speak, but his response was loud and clear. "You got that wrong, Howie. Don't worry your pretty head."

Howie's hand shot up to smooth one of the few strands of limp blond hair on his balding head. Once Sam was past, Howie's good humor evaporated. He'd thought Hal was in deep trouble.

I thought briefly of Precept Five. "Do not succumb to the temptation to confound those who appear to oppose you." I should have resisted temptation. But Howie Harris was a jerk.

I swooped down, delicately draped one longish blond strand over one ear, one over the other. The effect was, I think I may say with confidence, transforming. I hoped his new look remained with him all the way to the golf course.

Sam stepped into his office. As Sam opened the door, Hal turned from the window, slowly walked toward him.

Hal was dressed as he'd been last night—blue polo, faded jeans, sneakers. Light stubble covered his cheeks. His thick blond hair was neatly combed, but he had the appearance of a man who'd slept in his clothes, as I was sure he had. I wouldn't have expected Hal to appear bright and shiny, but the bleak emptiness in his eyes frightened me.

Sam closed the door behind him, took one look at Hal's drawn face. "Screw TV. As far as I'm concerned, you're in good standing and anything said to the contrary is scurrilous and may be actionable."

Hal's face softened. "Thanks, Sam. But"—he was grim again—"TV's the least of my worries right now."

Sam knew trouble when he saw it. "What's wrong?"

Hal held a couple of printed sheets in his hand. He walked to Sam's desk, slid the sheets across his desk. "I stopped downstairs on my way in, picked up the report on the beer bottle resting"—his voice was sour—"so very conveniently on the bank. The killer might as well have put up a sign with a red arrow pointing at the bottle."

Sam dropped into his swivel chair, which creaked at his weight. He picked up the sheets, read swiftly, looked up at Hal. "Somebody sure wants Deirdre Davenport to go to jail."

Relief, gratitude, and surprise transformed Hal's face. "I was afraid you'd say this clinched the case against her."

Sam leaned back in his swivel chair, hooked his fingers behind his head. "That's the intent. Sure, this looks bad. In fact, if you just looked at the facts, you'd say it was time to get the arrest warrant. Her fingerprints are on the champagne bottle that killed Knox." He tapped the sheet. "Now the lab says her prints are on a beer bottle with traces of Toomey's hair and blood. But let's give the facts another look. We know the history of the champagne bottle. We know Knox took the bottle and a couple of glasses to her room, put them on the coffee table. Davenport picked up the bottle and glasses, handed them to him as he left. Now"—he tapped the sheet again—"we have to find out why her prints are on a beer bottle Toomey held. We have to find out how somebody got hold of that beer bottle and used it to kill Toomey."

Slowly, struggling to keep his voice even, Hal said, "I know she's innocent because she's Deirdre. It doesn't matter to me what the evidence shows. How do you know?"

Sam made a fist, rubbed his jowl with his knuckles. "Sometimes it's better not to look a gift horse in the mouth."

Hal's back was to me. At the blackboard, I quickly sketched a horse with a halo, not that I claim any saintly qualities.

Sam looked at the blackboard, almost managed a smile.

"Gift horse?" Hal was puzzled.

After a tiny nod toward the blackboard, Sam said stolidly, "As I intend to put it to you and to anybody who asks, I'm acting on information received."

"Information received?" Hal was eager, hoping perhaps that someone had come forward and somehow cleared Deirdre.

"I can't say more. Confidential source. Deirdre Davenport's definitely out of it." Sam spoke with conviction. "A killer is using her as a stalking horse. I have some leads that we'll focus on. But we have to deal with the fallout from the TV smear." Sam's big mouth curved into a wry smile. "If you have the lady on speed dial like the news ticker says, give her a ring. We have to have an answer for the beer bottle. But first . . ." He grabbed his phone, tapped an extension. "Howie, Sam Cobb. Got a word for you. If you leak anything else about the Knox-Toomey cases, you're on an indefinite suspension. So like the big boys say, don't even think about it." He slammed down the receiver, drew in a breath. A red flush slowly subsided from his neck. "Okay, Hal, make that call."

"She's having breakfast in the lodge coffee shop." Hal hunched his shoulders and I knew his face was defiant. "I spent the night in her room. Like I told her, somebody's gone to a lot of trouble to frame her. She needs somebody with her all the time, because who knows what will happen next."

Sam's face was impassive. "Not a bad move. I like men who think ahead, take the initiative." There was the slightest flicker of amusement in his eyes. "If anybody asks, you've been detailed to keep an eye on her. That can blunt the innuendo on the news ticker and it will keep her safe as well. Probably better to keep her in view, not hover."

I imagined Sam foresaw other footage on TV if Hal stayed right next to Deirdre.

Hal nodded. "I told her to stay in her room or hang out around people until she speaks this afternoon." He paused. "Her topic's 'Upping the Ante for Your Hero.'" He managed to keep his voice expressionless.

Sam gave a quick bark of laughter. "She never knew when she wrote her speech that she would be living the reality. I'd say having her fingerprints on two murder weapons makes her an expert. And that's exactly where we need her help."

Hal pulled out his cell. He clicked Speaker, sat on the edge of Sam's desk, called. "Hey, Deirdre. I'm working with the chief and we need some information. Tell us about your contact last night with Harry Toomey."

Deirdre sounded tired, but composed. "Harry was sitting on the wall of the terrace with his dinner."

"What was he was eating and drinking?" Hal kept his tone casual.

Deirdre likely didn't understand his interest, but she responded immediately. "He had a paper plate with barbecue." A pause. "He was licking his fingers."

"Anything else?"

I wondered if she heard the tension in Hal's voice.

But her reply was quick. "A bottle of beer and a paper bowl with strawberry shortcake."

Hal silently exhaled.

Sam's face was intent. He made a quick note in his pad. I looked over his shoulder and read: *Davenport—No hesitation in mentioning beer bottle.*

Hal was pleased. "What happened next?"

"That redheaded writer came up." She took a quick breath.

Sam looked studiously down at his pad. Perhaps prompted by his subconscious, he drew the stick figure of a horse.

"Redheaded writer?" Hal's voice was odd.

Sounding only a little uncomfortable, Deirdre said hurriedly, "You know who I mean. Sometimes she's there, sometimes she isn't. She said her name was Judy Hope and she was working on a feature for a new online entertainment site. The *Rabbit's Foot*. She asked Harry if she could talk to him, get his insights on Jay's murder. I guess Harry thought he'd have a chance for some publicity, so he picked up his beer and dessert from the wall and put them on the ground by his feet. Of course, he was making a place for her, not me, but she told me to sit down and she'd go to the buffet and get some food for us. That left Harry with me. He wasn't pleased. But this gave me the chance to ask him about Thursday night. I told him I thought I'd seen him in the shadows by Jay's cabin. He acted odd. I got scared. I had the feeling he really had been there." Her voice was shaky. "He said a lot of people might be mad at Jay. He looked around the terrace one by one at Maureen Matthews, Liz and Tom Baker, Ashton Lewis, and Cliff Granger. He said maybe one of them was in the shadows. He seemed to think that was funny. Then he left."

"What happened then?"

"Nothing."

I could almost see Deirdre's shrug.

Sam intervened. "Ms. Davenport, Sam Cobb here. I'd like to take you through the next few minutes after Toomey left. Exactly what did you do? Did you sit there for a while, get up? Precisely what happened?"

"I sat there for a couple of minutes. I felt really unsettled by Harry, his attitude, the way he looked at me." Deirdre's voice held remembered discomfort. "Then I saw some people looking for a place to sit, so I got up. I realized Harry had left his trash, so I gathered everything up—"

Sam interrupted. "Describe the trash."

"Plate. Bowl. Bottle." Her voice reflected distaste. "The bottle was greasy. I put the dessert bowl on top of the plate and carried the plate and the beer bottle to a trash receptacle."

"Where was the trash can?"

"Near the steps leading down into the gardens."

Sam pushed up from his chair, walked around the desk

to the blackboard. I scooted out of the way. He erased the horse (quite feminine in appearance, I thought) with the halo, plucked up a piece of chalk. "Mr. Davenport, let's start with when you picked up the refuse. I understand that earlier Harry Toomey deliberately looked toward several people, implying they had reason to be angry with Jay Knox."

"That's correct. He looked at Maureen Matthews, Liz and Tom Baker, Ashton Lewis, Cliff Granger."

Sam sketched a long low wall, drew a thin figure at one end stooping to pick up a plate, bottle, and bowl. "Tell me where each one was on the terrace."

There was silence. I pictured Deirdre's long face tensed in concentration.

She spoke slowly. "Maureen was quite near me. She was sitting on the wall between Harry and me and the steps. Liz and Tom Baker were at a table a few feet to our left. I could see their faces. She looked desperately unhappy. Professor Lewis stood near the cash bar. Cliff Granger was at the edge of a crowd on the other side of the terrace but he was looking out toward the gardens."

Sam pinpointed each person on the blackboard. "Could any of them have seen you pick up Harry's trash?"

"Oh yes." The answer was quick and firm. "If"—her tone was wry—"any of them cared about Harry's trash, they could easily have seen me dispose of everything."

"What happened then?"

"I went to the ladies' room and washed my hands. I returned to the terrace and went through the buffet and carried supper up to my room. I didn't want to talk to anyone."

"What time was that?"

Deirdre thought for a moment. "It must have been almost eight. I ate, took a shower, and got ready for bed. I wrote some e-mails to my kids. Then Harry called. And I called Hal."

"That's helpful. All right, Ms. Davenport. Detective Sergeant Price will be returning to the hotel shortly. He'll be keeping an eye on you for your own safety. Do you have any questions?"

Deirdre asked uncertainly, "What difference does Harry's trash make?"

Before Hal could speak, Sam said smoothly, "It's important to establish all of Harry Toomey's actions. Please don't discuss this matter with anyone other than Detective Sergeant Price."

When the connection ended, Sam gestured toward the door. "She's safe enough having breakfast on the terrace. You look like a man who slept in his clothes. Better get home and shave, then go to the lodge. Don't tell her Harry was killed with a beer bottle. Better for her not to know."

Hal hesitated at the door. "How're you going to deal with the photos on TV?"

Sam's face hardened. "I don't care what a snotty stringer puts out there."

Hal started to speak, but Sam was brusque. "You got an assignment, Price. Hop to it."

When the door closed behind Hal, I decided to appear. I admired the shimmering blue of the beads on my shoes as I strolled around Sam's desk toward the sofa. "As they say in a different context: We need to talk."

Sam laughed. He reached over, touched the intercom. "No visitors until I buzz. Thanks, Colleen." He turned his swivel chair to face the couch, watched as I settled comfortably in a corner. He gave me a nod. "I forgot to tell you at breakfast: nice outfit. Claire says it's always appropriate to offer a compliment. And a thanks. I would be ready to arrest Deirdre Davenport if you hadn't tipped me off. Too bad you didn't see the person who mooched over to that trash can and filched out the beer bottle." But he looked hopeful.

I shook my head. "I wasn't looking that way when Deirdre put away the trash. But now we know Harry was a walking dead man when he and Deirdre talked."

Sam's eyes narrowed in concentration. "Exactly. The bottle was taken because Deirdre handled it. The decision to use the bottle as a weapon against Harry had already been made."

The killer was audacious. "The murderer thinks fast, moves fast. Using that particular bottle as a weapon tells us a lot." I held up my hand, paused to change the polish from pink to gold, a good match for the heels, and raised five fingers one at a time. "One, the killer was watching Deirdre and Harry. Two, Harry must have seen one or more of the following people at or near cabin five: Maureen Matthews, Ashton Lewis, Cliff Granger. He mentioned each of them to Deirdre, as well as Liz and Tom Baker. Three, Harry didn't know Liz's name until I described her Friday morning. Four, Harry knew who killed Jay. Five, Harry contacted the killer."

"Blackmail." Sam made it a statement, not a question.

"I think so." I remembered my surprise on Friday morning when I spoke to Harry and there was no evidence of despair at losing out on the job to Deirdre. Instead, he was in a good humor. He might have missed out on the job, but he was looking ahead to exacting some kind of boost from his knowledge. Either that or money. I ran over the names in my mind: two faculty members, an agent, a young writer and her husband. I made a quick decision. "Maureen Matthews, Ashton Lewis, or Cliff Granger might have been useful to Harry. Liz and Tom Baker, not so much."

Sam was judicious. "I'm not ready to count them out. Maybe Harry kept quiet, thinking he could use his knowledge one way or another. Maybe he wanted money, but the Bakers couldn't pay up. Maybe Tom Baker would do whatever he had to do to avoid being fingered as a murderer. What matters is that Harry obviously saw something Thursday night that linked one of them to Jay's murder."

I rushed ahead. "And then Harry contacted Jay's murderer. Perhaps he slipped a note under a door, perhaps he used a house phone. One way or another, he was in touch with either Maureen, Liz or Tom, Ashton, or Cliff. We don't know what Harry threatened, but he didn't come to the police, so he must have felt that he'd reached an understanding with the murderer—Harry would keep quiet in exchange for whatever Harry demanded." Harry was riding high Friday morning.

"Stupid kills," Sam said briefly.

I understood Sam's dark judgment. Cocky Harry saw knowledge of guilt as an advantage. He neglected to face the reality that anyone who kills will kill again.

Sam thought out loud. "Deirdre accused Harry of being near cabin five. I think he was in the shadows, watching. He saw the murderer and he may have seen Liz or Tom—"

I broke in. "He saw them both. When I talked to Harry Friday morning, he didn't know Liz Baker's name. But when I described her, he recognized her immediately and then he described her husband. That means Harry saw both of them Thursday night."

Sam looked discouraged. "A lot of people were apparently coming and going. Maureen Matthews may have asked Jay for her letters. Since Harry included Ashton Lewis and Cliff Granger, I think they were at the cabin at some point as well. That's why he looked at those five. Let's concentrate for now on the terrace last night. Deirdre and Harry talked. Harry left. Deirdre dumped his trash." He frowned. "What happened then?"

"The killer saw Deirdre pick up Harry's stuff, including the beer bottle. Maybe it was an association of ideas—how nice it was that the champagne bottle had Deirdre's prints, which made her a prime suspect, and wouldn't it be clever to use a bottle with her fingerprints on it to hit Harry."

I thought of each in turn: Maureen facing embarrassment, possibly even the loss of her job if the letters became public; Liz desperate to get the money back; Tom furious over Jay's treatment of Liz; easily angered Ashton outraged by Jay's sexual proclivities; Cliff lying about the tawdriness of last year's party at Jay's house. "When Deirdre left the terrace, the killer strolled to the trash barrel—"

Sam spoke fast, a picture clear in his mind. "The killer probably had a folded napkin in one hand. Drop the hand, fish out the bottle, take a couple of steps and be off the terrace and in the shadows. The rest seems pretty clear. The killer gets in touch with Harry, maybe asks what Deirdre had to say, realizes this can be used to trap Harry. The murderer persuades Harry to call Deirdre, set up a meeting." He frowned. "But what difference did it make that Harry saw Deirdre? She'd already told the police that she talked to him."

Lies have a tendency to come home to roost. I cleared my throat. "Under the category of information received and held confidential"—I definitely had Sam's attention—"here's the truth: Deirdre found the cabin door open. She stepped inside and found Jay dead. She panicked and ran. Very likely Harry knew this. The killer told Harry to call Deirdre, say he knew who was in the shadows, and this would entice Deirdre to come because she was scared she was going to be arrested. The killer convinced Harry it was a way for Harry to get Deirdre fired. When Deirdre came, all Harry had to do was tell her he saw her find Jay's body and ask her why she didn't call the police. The killer promised to hide nearby and tape the conversation and Harry could use the tape to get her in trouble at the college."

Sam's gaze was somber. "Clever. Harry was a fool."

"I imagine Harry was excited, pleased." Harry was sure he had everything under control. "He called Deirdre, said he knew who was in the shadows, and he wanted her help to prove it. He set the meeting for twenty minutes later. He went down to the pier with the killer. Maybe they talked for a minute, maybe the killer pointed under the pier, said that's a good place for me to hide. Harry looked. The killer struck. Harry went down. The killer shoved him into the water, maybe leaned over to keep his face under."

Sam slowly nodded. "I buy it. But proving it will—"

A heavy knock and Sam's door swung in. Mayor Lumpkin hurtled forward, as well as a woman nearing six feet in height and well over two hundred pounds can hurtle. Her blond coronet braids were a trifle askew, her green eye shadow too liberally applied, but the color rising in her square face was all natural—the bright pulsing red of sheer rage.

I disappeared.

Sam came to his feet. "Your Honor, what can I do for you this morning?"

She stood a few feet away, cheeks splotched, buxom chest heaving beneath a garish paisley blouse. "You told Colleen not to let anybody in." She stared at the couch. "I thought I saw a woman sitting there." Her tone was accusing.

Sam folded his arms. "I guess you've got double vision this morning. I know that must be disturbing. Have you had some coffee?" He looked up at the round-faced clock. "You're out early. Not quite eight thirty. I'll ask Colleen to bring—"

"I don't need coffee." Her flush deepened. "I see quite well."

Sam nodded quickly, as if agreeing with a disturbed person in hopes of encouraging restraint. "I'm sure you do." His tone was soothing, appropriate for anyone dealing with unreason. "Twenty-twenty vision." He gave the couch a passing glance. "But I'm here by myself. As anyone should be able to see." Emphasis on the noun. "I came in early. We have a double murder—"

"And scandal erupting. The honor of the Adelaide Police Department is in question. The news is all over the state that a police detective is closely associated with a criminal. I came at once. This shall be rectified immediately. A corrupt department will not be tolerated and this scandal shall not occur under my stewardship." Her voice took on the stentorian resoluteness of a politician at full bore. "I promised the voters of Adelaide that I would never countenance corruption at any level in this city. You must immediately dismiss that degenerate detective." She drew herself to her full height, quoted: "'Chief suspect in prof's murder has detective on speed dial.' I am disgusted. I am outraged. I am appalled. This is the result of incompetent leadership. That's obvious. I have long felt you have too free rein in the department. New blood is needed. Dismiss that detective immediately, arrest that woman. I will hold a news conference at eleven a.m. to announce that the department is ridding—"

"Hold on, Neva. You better listen and listen hard." Sam's heavy face was commanding. "Detective Sergeant Price has been assigned to protect an innocent woman—"

"It said she's the chief suspect!" Her voice was shrill.

"'It said' . . ." His voice dripped with sarcasm. "Was that an official announcement from police headquarters? Think again. The accusation is the creation of a sleazy third-rate stringer. It's a fantasy. The story is a fake. So, I've got a lot to do this morning, if you'll excuse me."

She had the look of a maddened bull pricked by the lunges of a picador. "I have it on good authority that the suspect and the detective were seated on a bench, obviously in disgrace."

"Good authority?" He shook his head. "I wonder who in the department wanted to cause trouble for me? Somebody who didn't bother to ask, yanked out a cell, called a stringer. Maybe you and I will have a talk about that another time. But right now, I'm telling you Ms. Davenport is innocent and Detective Sergeant Hal Price is discharging his duties in the finest tradition of the Adelaide Police Department."

The mayor's gaze was steely. Her deep voice was implacable. "At eleven a.m. I will hold a press conference. You will attend. You will announce that the woman pictured on TV has been arrested and the detective with whom she consorted has been put on leave or you will announce that you have solved the double murder and reveal the identity of the murderer." With that she turned and stalked to the door.

The door slammed behind her.

His face grim, Sam heaved to his feet. "What've I got? A little over two hours, then I'm toast. I better get out there and find a miracle."

I hoped St. Jude was listening.

Chapter 13

In the hallway outside Maureen's room, I quickly appeared. I smoothed the fabric of the French blue trousers. Uniforms provide an assurance of legitimacy. I needed to persuade Maureen this time that I was indeed Officer M. Loy. I touched the nameplate, then knocked.

The peephole opened.

"Officer M. Loy requesting a moment of your time." I spoke pleasantly though firmly.

Slowly the door swung in. Her stare was uncertain. "Who are you?" One hand touched the white chunky stone necklace that gleamed like alabaster against a black blouse. A black jacket with a white floral design of huge hydrangea blooms was striking. Slim black trousers and black slingback pumps completed her wardrobe. Her haggard beauty was apparent, but there was both sadness and suspicion in her eyes.

"I understand why you are confused. I used a pen name at the bar Thursday night. I would love to be able to launch an online entertainment site, but in real life"—one hand behind my back and two fingers crossed—"I'm a police officer. I can't use any of the material I picked up for a story since this has turned into an official investigation." I sounded regretful, career hopes dashed. "And, of course"—my shrug was casual—"the wig and dress were simply my undercover persona. But now"—I beamed at her—"I am who I am. And I'm here"—I was suddenly and truly grave—"seeking information about the party at Jay Knox's house last year and any other information you may have acquired, especially if you saw either Ashton Lewis or Liz or Tom Baker near cabin five Thursday night. You see"—I spoke with utter conviction—"we have very little time. Deirdre Davenport will be arrested at eleven o'clock unless the murderer is found."

Maureen brushed back of a lock of midnight black hair, held the door wide. "I will tell you what I know."

∽

I looked at Deirdre, and said glumly, "I don't see any way to prove what happened." After my interview with Maureen, I was almost certain I knew the murderer's identity.

Proof? Nothing, nada, zilch.

Deirdre again stood at the window of her room. She was lovely in a yellow shawl-collar tee and beige linen slacks and delightfully feminine beige strappy sandals. Despite bluish marks of fatigue beneath her eyes, her face reflected hope, her wiry russet hair was brushed and shiny, her makeup fresh. "Hal called and said everything would be all right. I saw him a few minutes ago"—she pointed out the window—"walking really fast across the terrace." She craned to look. "I think he went to the auditorium."

I wondered if she'd heard a word that I'd said.

"There has to be some way to prove guilt." I paced back and forth, glanced down at beautifully cut tumbled leather loafers that matched my lime linen jacket, but the restful colors gave me no peace. I might have been confident I knew the identity of the murderer. I could tell Sam. Sam could make an accusation, but this killer would never admit anything and there was no physical evidence.

I looked at the clock. Twenty minutes past nine. So little time. I didn't look at Deirdre. She was unaware of her peril, unaware of the mayor's determination to have her arrested. I knew and I was wild to do something, anything. "The only chance would be to ask Maureen to call, make a threat—"

Deirdre was untroubled. "Hal said everything's going to be all right. I trust him."

I gazed at her sadly. So little time . . .

A metallic scrape, rattles, a thump. "Attention, please." We looked at the grill over the bed.

"All hotel guests and staff are requested to come immediately to the auditorium. Adelaide Police Chief Sam Cobb will make an important announcement. Attention, please. All hotel guests and staff are requested to come immediately to the auditorium. Adelaide Police Chief . . ."

❦

The sudden rush of wind and clack of wheels shocked me. Casually dressed hotel guests, some casting uneasy glances about them, others excitedly chattering, streamed across the terrace. Hotel employees in their various uniforms looked concerned. All were oblivious to the thunder of wheels on rails, the scent of coal smoke, the deep-throated whoo of the whistle. I'd always loved the clarion cry of a train, that harbinger of journeys to take, adventures to enjoy.

But not right this minute.

Wiggins spoke too softly to be overheard. "No one will be at the pool. The diving board. Posthaste."

The roar of the engine was louder, the cloud of coal smoke heavier.

I dropped onto the platform, hoped Wiggins might take pleasure in the view—the sparkling blue water beneath, the bright towels casually draped on gay deck chairs, the umbrellas affording shade, the cabanas with closed curtains. "Wiggins, I'm so happy to bring you up to date—"

"Precept Five." Wiggins's tone was distinctly frosty.

"Mea culpa." Perhaps a humble admission of guilt would pacify him. Then I rushed ahead. "But honestly, Howie Harris is causing Chief Cobb all kinds of trouble and I thought it served him right."

"Draping scant hair over his ears was—"

Did I hear a faint rumble of laughter?

"—creative but reprehensible." Perhaps he found Howie unappealing as well, because he continued rather hurriedly, "And Precept Four: 'Become visible only when absolutely essential.' Bailey Ruth"—now Wiggins was clearly disturbed—"was it really necessary to be present when you spoke with Chief Cobb?"

"Wiggins, I wish I could always remain unseen." Heaven knows when we fib. I said hurriedly, "Let me rephrase. I truly felt Chief Cobb would feel more comfortable if we faced each other and shared information." Sometimes that inner voice of conscience can't be ignored. "And"—my voice was small—"I was wearing the most adorable white tunic and blue pants that really looked just like a Caribbean sea. And I had to convince Maureen Matthews she could trust me, and that's why Officer Loy appeared, and I had to appear just now in Deirdre's room. She finds it stressful to hear a voice and see no one. In fact"—I wasn't sure this was a plus, but I was desperate—"I thought it would cheer her to see this gorgeous linen jacket—" I broke off, clapped my hand to my lips. Bobby Mac always said if he let me talk long enough, the truth would out. Wiggins had no fashion sense, no appreciation of what it does for a woman to feel that she is splendidly attired.

"Now, now." Wiggins hastened to reassure me, his voice kind. "Lorraine finds your love of fashion to be very endearing."

I sent a Heavenly thank-you to Lorraine Marlow, the elegant, fastidious, and delightful ghost at the Goddard College Library who had turned out to be Wiggins's cherished sweetheart.

"We are," Wiggins said, I thought rather obscurely, "who we are. However"—a note of sternness returned—"I would have thought it incumbent upon you to summon the Rescue

Express when you realized you are no longer needed on earth to protect the good name of that fine young mother."

I saw my predicament at once. I'd insisted I must remain to prove Deirdre's innocence. Now that I had convinced the chief of police that Deirdre had no connection to the crimes, Wiggins was satisfied that my objective had been realized and my mission successfully completed.

The deep-throated mournful cry of the whistle, the rumble of the engine, the clack of the wheels, the scent of coal smoke signaled the imminent arrival of the Rescue Express.

I lifted my voice above the clamor. "Wiggins, there are extenuating circumstances. If I leave now"—I placed a hand over my heart, though I supposed I remained unseen; nonetheless I felt compelled—"many innocents will suffer. Our gallant police chief will be replaced by the odious two-strand Howie, who is a puppet of the mayor. Intrepid Detective Sergeant Hal Price will be relieved in disgrace. Innocent Deirdre Davenport will be arrested and charged by Sam's replacement, which will defame her good name, distress her helpless children, and thwart a tender and growing attraction between Deirdre and the detective sergeant." I paused for a breath and delivered the coup de grâce. "Picture Deirdre alone in a cell, defenseless, facing charges although she is innocent." I endeavored to create the pathos of an overwrought Victorian novel.

"It was such a simple assignment." Wiggins sounded perplexed. "You would draw on your background as an English teacher and help a writer find inspiration." A harumph. "Now you are caught up in what appears to be an almost impossible situation—a beleaguered police chief, a compromised

detective, a young mother in peril. Bailey Ruth, only you—"
A sigh. "Yes, only you. But as dear Lorraine says, your heart
is big, your goals are noble, though your means . . . Ah, well,
we must meet challenges as we can. Do your best."

The coal smoke, almost overpowering, whooshed past
me. The thunder of the wheels faded.

I would have hallooed my relief to the treetops, but there
was no time for premature celebration.

∽

Flanked by Dr. Randall and Detective Sergeant Price, Sam
Cobb stood at the podium on the stage. Sam, his blue suit
already wrinkled, bulked above both men even though Randall and Price topped six feet in height. Sam looked confident, self-possessed, and reassuring. Dr. Randall nervously
fingered the collar of his sport shirt. A clean-shaven Hal,
crisp in an oxford cloth shirt, open at the neck, and khaki
slacks, also appeared confident.

". . . wish to reassure all the guests and staff"—Sam's
deep voice was calm—"that there is no danger to anyone
here at the lodge. Our investigation reveals that last night's
victim, Harry Toomey, sought a meeting with the person
responsible for the death of Professor Jay Knox Thursday
night."

I hovered slightly above Sam. Today's attendance was
smaller than yesterday's. Possibly some conference-goers
found proximity to murder unnerving and had checked out
and left. There were perhaps seventy-five people, mostly
women, scattered among the seats. Deirdre was seated at
the end of the third row.

Gladys Samson was on the same row a few seats away. "Blackmail?" Her voice was strident, her sharp features quivering with excitement. Her jagged black hair made her look witchlike. She turned and stared pointedly at Deirdre.

It was Gladys who had eagerly described Deirdre as tense and upset on her way to see Jay Knox.

Deirdre returned Gladys's stare with a calm, measured look.

Sam was imperturbable. He gazed at Gladys. "Harry Toomey blackmailed the murderer. That's why Harry died. His murderer is in this room right now."

Gladys gasped, pressed fingers against her lips, shrank away from Deirdre.

Deirdre turned toward her, looking concerned. "If you know anything about the murders, I suggest you hurry to the police right this minute. I know"—she lifted her voice a trifle—"I've tried to help them. They've been very appreciative. I'll be glad to go with you."

I quickly scanned the audience. Ashton Lewis, lean and intent, stared at the stage with a level, cold gaze. Liz Baker's eyes flared in alarm. She turned and gave her husband a searching glance. Tom Baker nervously brushed back a lock of hair, hunched his shoulders. Smooth-faced Cliff Granger smothered a yawn. He glanced at his watch. Was he counting the hours until tomorrow and his flight home? As always, he was meticulously dressed. Bobby Mac would look terrific in Cliff's checked poplin dress shirt with a lavender background. Maureen Matthews was grave, her lovely face furrowed in a frown.

Gladys half rose. "Your statement is upsetting. If the murderer is in this room, why haven't you arrested that person?"

"We are putting together our case and we are hoping other concerned citizens like Ms. Davenport will come forth with more information. That's why I have called everyone here. This is what we know as a certainty. Toomey saw Knox's murderer arrive and depart from cabin five Thursday night. The next day, Toomey contacted the murderer."

A flash and click came from the side of the stage. Deke Carson lowered a Leica. "Is that why Deirdre Davenport was at the scene of the crime?" He was more presentable today—flyaway lank brown hair pulled back in a ponytail, a blue polo shirt, and jeans.

Sam's face hardened. "Press conference at City Hall, eleven a.m. No questions here."

"But, Chief"—Deke's tone was coy—"you just answered a question." He smirked and looked over his shoulder at the audience.

Sam pointed at a front row seat. "If you want to listen, it's a public meeting. There will be no more questions until the news conference." He nodded silent thanks to the *Adelaide Gazette* crime reporter who was writing furiously but keeping her mouth shut. "I'm here to communicate facts concerning a double murder. The first fact is that Harry Toomey was a blackmailer. The second fact is that Harry Toomey at some time yesterday spoke to Jay Knox's murderer. The third fact is that Harry Toomey contacted Deirdre Davenport at approximately twenty minutes to eleven last night. Harry Toomey hinted that he knew the identity of the murderer and wanted her help to set up a trap. He asked her to meet him at the pier. Instead, Ms. Davenport wisely contacted the police. That is why she and Detective Sergeant Hal Price discovered Toomey's body. However, the important fact for everyone in this room to understand—"

Sam was skating past the contents of Harry's call to Deirdre.

"—is the reality of Toomey's murder. Toomey blackmailed a killer." Sam let the words stand in a long silence. "Now he's dead. If anyone here has knowledge concerning the murders of Jay Knox or Harry Toomey, immediately contact police. And here"—Sam leaned forward, planted big hands on the podium—"is how each of you can help us. Think about each instance yesterday when you saw or spoke to Harry Toomey. We want to know about all contacts between Harry and any person at the conference. Obviously, most of those contacts were innocent. One or more were not. We need citizens to come forward."

He waited while a buzz of speculation rose and fell.

"Some of you may be able to offer other important assistance. We want to talk to anyone who was in the Silver Lake Lodge parking lot on Thursday night between eleven p.m. and midnight. We know"—a pause for emphasis—"that the murderer of Jay Knox took Knox's car out of the parking lot, drove to Knox's home, deleted material from his computer, returned to the parking lot, wiped the steering wheel to remove all fingerprints, left the keys in the car. Knox drove a black Mazda MX-5 Miata convertible. It may well be that someone in this room was entering or leaving the lot during this time period.

If you were at the lot during that period, if you saw Knox's car depart or return, please contact us immediately."

Now there was an undertone of excited whispers.

"In conclusion, we are exploring several avenues and believe the murderer will soon be apprehended. We are grateful for the cooperation of the Goddard English Department, especially Dr. Randall and Professors Matthews and Davenport. Again we are seeking help from the following possible witnesses: anyone in the parking lot Thursday night and anyone with knowledge of personal contacts made by Harry Toomey at any time on Friday. Please come directly to conference room A immediately after we close. Finally, we are requesting that every person, both guests and staff, who was present on the terrace last night between seven thirty and eight to report there at ten a.m. Thank you very much for your attention."

ℭ

Deirdre once again stood at the window of her room looking down on the terrace. The sunlight emphasized the buttercup yellow of her blouse. "Who knew being in mom mode would be my undoing?"

I looked at her. "Mom mode?"

"Like a happy robot," she said bitterly, "I automatically pick up book bags, carry dishes to the sink, clean up the back of the car, all the candy wrappers, squashed cans, discarded gum packages. I never thought the tidy instinct would put me in a cell. Why, oh why, did I pick up Harry's trash?"

"That's what mothers do." I had swift, happy memories

of beach towels and scattered clothing and errant school-work.

"Speaking of, my cell vibrated downstairs. It doesn't take ESP to know one of the kids is probably calling. Joey will lobby for me to come and get him tonight. Katie is having full-bore angst over how much the camp is costing." She pulled the cell phone from the pocket of her slacks, glanced down. "Katie. Voice mail." Deirdre swiped.

In a soft shaky voice, interspersed with sniffs, Katie said in anguish, "Mom, did you know you're on TV? This morning everybody was looking at me funny. I didn't know what was wrong until Gabby told me. Then I looked. Mom, what's going on? Are you going to jail? Will Dad come and get me, bring me home? If you're in jail . . ." She broke off, sobbing. The connection ended.

Her face tight with anger, Deirdre swiped.

Apparently the call was answered immediately.

"Hush now, honey. I'm all right. . . . No, of course not. . . . Breathe deep, honey. You have to get it together. Here I am and I'm talking to you and everything's all right and—"

I took the phone from her hand, backed away as Deirdre tried to snatch it from me. Recognizing a mother-defending-her-cub look, I disappeared and rose in the air far out of reach and talked fast. "Katie? You don't know me. I'm Officer Loy. I want to assure you that your mother's fine. She's been a huge help to the police department. She's working with us and with Detective Sergeant Hal Price. That's why her picture was taken with him. She agreed to be announced as a suspect so that we can close in on the actual criminal. She will be recognized publicly for her assistance, and it's fine for you to tell your friends that your mom is working with the police. She is in no danger, as one of us is with her at all times. A second murder has occurred, but the reasons for both crimes have nothing to do with your mother. The results of the investigation will be announced to news media later today. For right now, you get back to your friends and tell them you are really proud of your mom and so is everyone in the police department." I dropped down, handed the cell to Deirdre, and reappeared.

". . . happy to help the police. So, you go have fun. I'll text you this afternoon. . . . Sure. . . . Love you, too." Deirdre clicked off the cell, immediately swiped a call. "Hey, Joey. . . . Sorry I woke you up. . . . No, honey, I can't come until Monday, but there's a story on TV that's all wrong. It says I'm a suspect in a murder case here. They got the facts wrong. I'm helping the police in their investigation. . . . It's way cool. . . . And maybe I'll get to introduce you to some of the officers. . . . We'll stop at the Dairy Queen on the way home. . . . See you soon. . . . Love you, too."

She clicked off the cell, put it in her pocket. "How to start your morning with a buzz—tell your kids you aren't going to jail."

I wanted to give her a reassuring hug. I could have used a reassuring hug myself. If we didn't catch a murderer by eleven o'clock, Deirdre would be on her way to jail, but there was no point in upsetting her by revealing the mayor's ultimatum.

I kept my voice cheerful. "It's obvious where Sam's headed. He'd like to have a miracle—someone saw the murderer drive away or return in Jay's convertible. His next best hope is either a waiter or hotel guest who noticed someone at the trash."

Deirdre gave me a searching look. "So, what if someone says they saw Ashton Lewis or Liz or Tom Baker or Cliff Granger? You know what I'd do if I were one of them? I'd look surprised, maybe a little offended, and say, 'There's a mistake here. Certainly I put my trash in that can, but I didn't remove anything.'"

I understood her concern. What if a witness pointed at one of them? Where was the proof? We needed irrefutable, unmistakable, rock-solid proof. We needed the truth in black and white, signed, sealed, and delivered.

Black and white. Computer files. Photos. Love letters. Black and white . . .

I looked at the clock. Twenty-five minutes to ten o'clock. I'd have to move fast. "I know what to do." I disappeared.

ᔕ

Maureen Matthews sat on the terrace wall staring down into the trees and, I knew, a glimpse of cabin 5.

In the protective embrace of the long weeping willow strands, I appeared. No uniform this time. A deep purple blouse and a silky purple scarf were a nice contrast to white trousers. I chose a simple silver necklace, quite classy. Surely I wasn't very noticeable, though there is nothing a redhead can do about flaming curls. I wasn't focused on appearance, but there was one critically necessary item. . . . Eagerly, I opened the pale lavender purse, found a pad and pen. I drew them out, concentrated on my note.

To: Maureen Matthews From: Officer M. Loy

It is essential that we talk unobserved. Please go immediately to your room.

I strolled up to the terrace, paused next to Maureen, bent down, then rose. I held out the note. "I believe you dropped this." My eyes warned her to pretend we were strangers.

After the tiniest of pauses, she nodded. "Thank you."

I turned and walked away.

I heard footsteps behind me. In the hallway of the second floor, we walked together to her room. She used the entry card.

As she closed the door, she turned and studied me. "Where's your uniform?"

I met her suspicion head-on. "Did you speak with Chief Cobb, report our conversation? Tell him Officer Loy sent you?"

"I did." One hand again lifted to hold tight to the large stones in her necklace. "He was appreciative. But I wasn't able to give him any proof."

"That's why I've come."

"What do you expect me to do?"

I gazed at her lovely face. I saw sensitivity, a knowledge of loss and betrayal, a remembrance of good days. "Despite all that happened, despite the way everything between you and Jay ended, will you help me catch his murderer?"

She gazed down at her hands loose in her lap, gently twisted a golden band on her left hand. Her voice was low, almost inaudible. "You don't know much about me."

She was right. I didn't know her history, what happiness she'd known, what despair she'd faced, what mountains she'd climbed. I felt I knew that she was kind and caring, that she was generous. She'd welcomed Deirdre to the faculty even though she may have known that Jay Knox found Deirdre attractive.

Maureen spoke quietly, her violet eyes filed with sadness. "I came to Adelaide eight years ago after my husband's death. In Afghanistan. Kenneth was career military. He was a major when he died. I miss him every day. You have to live, but the pain never leaves. I'll see a baby in the park and remember when we were young, stationed at Fort Sill, how Kenneth would get up at night to feed Billy. Billy's at West Point." She brushed back a tangle of soft dark hair. "Billy is so like his father. And now, the way the world is . . ." She pressed her lips together, knowing that life is fragile, that youth and strength and leadership can end in blood and pain. She took a breath, continued, her voice almost inaudible. "I try not to think. I try to work as hard as I can and make every minute count. Now I teach." A faint smile. "A lifetime ago, I was going to be an actress. I met Kenneth at a dance when I was just out of college. After we married, I was an Army wife. I turned to writing, taught courses on various posts. When he was stationed in Korea, I finished my master's. An old friend from our Fort Sill days is retired and lives here in Adelaide and let me know when a faculty job opened up. I applied, and when the job was offered, I was glad. Adelaide was a nice place for Billy to finish junior and senior high. I enjoy teaching, and Adelaide doesn't hold memories that would make every day harder. So"—her lips trembled—"that was my situation when Jay joined the faculty. I was lonely. I hadn't been with a man since Kenneth died. Jay was the quintessential bad boy. I'm not a fool. I knew he was careless and selfish. But he was huge fun. He could make anyone laugh. And when he looked at me—but I don't need to explain."

She didn't. I know the spark that ignites passion, sometimes despite inner warnings of danger ahead.

Again she brushed back a silky strand of midnight-dark hair. Her haggard beauty was as striking as Hedy Lamarr's in *Algiers*. Many believe Hedy Lamarr to be the most beautiful woman ever to star in Hollywood—beautiful, brilliant, and shadowed by scandal.

"You understand"—I spoke quietly—"both love and passion."

"With Kenneth, I had both. With Jay . . ." A shrug. "I know now that he thought only of himself. I wasn't surprised when he threatened to publish my letters. He didn't care how destructive that would be for me, but he wasn't being cruel. He was being Jay. He wasn't thinking about me. He was thinking about himself. He had to stop me from telling Dr. Randall about that party. In a way"—her tone was forgiving—"that makes his threat easier to bear. He didn't want to hurt me; he wanted to save himself. He saw the world only in relation to himself. He didn't care that Liz Baker betrayed her husband. He didn't care if he seduced a student. He didn't care if he used the pictures from his party to force Cliff Granger to offer unsaleable books."

I spoke soberly. "Jay died because he was selfish, but his selfishness now affects others. Deirdre Davenport faces arrest if the police do not solve the murders. Detective Sergeant Hal Price has been accused of conspiring with her in the death of Harry Toomey. That suspicion was fostered by their obvious immediate attraction to each other. The police chief may lose his job and be replaced by an incompetent. Perhaps saddest of all, if Deirdre is arrested, there can be no future for her and Hal. Right now there is enough evidence to convict her. She is innocent, but the only way to save her is to trap a murderer who has left no traces."

Maureen looked at me in distress. "I told the police chief. Can't he . . . what do they say . . . announce a 'person of interest'?"

"There's no proof. We need evidence in black and white. I know a way." I looked deep into her hauntingly lovely eyes. "It all depends on you."

Chapter 14

Perhaps fifteen people milled about in the hall outside conference room A. Another ten or so occupied chairs along the wall. Sam Cobb definitely had a response to his invitation. I wondered if one of these people saw the killer climb into Jay's Mazda convertible or if one of them saw the killer stroll casually across the terrace, stop for a moment at the far trash can, ease out a greasy beer bottle.

I hoped so. Every additional piece of evidence would bolster the district attorney's case. But that information could wait. I had to contact Sam now. In fifteen minutes, staff and guests would gather on the terrace. I had no choice but to adopt desperate measures.

An officer—tall, gawky, thin, in his early twenties—stood next to the door.

I took the scene in at a glance. The officer was there to prevent interruptions to the police interviews. A few feet away, Deke Carson slouched against the wall, languidly fingered the keyboard on his laptop. His video camera rested next to his feet. Lean Joan Crandall, the *Gazette* reporter, tapped a stubby pencil impatiently on a notepad. Joan reported the old-fashioned way, with pen and paper and pointed questions. She ignored Carson.

I drew myself up to my full height, strode to the young officer, looked up into excited brown eyes though he kept his face solemn. I guessed he was a rookie, thrilled to be on the periphery of a double murder investigation and wanting to acquit himself well.

I spoke emphatically, though too low to be overheard. "Officer, notify Chief Cobb that Detective Loy must talk to him immediately on the terrace." I turned and strode away, head high.

Would effrontery carry the day?

∽

The honeysuckle arbor was warm, untenanted. I disappeared.

On the terrace, I hovered near the wall. What if the young officer hewed to his original orders? I was certain he'd been told to admit no one and to prevent any interruption. I was acutely aware of every passing second. People were arriving on the terrace, glances avid, conversations excited. How much time before the gathering began? Perhaps twelve minutes.

Sam strode out the door, shaded his eyes, scanned the surroundings.

At once I was at his shoulder.

I whispered, "Walk down the path toward cabin five. Appear to be deep in thought."

I waited until he was on the path, then, hovering at his shoulder, I talked as fast as I could. Even before I finished, he unclipped his cell, held it to his face, barked orders.

༒

Sam, his blue suit even more wrinkled, stood in the middle of the terrace, flanked by Hal Price and Judy Weitz. The sun turned Hal's blond hair cotton white. His handsome face was alert and intent. He held a brown paper sack in one hand. Judy's outfit today was much more flattering, a georgette shirtdress with white polka dots on navy and low-heeled white pumps. Made her look fifteen years younger. Now, if I could do something about her hair . . .

Perhaps forty-five people stood uncertainly on the terrace. Many looked uneasily at crime-scene tape that marked off about three feet of the terrace wall not far from a large gray plastic trash can. No one sat there.

Deirdre waited near a potted palm. She kept glancing toward the far trash container. In the bright sunlight, her russet hair shone. She was slim and lovely in her yellow top and beige slacks.

I stood just behind her, whispered, "Do not look toward the barrel."

She stiffened, hunched her shoulders.

"And don't look over your shoulder. I'm not here."

Maureen, as she'd been instructed, sat on the wall near the steps into the garden. She now wore sunglasses. She was dramatic in her black-and-white jacket, black blouse and slacks. One hand toyed with the chunky necklace of oblong white ceramic pieces. She seemed apart from the flurries of movement, the soft-voiced conversations, the shifting glances on the terrace.

Cliff Granger rested one hip against a pool table. He, too, wore sunglasses. His smooth face was expressionless.

Liz and Tom Baker sat as they had the previous evening, at a table a few feet from the wall. Liz was pale, her small features set, hands tightly clasped. Tom's eyes flicked nervously around the terrace, moving toward the officials conferring in the center, away, then back.

Ashton Lewis stood tall and straight near the cash bar. No bottles and glasses sat on the counter in the hot morning light. A portly bartender rested a hairy hand on the wood, fingers drumming impatiently. Had he been called back from his day off? That was the look he had. He was here and he wanted the cops to do what they were going to do and let him get back to his life. Lewis's expression was inscrutable, but every so often he gazed at Maureen.

Sam cleared his throat, held up a large hand. "Ladies and gentlemen, thank you for coming. I am Police Chief Sam Cobb. With me are Detective Sergeant Hal Price and Detective Judy Weitz. In a moment, I will explain exactly what we hope to learn. But first, I want to take you back to last night—"

I realized with bitter hopelessness that my plan was

doomed. I am no expert on recording devices, but I saw nothing in place that could serve to record the conversation I hoped would ensue between Maureen Matthews and our quarry. The necklace she wore was the one I'd seen in her room earlier today. Obviously, the jewelry belonged to her and was not fitted with a tiny recorder. Perhaps her purse . . . ? My gaze dropped to a braided raffia clutch bag resting by her feet. That had to be the only hope. I knew the chance was slim. That purse wasn't large enough to secrete the bulky recorder used by Detective Weitz. Moreover, a listening device might be able to pick up a whisper at ten feet, but I doubted one existed that could hear through cloth. Not even a doltish murderer would miss the retrieval of a recorder from a purse, and this murderer was clever and quick.

"—here on the terrace between seven thirty and eight o'clock."

Maureen cupped her chin in one hand, appeared to listen attentively.

"The murderer of Jay Knox and Harry Toomey was present. I will ask Professor Deirdre Davenport to come forward."

There was not a breath of sound except for the slap of Deirdre's sandals as she walked across the terrace, then stood facing the chief.

Sam half turned toward Hal. "Also assisting will be Detective Sergeant Price. He will stand in for Harry Toomey."

There was a rumble, and a large metal cart trundled through the main door onto the terrace, pushed by a tall man in an ill-fitting work shirt, faded jeans, and work boots. He was halfway across the terrace when Sam turned. "This area is closed until further notice."

"Look, buddy, I don't work for you. I got my orders." The tone was tough and abrasive.

I smiled and turned my right thumb up in a salute to Sam Cobb.

The workman, aka Detective Don Smith, was adamant. "I'm setting up for a deejay tonight, right over there." He pointed to a spot beyond the wall perhaps a foot or so behind Maureen. "I won't bother you any. All I need is to get over there and get my stuff arranged. I'll keep it quiet." He didn't wait for an answer, pushed the cart forward.

Sam looked combative for an instant, then, frowning, nodded approval. Sam waited until the cart was eased down the steps and in place behind Maureen, then gestured to Hal.

Hal opened his sack, pulled out a paper plate, cardboard bowl, and beer bottle, handed the empty sack to Judy Weitz. He crossed the terrace to the small area marked off by crime tape. He removed the tape, dropped it to the ground. He stepped to the terrace wall, sat down. He placed the paper plate, cardboard bowl, and beer bottle on the ground by his feet.

"Now," Sam spoke with emphasis, "please watch Professor Davenport."

Deirdre looked tall and thin in her yellow blouse and beige slacks and quite alone as she crossed the terrace, sat down beside Hal. They pantomimed conversation. Hal came to his feet, looked down at her, again made a pantomime of speech, turned, walked quickly away.

Deirdre remained sitting on the wall. She gazed after Hal's retreating figure, then shrugged.

I wondered how she felt, every eye on her, some suspicious and inimical, some puzzled and curious.

Finally, she stood. She turned and reached down, picked up the paper plate, cardboard bowl, and beer bottle. She walked swiftly to the trash receptacle, then paused with a hand outstretched.

The receptacle was overfull, the flap tilted up, jammed-in paper plates, cups, and napkins visible.

Deirdre's face wrinkled in distaste as she shoved the plate, bowl, and bottle into the overflowing trash can. The barrel of the beer bottle poked outward. She turned away, walked toward the exit. She stopped at the door, swung around to watch.

Avid glances darted toward her, then away.

Sam pointed at the receptacle. "You will notice"—his voice was calm, almost clinical—"how trash is wedged into the container. The flap is propped open. Professor Davenport picked up the refuse left behind by Harry Toomey, carried a paper plate, cardboard bowl, and beer bottle to that receptacle. There was very little room, but she shoved the items into the opening. Now, this is the important point." He spoke slowly, spacing the words. "Jay Knox's murderer observed the conversation between Harry Toomey and Professor Davenport, then watched as she picked up the trash and carried it to the trash bin." Sam gazed solemnly around the terrace. "At this moment, the murderer walked across the terrace to the trash can. The murderer, probably holding a napkin, stopped at the can, reached down, slid out the beer bottle. That beer bottle contained Harry Toomey's fingerprints and, of course, those of Professor Davenport. That bottle was used as a weapon later last night to stun Harry Toomey. The murderer struck Toomey, then pushed him into the lake, where he drowned. I want each person here to remember where you sat or stood last night at a few minutes before eight." He paused, waited for absolute silence. His voice was stern when he spoke. "Go there now."

There was a flurry of movement as people, shifting to other places, milled about the terrace.

I was close to Maureen when she rose. She placed her purse at her spot on the low wall, walked swiftly across the patio, stopped, looked up. "You'd better come with me." She gestured toward the wall and the raffia bag.

Cliff Granger looked down, his eyes invisible behind the dark glasses. "I wasn't sitting with you."

Her smile was cool. "I know. But I think you'd be well advised to join me now. If you don't want to be arrested for murder." She turned away, walked to the wall. When she was seated, her purse in her lap, she looked across the terrace, beckoned.

Cliff Granger slowly walked toward her. His face was hard, his lips pressed together.

Maureen made room for him beside her.

He sat down, turned toward her, his eyes hidden by the sunglasses. He managed a sardonic smile. "I don't think it matters where I sit, but I want to clear things up. You're confused about last night."

"Good try, Cliff. But I have you where I want you." Her

tone was silky, taunting. "I know about the party at Jay's house last year, you and the girl. You forgot that I spent a great deal of time at Jay's house. He showed me the video of you and the girl, said you were safe as long as you played ball with him. Having a conduit for manuscripts made him a lot of money. Almost fifty thousand dollars a year. We took a holiday to Bermuda. I can't afford to go there on my salary." Her lovely face reflected cupidity, greed, cruelty. "But if I do consulting work like Jay did, why, I can go wherever I want, buy whatever I want. It's simple. I'll take his place. No problems for you, no problems for me."

"I don't know what you're talking about." The words were pushed out, cold and hard.

She opened her purse, pulled out a color photo of a young girl looking up at Cliff with a slightly glazed expression. "You'll recognize her. And there are all the other photos. I'm sure you remember them."

Sam's voice was loud and clear. "Now that everyone is in place, look at the trash can near the end of the terrace where Deirdre Davenport placed Harry Toomey's trash."

Obediently everyone gazed at the plastic receptacle.

Everyone looked except Maureen and Cliff. She was gazing at him with a slight smile. His face was turned toward her, the muscles taut.

Sam continued ponderously. "Remember last night. Think back. If you saw anyone walk to that receptacle after Professor Davenport turned and left, come to conference room A. Do not share your information with others. It is important that you speak to the police first."

Cliff forced his body to relax. He managed a dismissive

smile. "I'm not worried about any photographs." His tone was contemptuous.

Maureen's quite lovely face was suddenly implacable. "You should be worried. Very worried. The photos are backed up on my laptop. Jay had you in a box. You didn't know she was only seventeen. But that doesn't matter. Nor does it matter that she's a year older now. She was seventeen that night. You can still go to prison for statutory rape. The law is quite clear in Oklahoma: No adult can legally have sex with anyone under age eighteen. Jay kept silent as long as you agreed to hawk those sorry books. But I didn't realize you'd killed him until just now. You see, I saw you get that beer bottle. Now, do you want me to talk to the police? Tell them about the beer bottle—and the party and statutory rape?"

Cliff's face turned an unhealthy red. His shoulders bunched.

She started to rise.

He reached out, grabbed her arm, pulled her down.

She stiffened, wrenched away from him. "Don't touch me."

"Maureen, we can talk about this." Now his face was smooth, unreadable, the flush of red fading away.

Her lips curved in a derisive smile. "I don't think so. I have no intention of engaging in tête-à-têtes with you, now or in the future. You have a couple of minutes to decide your future. I will keep what I know to myself"—she spaced the words—"on one condition."

"What is that?" He waited, muscles tensed—big, strong, dangerous.

Her face furrowed. "I need something to protect me."

"Maybe keeping your mouth shut will do that."

She reached up, touched her necklace. "Something specific." She gripped the stones, gave a decisive nod. "You won't dare come after me if I hold your confession."

He gave a short, ugly laugh. "You have the damn photographs."

"That isn't enough."

"What do you want? The truth? Jay pushed me too far. I told him I couldn't sell those sorry manuscripts and he had to back off. He laughed at me. I didn't have any choice. If he hadn't been greedy, he'd be alive. I picked up that bottle and hit him. He didn't make much noise when he fell." His voice held mild surprise. "Look, Maureen, we can work this out. I can't take the kind of books I was getting, but you can winnow them out, send me something that won't make editors mad. That's the deal I'll make. I'll even give you a cut of any earnings. That should be good enough for you."

Sam was still speaking. ". . . and again, let's take a moment for each of you to re-create that moment in your mind. Someone walked to the trash receptacle. . . ."

Maureen gazed at him warily. "It won't surprise you if I say I don't trust you. Your offer sounds okay. But I want something in writing." She opened her purse, drew out a pen and pad, handed them to Cliff. "Write down: *I, Cliff Granger, murdered Jay Knox and Harry Toomey.* Sign it. Date it. Hand it to me."

He sat immobile, the pad in one hand, the pen in the other.

Sam concluded, "And if you saw someone remove the

beer bottle from the trash can, please go directly to conference room A. Thank you for your attention." Sam turned away, strode across the terrace.

Though screened by people streaming into the building, I glimpsed Hal Price. He was poised to move fast, cover the twenty feet across the flagstones in an instant.

"Well." Maureen shrugged. "You've had your chance. I'll go to conference room A. I'd rather"—her tone was baiting—"plan a trip to Bermuda. But that's up to you." She rose.

"Sit down." Cliff spoke through clenched teeth.

She remained standing. "You have one minute."

He looked down at the pad, wrote in a savage jerky motion, looked up, thrust the pad at her.

Maureen read the words: *I, Cliff Granger, murdered Jay Knox and Harry Toomey.* His signature was a scrawl, the date overlarge.

She turned away.

He came to his feet, jammed his hands into his pockets, turned to head down into the gardens.

Sam Cobb waited in the path, taller than Cliff, heavier, big face implacable.

Cliff slowed, stopped, stared.

Officers were closing in, hands on the butts of their holstered guns.

Sam stepped forward. "Cliff Granger, you are under arrest for the murders . . ."

Cliff—tall, lean, at bay—swung around, his face malignant, fists clenched.

Hal Price—equally big, immovable, holding a pair of handcuffs—barred his way.

I murmured a thank-you to Saint Jude as the handcuffs snapped shut.

∽

A sandy-haired, thirtyish police officer patiently dusted powder on the doorjambs in Jay Knox's study. Sam Cobb obviously didn't intend to overlook any possibility. If Cliff Granger had touched a surface on his surreptitious visit Thursday night, those fingerprints would be found, catalogued, offered in evidence.

I admired the chief's forethought and diligence. I mightily wished he'd not been so efficient. I needed a moment alone in Jay's study. I looked at the handsome bronze clock on Jay's desk. The news conference at City Hall would begin in twenty-three minutes.

Grayish powder clung to the wood. The tech, careful and intent, bent nearer.

How quiet could I be? I eased open the center drawer of Jay's desk. I lifted the ornate fountain pen, rested the pen atop the desk. I reached for the checkbook, inadvertently moved a metal box of Altoids.

In the utter quiet, the sound seemed loud as a cymbal.

The tech straightened, turned to look across the office.

Would he remember that the surface of the desk had been bare?

He looked past the pen, the in/out box, the computer, the chair. Face crinkling in puzzlement, he swung around, stepped into the hall. "Yo, anybody here?" His footsteps thudded as he walked down the hall seeking the source of that sound.

I snatched up the checkbook. I looked at the check register, imitated Jay's handwriting, an almost indecipherable scrawl. I wrote fast, gently tugged to tear out the blank check. I returned the checkbook to the drawer, gently pushed the drawer shut.

I heard the tech returning. Quickly, I yanked open a lower drawer, grabbed an envelope and a sheet of stationery imprinted with Jay's name and address.

As the tech reentered, I kept my hands below the desk, folded the sheet, inserted the check, slipped the sheet and check into the envelope.

The clock read nineteen minutes to eleven.

I didn't have time to be subtle. I shoved Jay's desk chair backward and it careened toward a bookcase.

The tech swung around, watched the chair crash against the wall. His eyes wildly searched the room. A tentative step backward, another, a turn, and a lunge into the hall.

I pushed up the nearest window, unlatched the screen, raised it high enough to flow under and out into the air, the envelope in one hand.

I congratulated myself when I reached the entrance of Silver Lake Lodge. So far I'd moved the envelope high enough to escape notice. Now if I could find a spot to appear, all would be well. My undoing came in the lobby. I moved the envelope near the ceiling. Most people do not survey ceilings.

A little girl, possibly five or six, sat cross-legged on a

sofa. She looked up from her iPad. Her eyes widened behind thick lenses in sturdy blue plastic frames. "Hey Mom, look up. There's a woman carrying a letter up there," she said, and she pointed at the ceiling.

She saw me. A child's heart is open to more than adults ever know.

A distracted woman at the desk fumbled in her purse. "I know I've got that coupon somewhere."

"Mom." The girl now stood on the sofa, staring up with a fascinated gaze.

Without a pause, her mother called out, "That's lovely, darling. You can show me after I finish here."

"Mom!"

I dropped down, looked into magnified, intensely excited brown eyes. "Honey, do me a favor. When you talk to your mom, tell her you looked up at the ceiling and for a minute it was just like a movie, this woman was carrying a letter, and then she disappeared. And you and I will always know you really did see me, but if you don't tell anyone, do you know what will happen?"

She gazed at me with huge eyes. "What?" she whispered.

"I can take this letter where it needs to go and it will mean that someday not too long from now a wonderful young mommy and daddy will have a beautiful baby girl just like you. Will you help me?"

She nodded solemnly.

"I need to get this letter into the ladies' room. Will you carry it there for me?"

Her mother turned. "What's wrong, Abby?"

"Mom, I need to go to the ladies' room."

Her mother made a shooing motion toward the ladies'
room.

The little girl took the letter, clasped it against her chest,
and rushed across the lobby. Inside the ladies' room, she
held up the letter. "That's a pretty dress."

"Thank you, Abby."

The lounge area was empty except for us. An instant was
all I needed. I will admit to a touch of pleasure as I watched
the lovely white crocheted V-neck tunic appear. I did a little
jog to see the fringe sway. The light in the lounge didn't
adequately reflect the verve of the aquamarine slacks, but I
knew they looked like the shimmering sea at St. Croix. The
white leather stiletto heels gave me a lift, emotionally and
physically. I sat on the yellow-cushioned stool, fished out
the enclosed sheet. I quickly printed a note: *Dear Liz—As
requested, here is your refund for the book consultation.
Good luck with the book. Best Regards—Jay Knox.* I filled
out the check, signed it in a very nice imitation of Jay's
signature, wrapped the check in the sheet, placed it in the
envelope.

I turned to Abby. "Thanks a bunch. You're a hero."

Abby ducked her head, smiled. Then she looked at me,
blinked, her eyes owlish behind the thick lenses. "How were
you up in the air?"

"Sometimes, when I need to go somewhere in a hurry, I
just think what I might do and there I am."

"How were you not here, and then you were a bunch of
colors, and there you are?"

"Oh, it's just a way of arriving. Let's keep that our secret,
Abby."

She gave me a gap-toothed grin. "Sure."

I patted her cheek, then turned away.

Abby's thoughtful voice followed me. "Mama says I have enough imagination for six kids. I wonder what I can imagine next?"

I flashed her a smile. "Imagine you're a princess and nobody knows, but that's why good things happen all around you."

I hurried through the door. There was very little time left.

Chattering groups eddied back and forth in the lobby, some on their way to the main auditorium for a session, others headed to the meeting rooms in the wing. Perhaps it was my turn for luck. Or perhaps the fortuitous is divinely orchestrated. Your pick.

Liz Baker no longer looked haunted, but she still moved with dragging steps, all joy leached away. She clutched a notebook, was thumbing the conference schedule as she neared the exit to the terrace.

I caught up with Liz outside. "Mrs. Baker." I held out the envelope. "I have something for you."

Startled, she took the thin envelope in hand. She looked down and drew a quick breath at the address logo.

Before she could speak, I hurried on. "If anyone ever inquires, you received this in the mail and you threw the envelope away. I suggest you immediately deposit the check in your and Tom's account. The check will be honored, since it is dated before the death of the signatory. I doubt if there will ever be any questions asked."

She looked down, unsealed the flap. With shaking fingers, she lifted out the check, stared. "How—"

"Checks Jay Knox signed before his death are being sent to the proper recipients. As I said, if anyone ever asks"—I spoke slowly, forcefully—"you received this envelope in the mail, you didn't keep the envelope because you had no reason to keep it, and you are appreciative that Professor Jay Knox honored your request that he return the sum of five thousand dollars, which you paid for a manuscript submission that you later recalled. That's all"—I paused for emphasis—"you have to say. And now"—my smile was gentle—"you might want to share the good news with your husband. Bless you." I turned away.

She took several steps, caught my arm. "Who are you?"

I shook my head. "A friend. But as we both know, this moment never happened. You received a check in the mail."

Her eyes shone, her voice was tremulous. "How can I thank you?"

I hesitated, then said lightly, "Abby is a lovely name for a daughter." Then I moved fast, weaving my way across the terrace, plunging into the lobby. The little girl and her mother were gone, likely finally checked into a room. It was almost eleven. I had only minutes to spare. Most of the attendees were now settled in the auditorium or meeting rooms. I found the anteroom to the ladies' restroom empty, and I disappeared.

❦

The mayor's color choice was unfortunate. The bright red, tight-fitting suit added extra heft to her two-hundred-plus pounds. Her thick coronet braids were quite perfect and her makeup recently applied. Her expression oozed satisfaction.

She stood with one hand on the dais in City Hall's largest conference room. Detective Howie Harris was at her elbow, carrying a stack of printed sheets. Today he sported a pink-and-yellow bow tie, white shirt, and tan trousers. Very dressy for Howie.

Newspaper photographers and TV video crews jockeyed for space near the platform. Print reporters sat on the front row with laptops open. Shaggy-haired Joan Crandall leaned against a near wall, a jaundiced gaze on the mayor. She clutched a sheaf of copy paper and a thick-leaded pencil.

The bell in the tower tolled eleven o'clock; Mayor Lumpkin took a deep breath, surveyed the room. "True to my vows to the voters of Ade—"

The hall door swung in. Sam Cobb stepped inside, held the door for Maureen Matthews, who still wore dark glasses, and Deirdre Davenport, who looked years younger than the night I arrived at Silver Lake Lodge. Deirdre gazed about with interest.

Sam boomed, "Sorry to be late, Your Honor. I have some good citizens here who helped solve the murders at Silver Lake Lodge. Goddard Professors Matthews and Davenport assisted the Adelaide police in our investigation. We are also grateful for the outstanding work of Detective Sergeant Hal Price—"

Crisp and fresh, smiling, Hal came through the door.

"—and Detective Judy Weitz." Judy followed, looking pleased. "We've been at the station, our good citizens helping us flesh out the case against the accused."

As if marionettes on a string, the reporters, both TV and print, came to their feet, surged toward the door. Cameras flashed. Voices shouted. Video cameras were held high.

"Chief, who's the accused?"

"What's the charge?"

"Can you lay out some evidence?"

Sam was shepherding his charges toward the dais.

Mayor Lumpkin, her makeup now splotchy, watched grimly.

Sam genially waved Maureen, Deirdre, Hal, and Judy to the side of the platform, stumped up to join the mayor. He looked out at the press. "In case some of you have deadlines to meet, I'll lay out the facts first. Cliff Granger, a speaker at the conference and the literary agent for Jay Knox, has been arrested on charges of first-degree murder in the deaths of Jay Knox and Harry Toomey. We have proof that Knox was blackmailing Granger, which led Granger to kill Knox. Granger was observed at the crime scene by Harry Toomey. Instead of contacting police, Toomey attempted to blackmail Granger. Granger devised a trap for Toomey and killed him last night. Granger's attempt to implicate Professor Davenport failed because Professor Davenport's innocence had been confirmed by independent sources. Professor Davenport agreed to be publicly known as a suspect in order to facilitate our investigation. Professor Matthews made it possible for us to tape Granger as he made incriminating statements. I know"—Sam turned to the mayor—"Mayor Lumpkin takes great pleasure in recognizing contributions to the safety of Adelaide and will join me in recommending that Professors Matthews and Davenport be awarded Adelaide's highest honor, the Order of the Righteous Citizen."

Cameras flashed. Reporters surged forward.

I carried with me an indelible memory of the mayor's

face, an interesting mélange of colors—red, pink, and purple. Howie Harris slunk toward the door. I wondered if he carried printouts of his bio, suitable for passing out if he had been named to replace Sam.

I was alert for the clack of wheels on rails, the puff of coal smoke, the mournful summons of the whistle. But not quite yet.

Chapter 15

Deirdre burst into the hotel room. When I first saw her the night of my arrival, her frizzy brown hair was in need of a brush, her long face forlorn, sad, worried. Now her eyes were alight with joy, her face eager. She pulled her cell from her pocket, swiped. "Katie, everything's great. The police arrested the murderer, a man named Cliff Granger. You can tell everyone there that the police did a great job. And I was glad to help them. Maureen Matthews—you know, she's one of the professors in the English Department—she and I are being given awards for assisting the police. . . . Right. . . . And when you get home, I'll introduce you to some of my new friends. . . . His name's Hal and he's a detective sergeant and I've told him all about you and he's eager to meet you. . . . Two blue ribbons? Honey, that's swell. . . . Okay. . . . Love you, too."

Smiling, I swirled into being beside her.

Deirdre gave me a thumbs-up, swiped the cell again. "Hey, Joey, I helped catch the murderer. . . . Very exciting. . . . Nope, it was another professor who actually trapped him, but we are both getting awards. . . . I should get there by late afternoon, and I think a friend may come with me. . . . His name's Hal. . . . You'll like him. . . . See you then. . . . Love you, too." Deirdre wrapped her arms, whirled around the room to the window. "Hal said he'd come as soon as everything's all wrapped up. I'll make my speech and then he'll be here."

I beamed at her. "Everything ends as it should."

Deirdre's smile was incandescent, then it slipped away. Her long face softened. She stretched out her arms, hands open. "How can I thank you?"

"Why, I'll bet that now, with everything good again, you'll plunge into the new book."

Deirdre said uncertainly, "Do you think so? Maybe if I have her go up to the attic instead of to the window . . ." Her voice trailed off.

I remembered long ago, my grandmother's old frame house on Third Street, following her up narrow steps to a landing and a small door. She'd bustled directly to a leather-bound trunk, lifted the lid. . . .

Murmuring, I was at Deirdre's side.

Her eyes widened. "Oh. I like that." She rushed across the room to the sofa, picked up her laptop, plopped down, lifted the lid. In a moment, face tight with concentration, she began to keyboard (as they say these days, though it was typing in my day and typing should be good enough for anybody!).

I came up behind her and looked over her shoulder.

> Jane almost didn't go up into the attic, but Jane never ignored a duty. Jane might have been gorgeous—delicate features, dusky gray eyes, sleek black hair in a chignon—but her makeup was sparse, her gray cardigan slightly shapeless, her black slacks a little too large. Jane, in short, was kind, caring, honest, frumpy, tidy, serious, and seriously intense. She really wanted to go downstairs and fix a pot of tea and put the photos from the picnic in her scrapbook, not for the ephemeral album on her iPhone, but she'd promised Aunt Hortense she'd find her grandmother's lace tablecloth for the table with the punch bowl. Punch bowl . . .
>
> Did she really want to marry Richard? He was suitable. That's what everyone said. Suitable. Jane sighed. She felt a quick pang, resolutely suppressed. She'd met Richard's old friend last night. His name was Clive. . . .
>
> As she walked up the narrow steps, she had no idea that life would never be the same for her after she opened the old leather-bound trunk in search of the tablecloth. She knelt by the trunk, lifted the lid, saw a slender yellowed cardboard box. On the outside, it simply read: June.
>
> June?

Jane opened the box. Yellowed tissue paper. For some reason, she gently lifted the tissue apart, and there was a beautiful baptismal gown, delicate white lace on the cuffs and the hem. She picked up a small card inscribed in spidery writing: June's gown.

Jane lifted out the lovely gown.

A shaft of light, rather like exploding sparklers on the Fourth of July, dazzled Jane. She blinked, came to her feet in alarm. Standing on the other side of the trunk was a lively image of herself, but so different . . . dark hair in a jagged, sleek cut, perfectly sculpted dark eyebrows like wings, eyes dancing with laughter, cheeks flushed with excitement.

"I thought you'd never come."

The voice was Jane's own, but deeper, compelling. Oh, and the rich raspberry of a V-neck crepe dress and a necklace of silver and turquoise. Jane always wore brown or gray or black.

Jane scarcely breathed a faint, "Who are you?"

The vision placed her hands on her hips. "I'm June, your twin, and now I'm finally here. Oh, honey, are we going to have fun!"

Deirdre's fingers flew. A gurgle of laughter sounded as she paused, wrote again.

I smiled. "Have fun with Jane and June."

Startled, Deirdre looked around. "You're leaving?"

I smiled at her. "I'm done. Hal will be here soon. Good-bye, Deirdre." I disappeared.

The call was faint, receding. "Good-bye, good-bye. Thank you. . . ."

≪≫

I clung to the railing on the caboose, watched the blue orb of Earth recede. The wheels clacked *going home, going home, going home*. The deep whoo of the whistle lifted my spirit.

Wiggins was suddenly there. He stood beside me, large hands placed on the railing, feet spread apart to maintain his balance as the Rescue Express sped upward.

I turned, looked up at his kind face, felt welcomed. Though perhaps he had come to hold me accountable for not following a Precept. Or two. Sigh. Or three.

He cleared his throat. "In the main, satisfactory. A few mishaps, but the results amaze me. And just in time. My, that was close."

Silence.

Upward we climbed, the wind rushing past.

Another throat clearing. "I did have just one question."

I braced. "Yes?"

"Jane. And June. How does their story end, Bailey Ruth?"

Jane? June? I pictured Deirdre hunched over her laptop, fingers racing. I hoped she remembered that Hal was coming. I beamed at Wiggins. "I have no idea. But I did see Deirdre's working title."

He bent nearer.

"*Ghost to the Rescue*."

From *New York Times* bestselling author
Carolyn Hart

Ghost Wanted
A Bailey Ruth Ghost Novel

With mixed feelings, Heavenly supervisor Wiggins assigns irrepressible ghost Bailey Ruth to check out acts of vandalism and theft at a haunted library in Adelaide, Oklahoma. When an innocent girl is arrested, it's up to the spirited detective to book the real culprit.

PRAISE FOR THE SERIES

"Bailey Ruth . . . will delight readers."
—*Boston Globe*

"Blends an enjoyable fantasy with . . .
an engrossing plot."
—*Publishers Weekly* (Starred Review)

carolynhart.com
facebook.com/AuthorCarolynHart
facebook.com/BerkleyPub
penguin.com

FROM *NEW YORK TIMES* BESTSELLING AUTHOR

CAROLYN HART

DEATH ON DEMAND MYSTERIES

Death on Demand
Design for Murder
Something Wicked
Honeymoon with Murder
A Little Class on Murder
Deadly Valentine
The Christie Caper
Southern Ghost
Mint Julep Murder
Yankee Doodle Dead
White Elephant Dead
Sugarplum Dead
April Fool Dead

Engaged to Die
Murder Walks the Plank
Death of the Party
Dead Days of Summer
Death Walked In
Dare to Die
Laughed 'til He Died
Dead by Midnight
Death Comes Silently
Dead, White, and Blue
Death at the Door
Don't Go Home

BAILEY RUTH GHOST MYSTERIES

Ghost Gone Wild
Ghost Wanted
Ghost to the Rescue
Ghost Times Two

carolynhart.com
facebook.com/AuthorCarolynHart
facebook.com/BerkleyPub
penguin.com

Penguin
Random
House

M1323AS0715